Fearless Heart

Gail Cauble Gurley

World Castle Publishing
http://www.worldcastlepublishing.com

Fearless Heart© is a work of fiction. Any references to actual people, events, establishments, organizations, or locales are intended only to give the fiction a sense of reality and authenticity. Other names, characters, places, and incidents portrayed herein are either the product of the author's imagination or are used fictionally.

World Castle Publishing
Pensacola, FL

Copyright © 2011 by Gail Cauble Gurley.
ISBN#9781937085056
Library of Congress Control Number 2011928106

First Edition World Castle Publishing July 15, 2011

Licensing Notes
All rights reserved. No part of this book may be reproduced or reused in any manner whatsoever without written permission except in the case of brief quotations embodied in critical articles or reviews.

Front cover entitled "Shades of Winter" by artist Jeremy Sams, Archdale, N. C.
Website: www.jeremysams.com, E-mail: jeremy@jeremysams.com
Edited By: Beth Price

Author's picture by Rhonda Lester, Memory Lane Portraits, Archdale, N.C.
Website: www.rhondaswebsite.com

Fearless Heart

Fearless Heart

With love to, and in honor of
Ed, Denise, Charlie, Spencer, Madison, Molly, Murphy and Rusti

In Memory of
My parents and my grandmother

Gail Cauble Gurley

Fearless Heart

CONTENTS

PART I – TRIBULATION
Chapter 1   Hard Times
Chapter 2   Jake and Joe
Chapter 3   The Gift of Bob Julian
Chapter 4   The Pact

PART II – HOPE
Chapter 5   A New Beginning
Chapter 6   Snowed In
Chapter 7   Fulton Manor
Chapter 8   Illness

PART III – TRIUMPH
Chapter 9   Spring at Last
Chapter 10   Welcome, Dooble and Patches
Chapter 11   The Announcement
Chapter 12   Back to the City
Chapter 13   A Proposal
Chapter 14   A Wedding
Chapter 15   A Birth
Chapter 16   The Revelation

PART IV – LEGACY
Chapter 17   The Legacy

Gail Cauble Gurley

PART 1

TRIBULATION

Gail Cauble Gurley

Fearless Heart

Chapter One
Hard Times

A small group of men huddled around a 55-gallon drum containing a weak, struggling fire. They held their hands over the small blaze or crammed them deep into their pockets, dancing from foot to foot, in an attempt to create warmth. They glanced in the direction of the small office building on the side of the New York City dock, hoping that work would be available today. Unloading ships or a train, it didn't matter. Just as long as there was some sort of work so as to feed themselves and their families for one more day.

There would be three to twelve men gathered around the drum on any given day. The most regular group, however, included five that bonded through the cold days. There was Robert Blair who had become the one in the group depended on as a leader; Jake Fishel, the always despondent one; Bob Julian, who was the oldest at age fifty-two; Fred Barton rarely spoke but his presence comforted the others; and Joe Meechim, the youngest at seventeen and the most withdrawn. He and Jake had formed an alliance that was almost like father and son, and they were seldom apart. The two shared a room at the local night shelter. No one, including Jake, knew much about Joe except that he was from Ohio somewhere.

They became a brotherhood of sorts, partners in the poverty of late 1930 and had gradually shared their stories. It seemed to help knowing that they were not alone in their agony, so a certain camaraderie developed.

"I think what I miss most is my family," Jake declared one day.

"Where are they?" inquired Robert.

"They're in Kentucky. I came up here hoping to find work so I could send for 'em but it was for naught. I'm able to send 'em a few dollars each week but with four young'uns, that don't go very far, I'm certain. If I could find a place to live, I'd bring 'em on anyhow, but I can't 'spect them to live in the homeless shelter with me, even if it was allowed. That's jus' for men."

"Where they staying now?" asked Bob Julian. He had a constant cough and was finding it very difficult to cope with this lifestyle. He felt blessed, however, to have his family with him. His wife of thirty years and their oldest son as well as his only grandson waited for him in a tiny room at an old hotel several blocks from the docks. His son was in a wheelchair, the result of an accident at the mill where he had worked before the depression had started. After he became disabled, his young wife left him and their son, unable to handle the burden of caring for a baby and a man in a wheelchair.

"They're with her ma and pa. They live in a valley near the Stones Throw coalmine. Her pa worked there for most of his life but he's got black lung now and can't do nothing but sit and cough. They can't afford no doctor so he's on his own. Sure wish I could be there, especially with Christmas coming on. I miss my kids and my woman."

"What would happen if you did go back, Jake?" Robert wondered.

"We'd all most likely starve, I reckon."

Several of the group nodded their heads in understanding, making no comments but all aware of the predicament in which Jake found himself. The times had torn families apart, frequently destroying them completely. Their moods became decidedly gloomy as they related and compared their own situations to Jake's. They were helpless to control any part of their destinies, feeling as though they had failed their families. It was a bitter blow to their self-esteem and manhood.

"Tell you what!" Bob Julian stated cheerfully, changing the subject in an effort to lighten the mood. Everyone turned their attention to the storyteller among them who kept them entertained with delightful tales.

"I remember one time when I was a boy back in Illinois. We lived on a farm with my grandpa and grandma. Grandma had a flock of chickens and one old, mean rooster. That old rooster used to jump on me every time I went through the barnyard. And to add insult to injury, he woke me up every morning at the bust of dawn with that loud crowing of his.

"On my seventh birthday, my pa gave me a brown and white hound dog puppy and I named him Tick. That's 'cause he had two ticks on him when I got him. There was one on each ear. Looked like earbobs. I started to name him Sissy but Pa wouldn't let me."

The men chuckled at the pictures in their minds of this small boy and a hound dog wearing moving earrings.

"Anyhow, I was thrilled with that dog. The first time I took him outside, wouldn't you know that old rooster jumped on him. Sent him yelping all the way across the yard, that rooster riding his back and Tick scooted up under the house, scraping that rooster off on the edge of the wall as he went under. Took me more'n an hour to get him out from under the house, and that old rooster jumped up on the fence and crowed real proud like.

"Every time we went outside, that rooster would jump Tick. I got to carrying a stick to help knock him away. But everyday, Tick was getting bigger and that old rooster was getting bolder and cockier. He was the cock of the roost for certain.

"Tick stayed in my room at night and one morning 'fore dawn, he punched me with his paws, wantin' to get out. I opened the window and let him out. I was a little worried, thinking he might be sick. Well, I could barely make him out as he slunk along the ground in the dark real quiet like. I couldn't figure out what had got into him but I kept watching.

"Just then I saw that old rooster jump up on the fence near the barn, flap his wings and stretch up his head to let out one of his finest crows. All of a sudden, Tick made a flying leap at that rooster and knocked him clean off that fence. Feathers went flying everywhere and you never heard such squealing and squawking in your life as that rooster did. I like to fell out the window laughing. That old rooster got away and plumb forgot about crowing that morning. In a little bit, Tick came running back to my bedroom window and jumped in. He looked up at me pantin' and waggin' his tail to beat the band. I swear that dog was laughin', he was so proud. And I was laughin' and proud too! You know, that old rooster never did bother Tick again. Nor me neither!"

The men laughed heartily at Bob's story.

"Yeah," Jake interjected as the laughter subsided, "I remember taking my girls fishing one time. They was just little tikes but couldn't wait to catch all those fish down in the pond behind the house. They weren't allowed to go down there by themselves 'cause my wife was scared they'd fall in. Anyhow, we went down there one Saturday morning. They skipped and danced and hollered all the way across that field. I spoke to 'em kinda firm 'bout not making no noise when we got to the pond so as to scare off the fish. Seems like they forgot those directions when we got down there, they were so caught up in the excitement.

"The littlest one, Maybelle, was nigh onto five years old and she insisted on baiting her own hook. She was easing that worm on real slow like and I told her, 'Put him on there, Maybelle. What's the matter?'

"'I don't want to hurt the poor little thing, Pa,' she said. Well, I knew right there we weren't gonna get much fishing done."

The men all chuckled at the compassion of the little girl attempting to bait her hook without hurting the worm.

"Well, it wasn't but just a few minutes 'til Maybelle and Lorraine was both bored with the poles just settin' in the water, and they commenced to running up and down that bank, hootin' and hollerin' to beat the band. And when Lorraine started to throwin' rocks in the pond, I figured wasn't no point in sticking around there any longer. They'd done scared off every fish in the pond. So we packed up our fishing poles and headed back to the house. Of course, the girls were tickled pink. They'd been fishin' with Daddy and they were as happy as if we'd caught a whole mess of fish. When in actuality, we didn't catch nothing."

Jake's words caught in his throat and his eyes were red-rimmed as he finished.

"That's a nice story, Jake," Robert stated kindly. "Thanks for sharing it with us."

The men were silent for a few minutes, and then Jake said, "Well, guess I'll get on back to my room. Don't look like no more work today."

They had all worked for two hours earlier in the day when Josh Bennett, a benevolent supervisor for Bakersville Coal Company had called them over to Dock #4 to unload a barge of large, oak barrels. There were five men working that day, and it didn't take long but Josh split the work equally among every man who was present. He gave them each $1.00, which was much more than he should have paid, but he felt great compassion for them. He also felt a little guilty about his having a job when so many others didn't. He would pay them off in quarters as often as possible so that it seemed like more money, and at least, the men would have something in their pockets to jingle.

He paid them differently each day, depending on how much the owners of supplies being unloaded paid his company. Even though they were a coal company, they sub-contracted with every company shipping goods to the dock. This meant the companies did not have to hire anyone, and consequently, got the wares unloaded more cheaply.

As Jake and Joe moved away from the small group, Robert watched sadly. Jake's shoulders were stooped and his feet shuffled as he retreated, testimony to his great sadness and hopelessness.

"He ought to go home to Kentucky," Bob observed.

"Yeah." The others agreed.

"I was just wondering, fellas." Robert reflected. "How about if we try and help Jake get back home. Christmas is just a week away and if we could find a way to get him there, he should make it by then."

"Sounds like a good idea in theory," stated Fred, "but how we gonna accomplish it?"

The others nodded in agreement, shaking their heads in helpless bewilderment.

Robert thought for a minute, looked up and caught sight of Josh moving equipment around the dock. He looked at the men, they smiled encouragement as they realized that Robert had an idea, and the group moved toward Josh.

Robert explained about Jake's problem and how they'd like to help him get back home before Christmas.

"Do you have any thoughts about what can be done, Josh? And, uh, you know how close Jake and young Joe are. One doesn't go anywhere without the other."

"Well, let me think." Josh rubbed his hand across his jaw, frowning in deep thought. He looked out over the dock, his eye stopping at the railway which ended at the beginning of the docks. The train arrived almost daily with its meager load of goods to be transferred onto waiting barges and ships for transport to other cities. He knew that the train would be here tomorrow for sure but, according to the engineer, wouldn't be back again until after Christmas. The railway company had decided to shut down for a week as a cost cutting move and wouldn't be running again until December 27.

He saw the look of terror in the eyes of the group when he delivered this bit of news, and hastened to reassure them. "Oh, but there'll still be ships in here to be unloaded just like always but just not the trains." He was touched by the looks and audible sighs of relief escaping from the men.

"I know the men who work on that railway pretty good and they're a great bunch of guys. When they leave here, they head back to West Virginia and they're real close to the West

Virginia/Kentucky border. I've heard several of them speak of living in Kentucky so maybe they'd be willing to give Jake and Joe a ride. It's against policy but since it's so close to Christmas, maybe they'll make just this one exception. I'd be more than glad to ask them."

The men smiled broadly, thanking Josh, shaking his hand and slapping him on the back.

"Hold on, fellas, I said I'd try but I can't make any promises. It won't hurt to ask and I'm certainly willing to do that."

"Oh, that's okay, Josh, we all understand but just to have a ray of hope seems a blessing. We know it's a long shot but we'd sure like to get Jake back to his family." Robert spoke with gratitude and respect to their friend on the dock.

"What about getting them back here after Christmas?" Fred reminded them.

"You're right, Fred," Robert stated. "We don't want to abandon them with no hope of work."

They looked at each other, not sure what to do

"If the train takes them out, I'm sure they won't mind bringing them back," Josh assured them. "I'll be certain to ask. We don't want to send them to a situation more desperate than this one. Just don't say anything to them until we know for sure if this is going to work."

"No, we wouldn't do that. They might need a bit of money though, just in case."

"Yeah, can't never tell what they might run into, especially after they leave the train."

"They can have two of my quarters from today's pay," Bob offered.

A hat was passed and the total collected was $2.42. It seemed like a great deal of money to all of them so they felt confident this would get Jake and Joe to Kentucky and Jake's family. It should be enough to get them back to the New York docks as well.

♥♥♥

Robert shivered at the traffic light in the cold, damp evening a week before Christmas 1930, waiting for the light to turn red so he could cross the street. Ellen and little Stephen were waiting for him at their cold water flat in one of the many poor neighborhoods of New York City. His jacket, a leftover from more prosperous times, hung loosely over his now gaunt frame. He thrust his red, rough hands into the pockets in an attempt to ease the pain caused by cold weather chapping and manual labor.

He was 26 years old but felt much older. The worry of not being able to care for his young family, the guilt of not having steady work and the burden of responsibility weighed heavy on his countenance.

♥♥♥

Robert Blair had never been afraid of hard work and had gone to work in the steel mills of Pennsylvania when he was a lad of fourteen, after the death of his father. He worked each day after school until he graduated high school, and then took fulltime employment. He worked on the massive machinery, repairing the new gasoline motors. The labor was hot, noisy and intense, but the pay was good. After marrying Ellen Sims five years later, he decided to move his young wife to New York where he found work loading and unloading cargo ships on the docks. He enjoyed working outside, even in the cold, much more than working in the sweltering steel mill.

They lived in a tiny apartment belonging to Everlasting Warehouse Company, his employer. It was snug and comfortable with an inside bathroom and hot running water. A year later when little Stephen was born, they slipped a tiny crib into their cozy bedroom, and felt that they were settled for life. For three years, they were happy and content.

Then something called the Stock Market crashed and so did the tiny family's world. Ellen had saved a small amount of money in a large mayonnaise jar, but they knew little about such matters. Robert had a stable job, they had a nice place to live, were secure and had no reason to foresee the calamity which struck. Nothing in their experiences or history had prepared them for the dark days ahead.

Within a period of several weeks, Robert lost his job and the family lost their home. They were no longer able to pay the $35 a month rent, even if the company had not closed the housing unit. A company representative moved door to door in an attempt to do anything possible to help the families relocate.

The Blairs, however, had no place to go. They had no automobile in which to transport their possessions, no families to return to. Robert's adoptive parents were both gone and he had been on his own since age sixteen, after the death of his beloved mother. He had never known his biological parents.

Ellen's family had no room or resources to assist them. Her father had likewise lost his job in the Pennsylvania steel mill, as had both of her brothers. The brothers, their wives and a total of four children lived with the elder Sims in their two bedroom bungalow.

The Everlasting Warehouse representative gave them the address of the flat where they moved. It was twenty blocks away from the docks, and the streets were dirty and cluttered with garbage and destitute men, longing for work and begging for food. The red brick building was ancient and crumbling, and the family settled in on the fourth floor in a two room flat at the top of the stairs. The walls were streaked with dirt and dampness, the plaster cracked and peeling. There was one naked light bulb hanging from the center of the ceiling in each room but the bathroom was a community facility at the end of the hall. There was no one to officially clean it so the residents had to take the responsibility. It seemed that each time the Blairs visited the bath, it was necessary to clean it both before and after their use. The one redeeming grace of the facility was that it had hot water, a true blessing at bath time.

The kitchen was a small corner carved into the front room, containing dilapidated cabinets with no doors and broken shelves; a small countertop made of plywood, buckled and separating from water damage; a substantial sink with most of the porcelain worn away; and a single cold water faucet which dripped water constantly. The sink contained a large green stain from the persistent dripping. A small gas cook stove was no longer operational, but the oven served as a storage area for food and dishes and helped protect against the ever present roaches. There was an icebox but the windowsill in winter served them very well in storing perishable food. If it became too cold, large stalactite icicles attached to the eaves outside would be broken off and stuffed into the icebox. This prevented the food from being frozen and destroyed by the bitter, cold air. During hot weather, it was necessary to eat from cans and plan their meals carefully so as to have few leftovers. Lugging heavy blocks of ice up four flights of stairs was quite difficult and sometimes impossible as Robert frequently arrived home after the icehouse two blocks away had closed for the day.

The one source of heat in the apartment was a small, nearly ineffective coal heater huddled in the corner of the front room. The ancient radiators lining the decrepit walls had long ago ceased to operate when the coal fired steam central heating system in the basement of the building had given up the ghost. The landlord refused to replace the beyond-repair system, and had left the tenants to fend for themselves. Fortunately for the Blairs, the former tenants had failed to remove this small but precious appliance.

Their apartment was on the top floor of the building, which meant they were not disturbed by people overhead, but the ceiling was sagging dangerously due to the leaky roof. Robert brought scrap pieces of lumber home from the docks and nailed them to what was left of the ceiling joists so as to help ensure that the ceiling would not cave in on them. Most of the existing joists were nearly rotted through by water leakage, and two months after moving in, the wiring in the bedroom ceased to work entirely. Robert worried constantly about fire. Fortunately, he and Ellen were both light sleepers and kept a vigilant watch.

"Just be grateful we're on the top floor, dear," Ellen comforted, "At least it keeps us safe from most of the rats."

The only other redemption for the apartment was that the rent was just $8.00 a month. The coins and bills in the mayonnaise jar had totaled $118.32 when they first moved here, which seemed like a great fortune to the family in their present circumstances, so they guarded it carefully and passionately.

Robert blessed the cold weather because he didn't have to carry the heavy blocks of ice upstairs but worried about his small family being in the cold all day. He brought scrap wood home whenever he could find it but it was very scarce since the men burned it in the barrels on the dock to keep warm while waiting for work. And also, others had families to care for so they too coveted the tiny scraps. Coal was a luxury beyond their means so they did the best they could with wood and even cardboard or scrap newspapers picked up off the streets.

The few perishable groceries the family had in the winter were kept locked in a small wooden crate, chained to the fire escape outside the window. Meager meals were cooked on a rusty and bent electric hotplate or on the small heater when there was enough fire.

Each morning, Robert would rise at 5:00 AM and coax a tiny, cold flame from the heater in the next room. He would wash up at the small basin Ellen kept filled on the stovetop while she would find some sustenance for him before he started his day on the docks. It might be a cold potato, leftover biscuit or even a dried out piece of cake purchased for a penny from the day old store at the bakery down the street. She would pinch off any mold beginning to appear and attempt to heat whatever she had so as to make it more palatable.

By 5:30 AM, he left the flat and walked the twenty blocks to the docks, hoping to find work. Most days he found very little, but occasionally, there was someone who needed help for a whole day. He would stay there all day, waiting, hoping, huddled over large drums filled with burning scrap lumber, talking to the other men there for the same purpose. The day would really drag as the men began to drift away around mid-morning, but he enjoyed talking to them while they waited for work. Robert stayed most days until at least 4:00 PM, hoping for employment, no matter how meager or demeaning.

Gail Cauble Gurley

♥♥♥

Robert's heart was light but anxious as he waited to cross the street to his home. He was full of excitement about the possibility of sending Jake and Joe home to Kentucky. He just prayed that it would work out. It would be a wonderful Christmas present for them all, to be able to help their brothers in such a way. Life was hard enough but he couldn't imagine being without Ellen and little Stephen.

His steps lightened as he crossed the street and moved quickly to the stairs of the apartment building where his family waited.

Chapter 2
Jake and Joe

Little Stephen heard his father's whistling as he mounted the stairs. The lock on the apartment door was broken, and while Stephen and Ellen were home alone, one of the two ladder back chairs the family owned was wedged beneath the door knob for security. Robert had installed a hasp with a padlock on the outside, and on the rare occasions the family left the apartment together or Ellen and Stephen left while Robert worked, the padlock was placed in the hasp and securely clicked. Robert realized it wouldn't take much effort to force the hasp off the thin door but they all felt better knowing that what little they had was somewhat protected.

Also, when they did leave, their money was taken with them. Neither Ellen nor Robert had ever known such fear and doubt before, and they disliked intensely the feelings of distrust in their hearts, but these were desperate times. Many of their neighbors had been mercilessly robbed of what little they had, and the young couple had helped several families within their building as much as they possibly could after they had fallen victim to robberies. At least one family in the building was forced onto the streets as a result of their rent money being stolen. The landlord demanded the $8.00 rent on the first day of each month, before sundown, or the tenants were forced to leave immediately. The renters were not even allowed to stay until daybreak the next day.

Robert began whistling on the third floor so that Ellen and Stephen would know he was coming. Stephen stood by the door in glad expectation, waiting eagerly for his father's knock and voice. Only then could the chair be removed to allow Robert's entry.

No matter how cold or tired, Robert would scoop Stephen up, toss him into the air, and greet him with laughter and joy. Stephen squealed with delight, hugging his father hungrily. Ellen would smile, happily and proudly watching her son and her husband. She moved toward them and Robert kissed his wife warmly, so very glad for the comfort afforded by his small family.

♥♥♥

After supper, Robert told Stephen the story of Bob Julian's dog, Tick. They all laughed, and Stephen jumped up on the chair, pretending to crow like a rooster. Robert reached out, and with a deep growl, grabbed Stephen and tossed him to Ellen. The small room was warmed by their laughter.

Soon it was Stephen's bedtime so Ellen and Robert tucked him into their bed in the next room. They no longer had bedroom furniture as it had all been sold except for the mattress. The mattress rested on the floor and the few clothes they possessed were crammed into cardboard boxes lining the wall. They left him in their bed until they retired for the night and then moved him onto his small cot, which they set up near the stove in the front room.

Stephen dropped to his knees on the mattress, folded his tiny hands under his chin, closed his eyes, and said his prayers. His parents sat by his side, holding hands and listening to their son's words.

"Now I lay me down to sleep, I pray the Lord my soul to keep. And thank you for my parents and my bed and my supper. And thank you, God, for Mr. Bob's dog, Tick and for letting him get away from that old rooster. Bless us all and please help Daddy find work tomorrow. Amen."

The couple tenderly kissed their son good night, grateful for the darkness of the room so that he could not see their worry-filled eyes.

♥♥♥

One of the chairs was slipped under the doorknob. Ellen sat in the remaining chair and Robert pulled a wooden crate near her as they huddled around the stove.

Ellen waited, not wanting to ask the anxious question in her heart for fear of hurting her husband.

As if he heard it anyway, he declared, "I found a little work today but I just brought home fifty cents."

He seemed uncomfortable and somewhat guilty as he explained further.

"You see, Jake Fishel – he's the man from Kentucky who looks after young Joe Meechim – is really homesick. So much so that we – uh, me and the other men, that is – decided to try and help him get back to his family before Christmas. We spoke to Josh – you remember me telling you how good he is to all of us at the docks – anyway, we asked him if he had any ideas about maybe getting Jake and young Joe down to Kentucky. He promised us he'd talk to the men on the railway down there and see if maybe the two of them could hitch a ride on the train or maybe even work their way down and back on the train. So, we kind of figured that maybe they might need a little money along the way for some emergency, so just in case it works out, we took up a collection and I gave half of what I earned today." Robert dropped his eyes uneasily. "I hope you don't mind."

"Mind? Oh, my dearest, how could I mind, and I do love you so! There has never been anyone anywhere who is kinder and more compassionate and more unselfish than you. I'm so proud! I would have been disappointed if you had done anything else. No, I certainly do not mind! When do you think you'll know if it'll work out for them to take the train?"

"If it works out, it'll have to be tomorrow because the train won't be back until after Christmas. But, I'll probably still have work," he hastened to add, "as the ships are going to continue to come in daily except for Christmas Day."

Ellen moved quickly to the kitchen area in search of some morsel of food to send with the two men on their journey. She took their last two sweet potatoes and tucked them under the edge of the stove to bake during the night.

"I have almost a half loaf of bread and several pieces of cheese which aren't too dried out so I'll pack them each a sandwich. And there'll still be enough for you to have one."

She busily began to pinch off tiny pieces of mold forming around the edges of the bread.

"What about you and Stephen?" he inquired.

"Oh, there's still enough for us. I even have a little bit of macaroni noodles and can boil those on the stove and put the cheese in there. Stephen loves macaroni and cheese!"

Robert smiled tenderly as he held his wife close.

"There seems to be an epidemic of unselfish in this house," he murmured gently.

♥♥♥

He arrived even earlier than usual at the docks the next morning, eager to learn if it would work out for Jake and Joe to go to Kentucky. He clutched the package of cheese sandwiches and roasted sweet potatoes under his arm. The sandwiches and potatoes were wrapped in brown paper from a bag that had been torn apart, and the whole treasure was wrapped in a piece of newspaper.

He spotted the train at the dock a full block before he arrived and he broke into a run, eager to get there but fearful of disappointment at the same time. He slowed to a walk as he approached the gathering barrel where the men waited each day, straining to see through the early morning darkness, struggling to spy Josh.

He could see nothing, but a few minutes later, he caught sight of Josh stepping between two of the rail cars with another man. They were talking and laughing, and Josh reached out, shook the man's hand, then turned to leave. He caught sight of Robert standing by the barrel, smiled broadly and waved his hand, nodding his head vigorously in the affirmative.

Robert was ecstatic! He could hardly contain his relief and happiness, and fairly danced around the barrel. He could hear Josh's laughter at the spectacle, but wasn't the least bit embarrassed. His joy was too complete to hold inside.

The other men began arriving shortly afterward, and Robert ran to meet them, breathlessly giving them the wonderful news. It looked like Jake and Joe were going to Kentucky!

Soon Josh and the railroad man he had been talking to approached the small group. Jake and Joe hadn't arrived yet so the group anxiously awaited the news from the two approaching men.

"Fellas, this is Henry Bailey with the railroad. I spoke to him about your proposition and he has some good news for you."

"Morning, gents. Josh explained the situation to me and I'd be proud to help you out. The men can ride in the caboose with me where it's warm and they can help us with the uncoupling and shifting of cars when we stop at various stations. There'll be a little unloading and loading too but it won't be too much. We can't pay them but they'll get to ride for free. The train goes as far as Huntington in West Virginia. I live in Globe, Kentucky, and can take them as far as there with me in the car. Do you know where they're headed?"

"As I recollect," Fred Barton pondered, "he's from a little town called Poplar Plains. I remember it because my home's in Poplar Bluff, Oregon." The men looked around in surprise, as this was the most any of them had heard Fred speak at one time.

"Well, now, that's good news," Henry replied excitedly. "That's only about five miles from Globe. They should be able to get there okay. If nothing else, my boy can take them over. Sure don't want them walking if the weather's bad and it most likely will be this time of year. But you realize that the train leaves today at 4:00. And we won't be back for at least a week. It'll be after New Year's. We don't have a definite date yet."

The men missed the doubt and concern in Henry's voice in their excitement over his news.

"We're most grateful to you, Mr. Bailey," Robert declared, smiling and shaking his hand warmly. The other men gathered around, thanking and enthusiastically slapping Henry Bailey's back in appreciation.

"What's going on?" Jake asked as he and Joe approached the happy meeting.

"You're going home, Buddy," Robert announced, "and Joe's going with you."

Shock and bewilderment covered Jake's face, and he stood, momentarily stunned by the news.

"Whatya mean?" His voice cracked, his words disbelieving.

The men surrounded the two and quickly explained the plan, but it took several minutes for the significance of their explanations to sink in. Jake stuttered in confused amazement and even Joe looked shocked.

"Wow! For real?" Joe asked.

"For real, Joe, for real!" Robert assured him.

♥♥♥

The men worked quickly that morning, their spirits lifted by the wonderful news for their friends. They had the train unloaded by noon, and Jake and Joe hurried back to their room to gather their few worldly possessions for the trip home. They were back at 2:00, and the men gathered around the barrel to say their goodbyes.

Robert presented them with the food Ellen had prepared for them; Bob Fishel gave them their collection of $2.42; and Fred Barton handed them each a pair of wool socks.

"They ain't new but they got no holes," he explained. "I thought maybe you might have to do some walkin' and it gets mighty cold this time of year."

"I don't know what to say, fellas," Jake murmured. "This here's the nicest thing anybody's ever done for me. I don't know how I could ever repay you."

Joe made no comment but his eyes were glistening with tears. He quickly dropped his gaze, kicking at a dirt clod lying near the barrel. He cleared his throat and wiped his sleeve across his eyes.

"No need to thank us or even think of repaying us, Jake and Joe," Robert stated. "This is the greatest Christmas present for us too. With any luck, you'll be home no later than Christmas Eve and just remember us to your family. We're certain the two of you will be fine, and it looks like work is going to get harder to find here so you're probably leaving at a good time. Just be happy with your wife and kids."

"I'll do that, for certain! And thanks for including Joe in this. He'll be a big help to us back home." He glanced fondly at Joe, reaching over and patting his back.

The men shuffled uncomfortably and soon changed the topic of conversation to more superficial subjects. They had no work but all wanted to see the two men off.

"The train will bring you back after Christmas and you can tell us all about it," Robert assured them.

♥♥♥

Robert arrived home that night, eager to tell Ellen and Stephen the good news. Stephen jumped into his arms as he entered their door. His mother had told him about Jake and Joe having a chance to go home for Christmas.

"Did they leave? Did the train take them?"

"Yes, they sure did. And that was two very happy men! Actually, we were all happy. It was a wonderful present for us all, and Henry Bailey from the railroad will telegraph Josh when they get there and let us know that they made it safely."

"Yayyyy!" shouted little Stephen.

"Thank God!" whispered Ellen as she wiped away her tears. She hugged her husband tightly.

♥♥♥

The moods of the men were decidedly lighter for the rest of the week. Even the cold seemed less harsh as they talked about Jake and Joe and their trip home. The part they played in the drama brought them great pride and self-satisfaction.

As they prepared to leave after work on Christmas Eve, Josh approached them, waving a telegram.

"They made it!" he shouted.

The men laughed and congratulated each other eagerly as they received this welcomed news.

"Read the telegram to us!"

"It says: 'Arrived safely last PM. Stop. Delivered cargo to Poplar Plains. Stop. Welcomed warmly. Stop. Will report more January 3. Stop. Henry'"

It was going to be a great Christmas for them all as they rejoiced in the good fortune of their brothers. However, none of them missed the date of January 3 as a return date for the train.

♥♥♥

They left the docks, their hearts still warmed and their faces filled with smiles, after receiving the telegram, to return to their homes and families. It was going to be a grand Christmas after all.

As they said their goodbyes and parted, Robert noticed a long, black limousine parked a block away.

Strange, he thought. *Wonder who that could be?*

He was deep in thought as he walked the twenty blocks to his family. He was very happy for Jake and Joe but despondent that he had no gift for Ellen and Stephen, especially Stephen. He was four years old now and Christmas could be very special for him under more pleasing circumstances. His hand closed around the four quarters in his pocket. They had enough in the mayonnaise jar to pay the next two months' rent but not much else. They were planning to go to the soup kitchen for Christmas lunch. Maybe there would be a small gift there for Stephen. He raised his eyes and sent forth a silent prayer that his son would receive a small gift on this blessed holiday.

He approached the last block to his apartment building, and he spied Mona Dorsett set up on her corner. She was an elderly lady who so far as anyone knew had no home except the street. She was a fixture in the neighborhood, selling flowers and vegetables in the summer; nuts, holly, mistletoe and various other articles in the winter. She bothered no one but her salty philosophy and harmless sarcasm endeared her to all. She was apparently homeless but she wasn't helpless.

Robert's heart lifted as he saw her.

Maybe I can find something there. An orange or a few nuts. Anything, he thought.

"Evening, Miss Mona, how are you?"

"Very well, Robert, very well. Merry Christmas to you!"

"Thank you, ma'am. I need a little gift for Stephen. What do you recommend?"

"Got just the thing here. And they're on special."

He smiled at her standard response.

"Just look at these lovely birdhouses! Ain't they beauties? Not a rag in the lot!" She peered around to make certain no one could overhear, leaning forward, as if to divulge some secret information to Robert. "And they're handmade by Christmas angels!"

He smiled kindly at this information.

"They really are lovely, Miss Mona. But I'm afraid I can't afford one of them. They're much too exquisite for my budget."

"I told you they're on special!" she snapped, "And just $1.00."

She noticed his hesitation as he slipped his hand into his pocket. She heard the coins jingling and realized that he probably only had $1.00.

"But since it's Christmas Eve and I likely won't have no more sales tonight, I'm cutting the price by half. And I'm throwing in a surprise bag as a gift." She leaned behind her cardboard box stand, pulling out a small lunch bag with the top neatly folded over.

"What's in it?" Robert inquired.

"It's a gift!" she retorted.

Once again, Robert was caught off guard by this sassy and outspoken lady and he laughed with delight. He reached into his pocket and pulled out two quarters. "Okay, Miss Mona, you've made a sale."

"Well, I should hope so! You won't find no better deal anywhere and that's for certain! Now which one do you want?"

He looked carefully at the array of tiny structures, lined up neatly across the top of the cardboard box. One had a miniature front porch, another had a stone chimney, yet another was two stories high. There was one tucked way at the back, much smaller and cruder than the others. It was constructed of strips of bark, held together with tiny nails and twigs used as support beams. A bent twig curled gently around the opening so as to form a perch for a feathered occupant. It reached out to him, inviting him to pick it up, and, after all, it seemed selfish to take advantage of Miss Mona's generosity by picking the most elegant of the bunch. His hand closed around it and he felt instantly that this was the right choice.

"Ah, wonderful choice!" Miss Mona agreed. "And here. Here's the gift I promised you. Merry Christmas!"

"Thank you, Miss Mona. And Merry Christmas to you too."

Chapter 3
The Gift of Bob Julian

Robert approached the corner with his Christmas package tucked safely under his arm. As he prepared to cross the street to his apartment building, a truck roared around the corner from behind him. He stepped back, startled by its sudden appearance. The load on the truck shifted from the sudden turn, and two bundles crashed to the street, right at Robert's feet.

"Hey!" he yelled in an attempt to catch the attention of the driver, but the truck was gone.

Robert stood there helplessly, not knowing what to do about the two bundles lying in the street. He approached them and discovered that it was two bundles of small limbs tied neatly with twine.

Firewood! Blessed, blessed firewood!

He gathered them up and bounded up the steps as quickly as his load would permit, eager to reach his wife and son with this bounty. He began shouting to them on the third floor, and they both came to the door, anxious to learn what all the fuss was about.

He ran up the last few steps, laughing and shouting happily. "Merry Christmas, my two loves! Merry Christmas!"

They began to laugh as his excitement electrified them, and the door across the hall opened a crack with two small faces peering out curiously before the door was pushed shut by someone behind them.

He eagerly gave Stephen the birdhouse, hiding the small bag under his coat for tomorrow, and shared the story of the firewood, which seemed to fall from the heavens. His fervor was contagious, and they all were excited, with Robert tossing Stephen into the air and hugging Ellen.

He stopped suddenly, a look of inspiration crossing his face.

"Do you mind if I go down and see if Miss Mona can have supper with us, Ellen? That is, if she isn't gone yet."

"Well." Ellen hesitated only briefly. "We don't have much but you know she's more than welcome if she doesn't mind sharing what we have."

He hugged her quickly.

"I'll be right back!" he promised as he dashed down the steps, hoping to catch Miss Mona before she left her spot.

He observed her packing up her remaining birdhouses and shouted to catch her attention as he ran toward her.

She turned and waited as she recognized who was calling.

♥♥♥

Soon Miss Mona sat in the small room with the Blair family, sharing their meager meal. Her cardboard box rested beside the door, and they talked as if they had known each other for years.

"Where do you live, Miss Mona?" Stephen asked with childlike innocence. His parents glanced at each other uneasily, embarrassed by their son's unintentional boldness.

"Oh, here and there, Sonny, here and there. Old Mona makes out just fine, don't you worry none. However, I almost lived with a police officer once." She chuckled as the others prepared to hear what they perceived to be a story.

"You know Officer Dan, don't you? He's the policeman that patrols this neighborhood. He's a nice enough young man but when he first started back eight or nine years ago, he was stiff with starch, that one was. Was going to single-handedly stamp out crime in this area."

They all knew Officer Dan and were interested in hearing Miss Mona's story. He had always been very kind to them all, and the children particularly liked him. He would let them hold his nightstick, and he gave them all small replicas of his badge, which they pinned on their shirts as they played on the sidewalks in front of their buildings or in the small park across the street.

"Well, don't you know," Miss Mona continued, "I was set up down there at my spot on the street, selling the first flowers of spring. They was lovely things, too. Tulips and jonquils and yellow bells. Just lovely! This young police officer approached and I greeted him. Thought I was going to make a sale.

"Anyway, he said, 'Where's your peddler's permit, ma'am?'

"'My what?' says I. I thought he was kiddin'. But I soon learned he wasn't kiddin'. No, sir, not that one!

"Well, we argued back and forth for a few minutes and he told me in no uncertain terms that he was shuttin' me down until I got a peddler's permit. I told him he couldn't do that and he told me he could.

"So I shut down everything and just sat there, waiting for him to get off work. When he left, I followed him. He lived only about four blocks from here and I was grateful for that since I was carrying my cardboard box with me. And it still had flowers in it, too.

"I think he got a little nervous as I followed him but he didn't say nothing. When we got to his building, he went in and so did I. He stood there a little confused like and then he pushed the bell on 208. His wife came on the speaker and he told her he was home. And I chimed in and said, 'And he brought home company.'

"Well, he like to fainted. He told me I couldn't go up with him and I told him I could. By then, his wife came downstairs to see what was going on and I explained to her that he shut down my business and I had no money to buy food nor to pay for a place to stay so I was going to stay with them.

"She was a pretty little thing, very kind and flustered too. She really didn't know what to do. Others had started gathering outside to see what was going on and I was quick to explain to them. Officer Dan was red as a beet. Stood there just kind of sputtering and twitching around, real nervous like. Finally, his wife invited me up. Officer Dan told me I could eat supper with them but then I'd have to leave.

"I told him, 'I ain't going no where. This here's home now. You done destroyed my livelihood. You wouldn't put an old lady out on the street, now would you?' I'm certain he could have probably choked me.

"Anyhow, I spent the night on their couch that night. Took a bath in the bathroom. I could tell his wife was real uneasy 'cause in all truthfulness, it'd been awhile since I'd had a full bath. I thought I might as well do it, wouldn't hurt nothing, so she drew me a good, hot bath in the tub. Even gave me some shampoo so I let my hair down and washed it too. It was a warm evening so I sat by the window and let it dry. She and I talked and she was a real nice lady. But she was still confused as to what to do with this old trespasser.

"I had breakfast and left around 7:00. I said 'Thanks ever so much, I'll see you tonight.' And I left. I can just imagine the conversation between those two after I went downstairs." She chuckled at the memory.

Little Stephen was delighted and eager to learn what happened next.

"Well, I sat on the steps and waited for Officer Dan to come down on his way to work. He stopped when he reached the steps and said, 'Why are you still here?'

"Got no place to go,' says I. 'I'm out of business.'

"He sort of stammered around for a bit and then said, 'Well, I guess there's no harm in your selling flowers but just don't make a scene.' I agreed. 'And will you go back to your own home tonight?' He glanced up toward his apartment so I knew he'd caught what for from his wife. 'I'll be going back to my own place tonight, thank you very much. You can be certain of that. And I appreciate your hospitality last night. You and your Mrs.'

"Needless to say, I wasn't ever told I'd have to have a peddler's license again!"

They all laughed gleefully at Miss Mona's story, the adults shaking their head in amazed disbelief.

"Well, I got to go before it gets any later."

"Stay the night," little Stephen pleaded. And his parents eagerly agreed.

"Oh, no, that's mighty kind of you but I got to go. Tomorrow's Christmas and I got plans."

"You're not going alone. I'll walk with you," Robert insisted.

"It ain't far. Just on the other side of the park."

"I'll walk you, Miss Mona."

♥♥♥

Ellen and Stephen stood in the hall saying their goodbyes to Miss Mona and inviting her to come back again soon. Robert held her cardboard box, and as they prepared to descend the stairs, the door across the hall opened once again and the two small faces peered out.

"Hello," Miss Mona called. "Merry Christmas."

They made no reply and closed the door. She reached inside the cardboard box, pulled out two lunch bags and moved to their door. She knocked boldly. There was no answer. She knocked again, louder this time, announcing, "I know you're in there so you might just as well open up. I ain't leavin' 'til you do!"

The door slowly opened, she leaned down, and stuck the two bags through the small crack.

"Here!" she greeted. "God bless you. Are there anymore young'uns in there?"

The tallest child, who was a small boy, shook his head.

"Well, then, take this and enjoy!"

The two smiled shyly, looked across the hall to Stephen who smiled and waved, and then they closed the door. It opened again almost immediately, and a man and woman stood there.

"Thank you. We're beholden to you," the man spoke gratefully.

"Yes, thank you, and God bless you," the woman echoed.

♥♥♥

"Exactly where do you live, Miss Mona?" Robert wondered.

"Just over there in that building." She casually motioned with her hand.

I thought that building was empty, he thought. But he wisely kept his thoughts to himself and made no comment. He walked her to the steps.

"I'll go in with you," he offered.

"Oh, no, I'll be fine. I know you think the building is empty but things ain't always the way they appear on the surface, young man. I appreciate your concern and your worryin' but I assure you, I'm fine. The Lord has always taken care of me."

He smiled, humbled by her words. "Of course, you're right, Miss Mona. Good night."

Just the same, he stood outside for a few minutes after she entered to make certain she didn't slip back outside into the cold.

As Robert returned to his building after walking Miss Mona home, he noticed what appeared to be the same black limousine he had seen at the dock earlier. It was parked on the street on the far side of the park. He stopped, looked in that direction and wondered at its presence. As he watched, the car moved slowly away.

Strange, he thought.

♥♥♥

Christmas morning dawned bright and clear. The sun sparkled off the icicles hanging from the roof and the frost stars bunched on the windowpanes. A light snow had fallen during the night and nestled against the window frame, adding to Stephen's delight and joy. Ellen had taken three pieces of their precious newspaper, rolled it together and torn it down about a foot into strips, then pulled it up like a telescope to fashion a Christmas tree. Stephen was enchanted.

"It's the best Christmas tree I've ever had in my *whole* life!" he declared.

His parents' surprise at this statement of wisdom and purported age from their four year old filled their tiny room with happiness and pride.

The small lunch bag set under the newspaper tree, waiting to be opened by Stephen. As he eagerly poured out the contents, a big red apple, an orange, several nuts and seven shiny marbles rolled out. The young boy squealed in ecstasy. The marbles were blue and green and red and there was even one coveted tiger's eye! It was a treasure beyond his wildest expectations.

The room was enveloped with warmth, from love as well as the wood burning brightly in their stove. The morning sped quickly by, and soon it was time to go to lunch at the local soup kitchen. Stephen skipped eagerly about, the air filled with expectant hope and faith. He was certain their good fortune was only just beginning.

"Oh, to have the faith of a child," Robert mused.

As they entered the hall to walk to their Christmas meal, the door across the hall opened and the two small children from the night before emerged with their parents. The boy appeared to be about six years old, and the girl could have been no more than three. The parents were young but had the haunted look of age created by poverty, hardship and worry. They hesitated as the Blairs entered the hall, and took a step back as if to retreat into their room.

"Hello," Robert greeted joyfully. "Merry Christmas! It's good to see you again."

Ellen and Stephen moved forward, smiling, greeting them warmly.

The small family relaxed somewhat, responding to the obvious acceptance by the Blairs. The man introduced himself as Cletus Danton, his wife Birdie, son Carson and daughter Julie.

"Hey, your name is Birdie!" Stephen exclaimed excitedly. "Maybe you can live in my birdhouse!"

He clutched the small frame firmly, refusing to leave it behind as they left. The adults all laughed and Ellen scolded Stephen gently.

"Stephen, this is Mrs. Danton, we don't call adults by their first name. Mind your manners."

The Dantons were on their way to the soup kitchen as well. "Mind if we tag along, Mr. Danton?" asked Robert.

"Glad for the company. And, please, call us Cletus and Birdie."

The two families chatted cordially, the children eagerly showing the treasures retrieved from the lunch bags given by Miss Mona the night before. Julie had a set of jacks and a small red comb. Carson had received a whistle and a candy cane. Both had oranges and large red apples, just as Stephen had received. Carson blew the whistle, playing one-noted Christmas songs as they walked through the fresh, Christmas snow to their lunch. Stephen and Julie skipped and danced, singing Jingle Bells to the tune of the whistle.

"We may all be sorry he received that whistle in a day or two," lamented Birdie.

The adults agreed, saying nothing to stop the exuberance of the children. Socializing was rare for the two families lately and they reveled in the comfort of it.

The Salvation Army served a hot, hearty meal of cornbread, pinto beans, Stephen's favorite macaroni and cheese, and Cole slaw. The children were given chocolate milk and the adults had delicious cups of rich, black coffee. None of them had enjoyed this treat for many months. A piece of peppermint candy topped off the feast and offered a welcomed dessert.

The small Salvation Army band played Christmas carols and the children, especially Stephen, sat in awestruck wonder at the beautiful, although sometimes off key, notes and golden ringing escaping from the trumpets and tambourines. Stephen had never experienced such amazing sounds and he was enchanted.

The workers at the center organized games for the children, and they all shouted with delight as they played musical chairs, drop the handkerchief, and Red Rover. Too soon, it became time to leave as the long winter evening quickly approached. Amid complaints of not wanting the festivities to end, all the new friends bade each other Merry Christmas and good night as they prepared to leave the warm center to return to their mostly cold homes. The spirit of the celebration, however, kept them warm and comforted and filled with hope for better tomorrows.

The group gathered in a circle, hand in hand, and sang Christmas carols as a grand finale. With the notes of "Silent Night" echoing in the large hall, the group reluctantly moved to the exit. A smiling and gentle lady stood by the door, tucking a small but bright red apple into the hand of each person.

"Merry Christmas and God bless!" she beamed to every person.

The Blairs and Dantons relived each moment of the magical afternoon on the short trip home, the children not quite as energetic as on the walk to the center several hours earlier. Also, the pangs of hunger had been chased away by the ample meal, and they felt very comfortable. They would all sleep well tonight.

"This has been the best Christmas ever," Carson declared.

"Yeah!" Stephen and Julie agreed.

"And we got these great gifts too," Stephen explained.

"The gifts are wonderful, Stephen, I agree," Birdie spoke warmly to the child, "but I think the most wondrous gift of all is the gift of new friends."

"Amen." The other adults quickly concurred.

♥♥♥

"Please come in and stay for awhile," Ellen invited their new friends. "It's been so good to share fellowship with someone again. We've been so caught up in our problems that we've forgotten how comforting others can be."

The Dantons exchanged a quick glance.

"Well, for just a little while," they hesitated. "But we know you have to go to work in the morning and we don't want to be a bother."

"Ohhhh, it feels so good and warm in your house," little Julie exclaimed as they entered the Blairs' home. "It's not cold like ours."

"Shush, child," Birdie admonished. "You'll have to excuse her, she's still our baby," she explained with embarrassment.

"Don't you have a stove?" Stephen questioned. "If you do, you can have some of our wood. We got plenty. Some fell off a truck last night when Daddy was coming home."

After an awkward few seconds, Cletus explained that they used their hotplate to heat the room.

Soon the children were playing and the uncomfortable moment was forgotten in the joy of romping, laughing and talking together.

While conversing, it was revealed that Cletus was not working and Robert was certain their situation was probably critical.

"Cletus, I can't promise you anything but would you like to walk down to the docks with me tomorrow to see if there is work available? We lost two men the other day when they left to go home to Kentucky so it's probable there's something you might like to do. That is, if you're interested." Robert felt somewhat uneasy in making the offer, hoping he wasn't intruding in their business or hurting his new friend's pride.

Cletus' face brightened and he straightened his back in grateful anticipation. "Oh, yes, that would be great and I'd be most appreciative. I know you can't make any promises and I won't hold any hard feelings toward you, but I'd be beholden to you for the chance."

Relief also flooded Birdie's face, and the Blairs were touched by their gratitude.

"I leave here by 5:30. It's twenty blocks down there and it gets pretty cold but there's usually a fire in a drum when we get there so we have time to warm up before the work starts. And Josh is a good friend of all the men who go there everyday so he'll treat you fairly. He's the supervisor at the docks and is the one who builds the fire for us each day. If there's any work, he'll see that we all get a chance. Is leaving at 5:30 okay with you?"

"Oh, yeah, that's just fine!" Cletus exclaimed. "I'll be ready, you can count on me."

He turned to Birdie. "We'd best be going, Birdie. We all need our rest so we can get up early in the morning."

"Yes," Ellen agreed, "we've all had a busy day. We've been especially blessed to find such good friends, and just right across the hall! You've been a special Christmas gift to us. And, Birdie, please bring the children over tomorrow to play. Stephen and I get pretty lonely here all day alone."

Birdie hesitated briefly but upon seeing the look of eager anticipation on her children's faces, she relented. All the children danced happily around the room, anxious for the next day to arrive.

No one objected as they were soon tucked into bed, the warmth and joy of this special Christmas comforting them, giving hope for better times to come.

♥♥♥

Robert exited his door a few minutes before 5:30 the next morning, prepared to knock on the door across the hall to retrieve his friend. He was only mildly surprised to find Cletus sitting on the top step of the stairway, waiting for Robert to appear. He jumped to his feet, his face glowing with excitement and anticipation. It touched Robert and he raised a silent prayer that this good man would find work and sustenance for his family.

"Good morning," he beamed as he jumped to his feet. "Good to see you! I'm ready to go." He grasped a small bundle wrapped in newspaper, which Robert recognized as his lunch.

Soon the men were on the street and headed for the docks. Conversation came easily and comfortably between the two, with no self-consciousness or awkwardness, just a mutual acceptance of, and respect for, the other.

The twenty blocks quickly melted away under the footsteps of companionship, and they arrived at the docks, the friendly metal drum blazing and sparking a warm glow of welcome, true to Robert's prediction.

"That was quick!" Cletus seemed to echo Robert's thoughts. "Guess it's because you're such good company."

"Same to you," Robert concurred.

They were the first to arrive but were soon joined by the others. Cletus was the only new one and after introductions, they shared their Christmas experiences and recalled their joys at the good fortune of Jake and Joe. Cletus listened with interest and delight as they shared stories about their two friends in Kentucky. He was struck by the genuine concern and care demonstrated by this group of men. It was testimony to their strong characters that their personal hardships in no way prevented their humanity in assisting their companions. They derived strength and courage from each other rather than becoming caught up in their own personal worlds of tragedy and discomfort. There was no room for self-pity and bitterness among these men.

Bob's cough was worse this morning and the men glanced uneasily his way as he struggled to maintain control and participate in the conversation. He was also having a difficult time standing.

Josh soon arrived, greeting each man individually and warmly welcoming Cletus. They were all soon busy unloading a barge loaded with bags of potatoes, onions and garlic, and the heavy bags helped them stay warm. Within an hour, Bob was coughing so violently, he could not stand upright. Robert hurried to his side and was alarmed to see blood trickling from one corner of his mouth.

"Bob, you need to go home, buddy, and go to bed. You're really sick."

"Nah, I'm okay. Gotta work. We need to eat whether I'm sick or not."

Josh approached the men, likewise concerned about Bob. He had noticed his distress and the others' worry and witnessed the attack which brought blood from Bob's mouth.

"Bob, I'm going to send you home. You're too sick to be here and you need to be home in the bed. We don't have much work today and with Cletus, we have an extra hand so you just go on home and take care of yourself."

He waved away Bob's objections. "No, this isn't an option; we're all worried about you. You just go on home and get some rest. Maybe you'll feel better in the morning and can come on back. Here's your wages for today so you just go on."

He reached into his pocket and pulled out a dollar bill, pressing it into Bob's hand.

"Do you need someone to walk home with you or can you make it on your own?"

"I'll be okay," he muttered, still disappointed that he had to leave. "I only live about two blocks from here. I don't want to take anybody else away from their work."

"I'll walk you home," Robert insisted, "It'll only take a few minutes."

The two moved slowly toward the Julian home, having to stop frequently as Bob was seized over and over by a violent attack of coughing. Robert supported his friend's weight as they climbed the six steps to his building, pushing the door open for Bob to enter ahead of him.

They were soon knocking on the door to his room. A voice behind the door inquired, "Who is it?"

"It's Bob and a friend, Robert Blair, Mrs. Julian. I've brought him home."

The door immediately swung open and a heavy woman reached out for her husband. Her gray hair was pulled back into a bun at the nape of her neck, and her faded dress was clean but much too thin for the coldness. A dark sweater with tattered sleeves and a hole in one elbow covered the thin, worn material.

"Oh, my, oh, my," Mazie Julian cried. "I was so afraid he was too sick to go to work today but he insisted. Please bring him on in and put him on the bed. I thank you so much, Mr. Blair, for bringing him home. It was most kind of you."

There was a weak fire in a fireplace across the room and their son's wheelchair was pulled close to it. Their grandson sat on his father's lap in the chair, snuggled together for warmth. Robert made a mental note to drop off some wood to the family after work today.

"Do you have a doctor, Mrs. Julian?"

"Mercy, no, we don't have no doctor but the Salvation Army helps us out some. I'll run down to their office and see if they have some cough syrup for him. And I'll keep him wrapped up real good. I have some soup too so that'll be mighty good for him."

"I'll stop by after work and bring some wood for you. We have some at the dock and I'm certain they won't mind if I bring a little by here. Is there anything else that I can bring or do before I go back to work?" He was reluctant to leave the small family.

"Oh, no, sir, that's mighty kind of you and we'll certainly appreciate the wood, but there ain't much else anybody can do right now. I'll just go on down to the Salvation Army right away, and I thank you again for your kindness in bringing him home. He's a good man but a bit stubborn. Of course, he's worried to distraction about his family. These are trying times, Mr. Blair, these are trying times."

Robert nodded his agreement as he turned to his friend, touching his arm. "I'll see you later this afternoon, Bob. You rest and do what your wife says."

"Thanks, Robert. I'm much obliged," he gasped as he was seized by another storm of coughing.

Robert slowly left the room, his heart heavy with worry and concern for his friend.

♥♥♥

The day passed quickly as the men labored with the heavy cargo, the heaviness a blessing that warmed them against the December coldness. Soon the work was completed and it was time to leave. Josh paid them each $2.50, which seemed like a fortune, and gave them all bundles of firewood to take home. He gave Robert an extra bundle for Bob.

"Many thanks, Josh, they'll really appreciate it."

He also gave each man potatoes and onions from bags which broke open in the cargo bins. Not wanting to forget Bob, he gave extra ones to Robert for delivery to the Julians. Robert was anxious to leave, not lingering as he normally did, hoping for more work. As he and Cletus left, Cletus offered, "They can have my firewood, Robert, unless you and Ellen need it. I don't have no use for it since we don't have a stove."

"That's very generous, Cletus, and please, just give it to Bob and his family. The Lord blessed us on Christmas Eve with the two bundles that fell off that truck, and with this bundle, we'll be fine for several more days."

Mrs. Julian opened the door to their knock and invited them in, grateful for the gift of firewood.

"How's Bob?" asked Robert.

"Not much better, I'm afraid. The Salvation Army lady gave me some cough syrup. She's a nurse and she's coming by in a little while to check him out. She's going to bring us some food too so we've been blessed this day after all. I think we'll be fine, but please just pray that Bob's gonna be okay. And we appreciate again all your kindness and worry. He has some wonderful friends." She began to weep, overwhelmed and overcome by the emotions of worry, hopelessness, helplessness and fear.

"We brought a few potatoes and onions also. Josh gave them to us at the docks today and wanted to be certain you and your family received some," Robert explained. "We thought maybe Bob might feel better with some of this. My mother always used to call potatoes and onions food that strengthened the body and soothed the soul. She said it was simple fare from God that nourishes all mankind better than any fancy food."

Mazie was extremely grateful for their gift and thanked them profusely.

"No need for thanks, ma'am," Cletus smiled. "It's the least we can do, and we just pray it makes him feel better."

"It'll make us all feel better, sir," she whispered gratefully.

They spoke briefly to Bob as he lay in his bed, and he rallied somewhat at their presence. He thanked them for coming and for their kindness in bringing food and firewood. They both felt inadequate and helpless as they peered down at their stricken friend. Life was hard enough without having a serious illness to make bad matters even worse.

Robert reached out to gently touch the young grandson standing shyly behind his grandmother. He looked to be about five or six, and his eyes bore the same haunted look of poverty as his grandmother's. Robert thought, I wonder if that's how the eyes of my family look.

The child stared glumly at the two, making no attempt to respond to their gestures of kindness.

"We'll pray for you, Buddy," Robert called to Bob.

"Thank you, fellas, thank you so much. I appreciate it. Hope you can accept that until I can do better. I'm gonna try to be at work tomorrow for certain."

They left the room, doubt for his ability to return to work tomorrow heavy on their hearts.

♥♥♥

Robert whistled as they reached the fourth floor of their building, and he heard shouting from within his apartment as Stephen recognized his father's signal. The door burst open and Stephen, Carson and Julie all tumbled out to greet their fathers. Birdie and Ellen stood behind the children, smiling at their enthusiasm.

"Hey, hey, what have we here?" Cletus laughed. "Has my family left me?"

"No, Daddy," his children giggled. "We've been playing over here 'cause it's warmer than our house."

"Well, not for long if we don't all get out of this cold hall," Ellen warned.

Soon both families were snuggled into the small Blair apartment, laughing and talking.

Stephen, Carson and Julie played with the birdhouse. Each had a small bird made of folded newspaper and they would stand them on the roof or the perch on the front. They ran around the room, swooping and gliding their birds, lifting the birdhouse to shake them out after they slipped the birds inside.

As the afternoon waned, the two families decided to have supper together. The potatoes and onions were a treasure, and with the bread, cheese and cake they put together, it felt like a feast. Good company and laughter allowed the evening to speed along, and all too soon, it was time to say good night. The warmth of kindness shared soothed all of them into a deep and restful sleep soon after retiring for the evening. Neither family, however, forgot to mention Bob Julian in their prayers.

♥♥♥

"Do you mind if we stop by to check on Bob on our way to the docks this morning, Cletus?"

"No, no, not at all. I was hoping you'd want to do that. I'm worried to distraction about Bob and his family. You think you have problems 'til you see somebody else. It sorta puts things in their proper order."

"You're right, I'm afraid, Cletus."

♥♥♥

The two men stopped by the Julian apartment, and the door was opened by a stranger. Bob's son sat leaned over in his wheelchair, his face buried in his hands, his shoulders stooped. Mazie was on the sofa, her grandson in her lap and her eyes red and swollen from weeping. She regained her composure somewhat as she recognized the two friends standing there.

"Come in, come in, please," she requested.

"We're so sorry, Mrs. Julian," Robert attempted to comfort her. "We truly are. What happened?"

"God bless you both, you've been so kind. He died right before midnight. His heart just gave out, he had coughed so much. This here is the Salvation Army nurse, Miss Katie Brock. She has been an angel of mercy. She came over last evening right after you two left and was so worried about Bob that she brought a doctor back. The doctor said he had pneumonia and there wasn't nothing he could do for us. He wanted to send Bob to the hospital but we didn't want that. Bob said he wanted to be with us. Miss Brock stayed with us until the end and she got a funeral home to take him away for us." She paused as a new wave of grief overwhelmed her. The two men stood awkwardly by, waiting to listen to her account of their friend's last hours.

"He was able to eat some of those potatoes and onions you brought us yesterday, and he commented about how delicious they were. They was a fitting last meal, and we thank you for it. Wasn't much nobody could do. He was just too sick.

"Miss Brock got here a bit ago. She's tryin' to help us, but I just want to go back home. This city's just too harsh and now it's killed my man. I just want to take him back to my home in Oklahoma. I don't want him buried here."

She broke down into bitter sobs as Robert and Cletus stood helplessly by. Miss Brock hastened to her side, slipping an arm around her shoulders.

"I'm going back down to the center and see what kind of arrangements I can make to help you out, Mazie. Exactly where in Oklahoma are you from?"

"It's a little town called Fellows. Not close to nothing, really. The railroad runs to Oklahoma City which is about fifty miles away. But it's the prettiest, friendliest little town you would ever want to see. Folks care about one another and look out for one another. 'Course, so do Bob's friends at the dock," she was quick to add as her eyes fell on the two men standing there. "But in Fellows, we're all family and that's where I want to be. I want my son to be home with me and we'll raise my grandson. We won't be cold no more and hopefully, we won't be hungry no more."

"We'll do everything we can for you at the center, Mazie. I'll be back directly, I promise. Will you be okay until I get back?"

"Oh, yes ma'am, we'll be fine."

"Is there anything we can do, Mrs. Julian?" Robert inquired.

"No, you two just go on to work. You got families to care for and there ain't nothing that can be done here. Just thank everybody at the docks for all their kindnesses and prayers for Bob. He was real fond of every one of you. Spoke kindly of the men down there quite often and really loved the stories you all shared."

"Yes, and we all greatly enjoyed his story about his dog named Tick. My family was delighted when I shared it with them. He gave us a very special memory to remind us of joy we shared. That's a beautiful legacy for anyone to leave."

♥♥♥

It was a gloomy day for all of them that day. They couldn't think very much about their own problems for grieving over Bob and worrying about his family. Each one spent the majority of the day deep in silent prayer for the small family. They were down to three now, counting Cletus, and they still completed emptying the barge of fertilizer by 1:00. Josh gave them each a stack of wood rescued from the pallets under the fertilizer along with $1.00 for their work that day.

Fred and Josh moved along silently with Robert and Cletus as they all stopped by the Julian apartment on their way home. They felt drawn to it, with the remote hope that there may be something they could do for them.

Mazie let them in and seemed in better spirits than early in the morning. She was still crying but there seemed to be less stoop to her shoulders, and the lines on her face appeared less deep than this morning.

"Thank you, men, for coming by again. This is mighty thoughtful of you.

Miss Brock from the Salvation Army came back this morning and they've made all the arrangements for us. We're going home to Oklahoma! All of us! They're taking Bob on the 8:00 passenger train tonight, and we're going to all get to go along. And we're not coming back! Isn't that wonderful? We'll give Bob a proper Christian burial at our church back home, and then we'll manage somehow. I'm just so happy to have our son and grandson with me and that we're all going back home. I'm just sorry Bob had to die to get it to happen, but he'd be pleased to know that we've been given this chance."

"Do you need any money, ma'am?" Josh asked.

"No, no, we'll be fine, really we will. The Salvation Army is paying for our tickets. It'll take us three days to get there and we'll eat food the Salvation Army gave us for the train. We'll have to sleep in our seats since our tickets don't pay for a sleeper but that'll be just fine. At least we'll be warm on the train. And they've arranged for a car from the funeral home in Fellows to pick us up and carry us home from Oklahoma City. I just want to get my man back home. He was a good man and I'm going to miss him so." Her tears started anew as Robert slipped his arm around her shoulders.

"We're mighty grateful to have known him, ma'am," Fred stated softly. "We'll miss him too."

"Yes," Robert agreed, "he was a good friend and brought us much happiness. A man can do no better in this life than to bring happiness to others."

Chapter 4
The Pact

The next two days sped by as the men worked silently, their minds and thoughts on the loss of their friend, Bob.

Birdie, Carson and Julie spent the days with Ellen and Stephen, and the children thrived under the companionship of their peers. The women shared their chores, and even the laundry was easier when tackled with a friend. Their meager food supply seemed to go further too, as they combined their resources daily.

And Stephen never forgot to thank God for his new friends and blessings when he said his prayers or when the food was shared. The group learned to wait until he had offered his gratitude before they continued with their activities. His confidence and trust in God's strength through their troubles was heartwarming and inspirational to all the others.

"Ah, to have the faith of a child," Birdie whispered after his blessing at the dinner table one night.

The other adults smiled their agreement and the children missed the exchange completely. They accepted Stephen's faith without question or doubt.

♥♥♥

Robert and Cletus walked to the docks, discussing their families and their fears for the uncertainty of the future.

"I guess it serves little purpose to worry about tomorrow," Robert observed, "when we're so uncertain about today. Maybe we should concentrate more on that and let heaven handle everything else for us."

"Yeah, you're right, but it's mighty hard. I guess I'm worrying about things that may never happen, but I can't help but be scared about one of my family, or even me, getting sick. It scares the daylights out of me that if I couldn't work, Birdie and both the kids would be in dire straits for sure. Seeing Bob's illness and the effect on his family really scared me." Cletus was obviously worried.

"Yep, same with me. But we have to have faith that the Lord will not let anything happen to us that we can't handle or work through. I guess all this trouble is part of His great plan for us so we just have to be patient and wait. That's the most difficult part."

They walked on in silence for a few blocks, watching the weak January sun struggle to begin its anemic ascent into the gray, smoke choked skies of the city.

"Let's make a pact, Cletus," Robert declared. "As long as we're all together, we'll look after each other. Any blessing we receive will be shared with the other, and likewise, any trouble we suffer will also be shared. I think that God put our two families across the hall from each other to help one another. I've never believed that people are put together through chance or coincidence. I think we're all led and guided to each other."

"You're right, Robert," Cletus agreed. "And thanks for putting it in such good words. I don't have your gift for putting my thoughts and beliefs in words but I agree with you 100%. And I think that making such a pact is a wonderful idea. I, of course, will do everything that I can should you and your family have a need. However, it seems to be all one-sided at this point in time as your family has already done so much for us. I can't begin to thank you. You found us at the very lowest point in our lives, and I'm not sure where we were headed at that particular time."

"We didn't find you, friend, we were led to you. And don't even say such a thing as our friendship being one-sided. Every gift shared is equally special, whether it be a smile, a crust of bread, a bundle of firewood or a kind word. And you and Birdie and Carson and Julie have brought much joy into our lives. We are so grateful for your presence.

"So, it's settled," he continued. "We have a pact. The Blairs and the Dantons have made a pact of friendship and cooperation to be there for each other, regardless of what trials we may face. And I'm sure our wives won't mind that we've made this pact without consulting them."

They both laughed as they realized they had committed their wives without prior approval, but they were correct in assuming they had the blessings of the women in this endeavor.

♥♥♥

The metal drum burned brightly as they arrived at the docks, and they were soon greeted by Fred. Three other men showed up but stayed only long enough to get warmed up. One explained that he was waiting for a train, or any form of transportation, so that he could hop on and leave the city.

"Where you going?" questioned Cletus.

"Don't know. Don't matter. Just out of town. Can't be no worse anywhere else, I reckon."

They stood silently, neither willing nor able to dispute his words as the three strangers moved away from the group.

After about an hour, Robert glanced around uneasily.

"I wonder where Josh is this morning? Sure hope he's not sick."

"Maybe we'd better go over to the shack and check," Fred offered.

They looked toward the building where Josh had his office. The lights were on so they assumed he was working.

"Maybe he's on the phone," Cletus suggested.

As they became more uneasy and began making moves toward the building, the front door opened and Josh stepped out.

"Here he comes!" Robert couldn't hide the relief in his voice.

Josh moved slowly forward, his eyes avoiding contact with them.

I don't like the looks of this, Robert thought anxiously. *I have a bad feeling all of a sudden. God, give us strength to accept what You have in store for us.*

♥♥♥

Josh reached the three men, reached out and shook each hand, giving them an extra warm greeting. This was very strange behavior, never before performed, so the men waited with dread to hear what their friend had to share with them.

"Fellows, I don't know how to say this except to just come out and say it. The railroad has decided not to come back down to these docks anymore and the shipping company is forced to move the barges to the other side of the island. I'm going over there but it's almost ten miles away so I know that makes it especially hard on you. You will, of course, have a job if you can move over there. I'll see to that. I'm just real sorry, fellows. I was shocked by all this. The owner of the company called me this morning and let me know. We didn't have any warning at all. I'm really sorry. We will pay you $2.00 for today but that's the most we can do right now. Is there anything else I can do for any of you? Do any of you think you can move over there?"

The men stood in stunned silence, struggling to absorb the shock of this news, unable to respond at once.

"Guess I'll just go on back to Oregon," Fred blurted. "Ain't nothing for me here and I got nobody depending on me. I got a sister back in Poplar Bluff, and I'm certain she'll let me stay there for a while. I can help her out too. She's got a couple of kids."

Robert couldn't help but look at Fred. That was the most he had ever learned about the quiet man.

"Well, I can't move my family ten miles, even if we had a place to live," Robert decided. "We have no way to move so we'll just stay where we are. And, please, don't worry, Josh. We just appreciate your generous kindness to all of us. You've been just wonderful and this $2.00 is greatly appreciated. We know you wouldn't have to do anything, and we also know this isn't your fault. No more than it's our fault or anyone else's. That just the way things are right now. God will provide for us just as He always has. This is just another test of our faith."

"Me and my family will stay where we are too," Cletus said as he moved to the side of Robert. "We got no means to move either. I haven't known you very long, Josh, but I'm much obliged to you for all you've done. You're a most kind and generous man. I'm just grateful to have known you and I'll never forget you. You can count on that."

"I guess it's good that Jake and Joe left for Kentucky when they did. Things couldn't be any worse for them there than they would be here and at least they're with family." Josh ran his hand through his hair as he commented on the two friends the others were thinking of. "You fellas did a good thing, sending them home when you did."

Josh watched with a sad heart and troubled mind as the men slowly left the docks for the last time, moving back to their homes and an uncertain future, their $2.00 in their pockets and a bundle of firewood tucked securely under their arms.

♥♥♥

"Well, I reckon it was providential that we made our pact this morning, Robert. But if you want out of it, I certainly understand and will hold no hard feelings toward you."

"What do you mean, want out of it? Of course, I don't! What kind of person would tuck tail and run at the first big problem that comes up? We'll stick together, friend. And together we'll get through it, the good Lord willing."

The men were relieved by each other's declaration, and the loyalty pledged brought comfort to them both.

"I guess Birdie and the kids'll be over at your place but I really need to get to the store for some food while we still have this $2.00. We have enough for next month's rent and I want to get on the streets to look for a job as soon as possible. I'll buy some food and bring it back, and then I'll strike out to look for more work. I might be out late, depending on how far I have to walk, so I'll make certain the family has food before the store closes. Will you be okay for me not to go up with you or should I go so we can both explain what happened?"

"No, you go ahead, I'll tell them. I'll explain to Birdie that you've gone to the store so you can start looking for work as soon as possible. I'm sure she'll understand."

"Did you need to go to the store first?" Cletus asked.

"No, Ellen went yesterday so we're fine. You go ahead and I'll go upstairs and explain it to everyone. I want to go ahead and get out there to beat the pavement too and I'll see you upstairs later."

They arrived at the building and parted ways. Cletus shook Robert's hand warmly.

"Good luck, Robert. I guess we've been in worse spots, although I can't rightly remember when, so I'm certain we'll get through this too. I'll see you back home either later tonight or tomorrow."

"Thanks, Cletus. Good luck to you too. And you're right, we'll get through this." Robert struggled to hide the doubt and fear in his voice as he spoke.

♥♥♥

Ellen and Stephen looked up in surprise as Robert entered the apartment, opening the door without his customary announcement. There had been no whistling on the third floor that day.

Before Ellen could speak, he asked, "Why was the door open?"

"What's wrong?" she asked in alarm, ignoring for the moment his concern for fear that he had been injured or was sick. Her alarm turned to fear and then resignation as he explained why he was home so early.

"Try not to worry, dear," she comforted. "We'll manage somehow. We still have a little money left, and we have enough saved for a couple more months' rent. Maybe I can find a job too."

"No!" Robert retorted, immediately regretting his tone. "I'm sorry, Ellen, I didn't mean to snap, but I don't want you working. You need to be here, taking care of Stephen."

He strode around the room, running his fingers through his hair, scared, confused and angry.

"I've got to go tell Birdie, too. Cletus went to the grocery store before he starts looking for work. I feel like I let them down too. Where are she and the children?" He looked around the room as he realized they were not here.

"She's giving the children a bath. She just left a few minutes ago and that's why the door was unbarred. And don't start blaming yourself," she scolded. "You had no control over what happened, and they certainly know that. It's nobody's fault, Robert. It's the times. At least we're together, and God will provide what we need. We just have to ask Him."

Robert hesitated, his faith shaken, when Stephen ran to his parents.

"Here," he commanded, as he held onto the hand of each parent. "Pray."

The small family joined hands, Robert holding on tightly to the two hands he loved so dearly. He sat there for a few seconds, not knowing how or where to start.

"God," Stephen declared, "my daddy needs to ask a favor. I hope you're home to hear it. Go ahead, Daddy."

He gently squeezed his son's small hand as he began.

"God, thank You for all our blessings and for our health. You know that we're in a real mess right now. There are others who are much worse off than us, but I hope You won't mind if we ask for Your help. I need a job and so does Cletus across the hall. You know our needs better that we do so I give it to You and ask that You guide me in the right direction. Be with Cletus also as he looks this afternoon. If only one of us can find work, I thank You for sending the Danton family to us. I pledge to You that we will look after them should I find a job before Cletus does. Give me the courage and strength and wisdom to face what You have planned for us, and bless my beautiful wife and my loving son and our friends across the hall. Keep them all safe from harm and cold and hunger, I pray. Thy will be done. Amen"

Robert waited to tell Birdie when she and the children knocked on their door, the bathing completed. As soon as he opened the door, Birdie knew. She placed her hand over her mouth, making no sound in front of the children and turned away to regain her composure.

Soon Robert left the two women and the children as he descended the stairs to the street in his quest for work.

♥♥♥

He stepped off the small stoop outside the building, stood on the sidewalk, looked first to the left and then to the right. Which way should he go? Where could he start? As he struggled with his decision, a vehicle moving toward him from around the corner caught his attention. It was the black limousine he had noticed on several occasions. He watched with curious interest as it moved slowly toward him and was surprised to see it pull over and park at the curb where he stood. He stepped back to get out of the way as the driver's door opened, and a tall, dignified looking man in a black coat and chauffeur's hat exited the car into the street. He moved around the front of the vehicle, passed Robert, tipping his hat and nodding his head as he passed, and opened the back door. He reached inside and assisted a small woman out of the back seat.

She supported herself with a cane but moved with assurance, confidence and strength of determination as she approached him. He moved back further, his curiosity increasing as he realized that she was not only coming toward him, but was making eye contact. He felt somewhat anxious and uneasy because she obviously intended to speak to him, and she appeared to be a refined lady of means. He pulled his hat from his head, holding it at his waist.

"Young man," she summoned, "my name is Molly Fulton. I'm looking for some help at my home. Are you interested?"

"What? Well, uh… yes, ma'am," he stuttered, unprepared for her directness as well as her request. It had literally fallen into his lap out of the blue. This was probably just a one-day opportunity, but he was indeed grateful just the same.

"What's your name?"

"Robert Blair, ma'am."

"Well, Robert Blair, I need help in my yard and garden. Just mowing and trimming and weeding when spring arrives, but I need someone now who can do minor repair work – fix a fence, build some steps, pick up limbs and branches, that sort of thing. Are you interested?"

Robert felt flustered and confused. This job had literally fallen out of the sky, and he had never turned down work, but he was also an honest man with great integrity. He just wasn't sure he could handle this type of work. He knew almost nothing about plants, and even though he could operate a saw and hammer, he was no professional.

"Miss Fulton," he stammered, "I'm very interested but I won't lie to you. I know very little about gardening but I can certainly mow when the spring comes. I can drive a nail and use a saw but I'm no great carpenter. I'll work hard," he quickly continued, fearful that she would withdraw her offer, "and will be there everyday, but I don't know if you'd be satisfied with what I do."

"I appreciate your candor, Robert, and I don't need a great carpenter," she assured him. "I'll give you a chance, and if it doesn't work out, we'll know it. This is my chauffeur Walter Monroe. He'll pick you up tomorrow morning at 7:00. Is that too early?"

"Oh, no, ma'am, that'll be just fine. And I appreciate it so much." He was still in shock over the events that had transpired over the past few minutes and thought maybe he might be dreaming.

"I'll pay you $3.00 a day. Is that satisfactory?"

Robert was certain his mouth flew open.

"Oh, yes, ma'am, that's most satisfactory!"

"Good, it's settled then, and we're glad to have you. Now we'll take you home so Walter will know where to pick you up."

"No need, Miss Fulton, I live right here in this building. Up on the fourth floor. And I'll be out here in the morning at 7:00. Thank you once again for your kindness."

As she turned to enter the car, he asked, "Ma'am, do you mind if I ask you a question?"

She looked at him and nodded slightly.

"Why me?"

"Walter has been driving around the city looking for somebody who looked trustworthy. He's seen you down at the docks, and he said you stay long after everybody else leaves. He's also seen you there early in the mornings when nobody else has arrived, and he's seen you walking on this block, so we felt that you probably lived in this area. We took a chance on finding you here today. I need somebody who is reliable and hardworking and will give me an honest day's work for the pay."

"Oh, I will that, ma'am, I assure you," he eagerly stated. Now he understood why he had seen the limousine in the area several times.

"Good." She smiled, turned and entered the car. Walter closed the door, tipped his hat to Robert and winked.

"I'll see you in the morning, Robert."

♥♥♥

He stood in disbelief as the long, black limousine disappeared around the corner and down the street. He was trembling, reluctant and almost afraid to trust what had just happened. He finally regained his composure, turned and went back inside the building. He started up the stairs, his excitement mounting as he approached each floor. By the time he reached the fourth floor, he was bounding up the steps, two at a time. He tried to whistle but his lips were too dry, his lungs and heart pumping too fast with the fervor of this miracle which had been bestowed upon them.

He tapped on the door excitedly, calling eagerly to Ellen and Stephen. They quickly opened the door, alarmed by his sudden return. He swept into the room, picking Stephen up and throwing him high over his head, laughing and twirling around the room, his laughter echoing off the walls.

Stephen and Ellen were confused but laughed along with him, his contagious joy taking control of them. They had no idea what was happening, but Robert was obviously happy and that was enough for them.

"I have a job!" he finally managed to gasp. "I have a job!"

♥♥♥

"Praise God!" Ellen beamed and Stephen grabbed his father's leg, shouting with glee. After a few hysterical minutes, they managed to settle down so that Robert could explain what had just occurred on the street below.

Birdie and her children stood silently, smiling kindly but not wanting to impose on the family's triumph. She herded the children silently and moved toward the door so as to allow the Blairs to share their good fortune in private.

"Hey, where you going?" shouted Robert as he realized they were moving toward the door.

"We'll go home so you can have some time alone," Birdie explained, "and congratulations, Robert. I couldn't be happier." He could tell she was sincere.

"Come on back here, Birdie. You and the kids. I want to explain something to you. Cletus and I made a pact that we'd stick together and help each other out, and this morning before I left to look for work, I made a promise to God that if I found work before Cletus, we'd take care of your family until you can get on your feet. And less than ten minutes later, I had a job! Now don't tell me that wasn't divine intervention. I asked that His will be done and so it has been. And you can rest assured that you and your family will be taken care of just as He has blessed us."

She smiled warmly through her tears of gratitude as she moved to embrace Robert and Ellen and Stephen.

"I don't know what to say," she whispered hoarsely, "you are the kindest people I've ever known."

As they stood there rejoicing in their good fortune, the door flew open and Cletus rushed in.

"I found a job!" he beamed.

Gail Cauble Gurley

PART II

HOPE

Gail Cauble Gurley

Chapter 5
A New Beginning

Cletus explained that he was paying for his groceries and talking to Mr. Schmidt, the storeowner. Mrs. Schmidt wasn't there as she had gone upstairs to their apartment, unable to work due to her rheumatism.

"Mr. Schmidt mentioned that he didn't know what he was going to do because his wife just isn't able to work anymore and moving the heavy boxes of canned goods around is getting hard for him too. He said he guessed he was going to have to try and find some kind of help, but it was going to be hard because he couldn't pay much.

"I couldn't believe my ears. I told him, 'Mr. Schmidt, I don't have a job right now, and I'd be proud to work for you.' He looked at me kind of stunned like and then he laughed.

"'Well, I'll be dogged,' he said. And then he explained that he couldn't pay me much but I could have all the damaged and outdated merchandise, and he guaranteed we won't go hungry. I explained about our rent and he assured me I'd make $2.50 a week and with his giving us food, we should be just fine."

"I know that when God closes a door, He opens a window, but this time He opened all the windows plus the doors and even rolled the roof back!" Robert observed happily.

♥♥♥

Robert waited eagerly the next morning for Walter to appear. He stood just inside the hall out of the cold and watched anxiously down the street. A few minutes before 7:00, the long, black limousine pulled up in front of the building, right on schedule. Robert ran outside as Walter stepped out of the car.

"Sit in front with me, if you don't mind."

Robert hesitated briefly as he felt unworthy to sit in the front seat of such a magnificent vehicle. "Are you sure?" he asked meekly.

Walter opened the passenger door and motioned for Robert to enter.

They talked pleasantly as they traveled the streets out of the city. It was very warm and cozy, and Robert struggled to stay awake. He certainly didn't want to fall asleep, especially on his first day!

The sun slipped over the edge of the sky, appearing to rise from the bay waters. The sky and water were splashed with deep crimsons and rich golds, as it began its daily journey around the world.

"Looks like we may have some weather soon," Walter remarked.

Robert gazed curiously at the sky, unmarked by clouds, and wondered at Walter's comments.

"Let's see if I can remember. 'Red skies in the morning, Sailor take warning; Red skies at night, Sailor's delight'." Walter looked thoughtful as he recalled the adage.

"Oh, I think I remember that but it's been a long time ago. I had forgotten."

"Well, actually, it may be the other way around. Maybe I got it backwards."

They chatted pleasantly for a while, and Robert began to notice that they were moving further and further away from the city. He became somewhat uneasy, as he had no idea the job was so far away. This could present a problem since he had no transportation, and surely, Walter wouldn't be expected to be his taxi everyday.

His uneasiness increased as 8:00 approached. He shifted nervously in his seat and cleared his throat.

"It's a pretty good distance out here, isn't it, Walter?"

"Yes, but it's quite lovely and peaceful. You're going to like it, I'm certain. We'll be there shortly." Walter missed the concern in Robert's voice.

At 8:10, Walter pulled up to a large iron gate attached to a stone wall nearly eight feet high. He walked to the gate, unlocked it and pushed it open. He reversed his actions after entering onto a paved drive, and they proceeded through a wooded area. Robert watched as they drove along, not certain where they were, but enjoying the beauty and serenity of it.

They traveled for approximately a half mile when he spotted a large, gray stone house rising in the early morning frost. Wisps of Christmas snow clung to the dormers and roof tiles, and small mounds of it remained along the driveway, testimony to vigorous shoveling and scraping to clear the drive. Robert gasped at the majesty.

"It is rather impressive, isn't it?" Walter laughed. "Now you can see why Miss Molly needs help."

"I hope I haven't bitten off more than I can chew," Robert commented without complaint. "But I'll sure try, and you can rest assured I'll work every minute. I don't want to disappoint Miss Fulton."

"I doubt that'll happen," Walter smiled, glancing over at his passenger. "Besides, we're going to try and get more help from the village in the spring. It's just a couple miles further up the road from where we turned off into the driveway, but there aren't many people left there anymore. We were lucky to find someone to shovel the drive when it snowed at Christmas. Most everyone has left because of the bad times and gone to the city to find work. About all that's left are the retirees who are too weak to work anymore. And there are a few families left with small children, but the men have left the area, looking for work. We're very glad to have found you, Robert. Trust me. Just relax and try to enjoy yourself.

"It's a beautiful estate even though it's getting a little ragged around some of the edges. We haven't found anybody to work it for nearly two years, since times got so hard. I do what I can but Miss Molly needs me to help her with the business of running the house and her company, Fulton Engine. She has a housekeeper, Miss Sophie, but she's having really bad health problems, as is her husband in the village, and we're not certain how much longer she'll be able to work. She's been here since before I was born so she's like family to Miss Molly. Of course, Miss Molly treats all her staff like family. She's a very kind lady. A bit feisty but good as gold and very fair."

♥♥♥

They entered the house and Robert peered around shyly as his eyes grew accustomed to the darkness of the interior. The foyer was two stories high, reaching to the roof, and the floor was Italian marble. A large rotunda on the ceiling was filled with an elegant stained glass window, depicting cherubs and doves in settings of the four seasons. A massive staircase ascended to the second floor, rich mahogany handrails gleaming brightly, and opulent carpeting covering the center of the generously wide marble steps.

Walter slipped two heavy mahogany pocket doors into the walls and invited Robert inside to wait for Miss Fulton. His eyes moved slowly around the room, which was obviously a library. Tall bookcases heavy with leather bound books lined the end and one side of the room. Three tall windows reached from floor to nearly the ceiling and were covered by rich, velvet curtains in a royal blue with gold tassels. A fireplace at the far end of the room was likewise surrounded by high bookcases. A fire popped and crackled invitingly, and Robert moved toward it. He noticed that coal was used as fuel, and a large bucket of it set on the hearth, ready to feed the hungry flames as they diminished.

The space was furnished with elegant Victorian furniture. A sofa with hand carved arms and legs and burgundy velvet fabric faced the fireplace. Two wing back chairs covered by exotic gold damask flanked the sofa. Ornate, delicately carved tables were set in various areas around the furniture. A massive desk filled the end of the room opposite the fireplace. A large Oriental rug graced the rich wide floorboards. Expensive wood paneling embraced the walls where huge portraits of men and women, presumably Fulton ancestors, were displayed. Most of them were unsmiling and somber. One particularly austere gentleman, looking quite menacing, glared down from the far corner behind the impressive desk. Robert instinctively shuddered and immediately scolded himself for his callousness.

He was reluctant to sit in any of the expensive furniture. He had never encountered such wealth and beauty, and he was uncertain of exactly how to behave. He didn't want to damage anything.

The door from the foyer slid open and Walter stuck his head in. "Come on down to the kitchen, Robert. Miss Molly wants to speak to you there before you start work."

He soon found himself in a warm and cheerful kitchen lined with ample cabinets and various appliances. A large island in the center of the room was surrounded by barstools. A large elderly woman sat in one, a bowl of potatoes in front of her. She looked up from her work of peeling just long enough to nod slightly at Robert.

"This is Miss Sophie," Walter introduced her.

Molly Fulton sat in a rocking chair by the fireplace, and she stood, smiling warmly in greeting her new employee. "Good morning, Robert. I trust you had a nice drive up this morning."

"Yes, ma'am, it was very pleasant, thanks to Walter's gracious kindness. It was a bit long, however."

She made no response to his remark and offered him a chair in front of her rocker.

He expected her to give him his duties for the day. He was anxious to get started. He felt that most of the morning was already lost; it had taken so long to get here. Also, he was most concerned about the long distance from here to the city.

"Tell me about your family, Robert," Miss Molly settled back in her chair, seemingly ready for a friendly chat that Robert was unwilling to share at this particular time.

He was somewhat shocked and impatient, and before he could stop himself, he blurted out, "I beg your pardon, Miss Molly, and thank you for asking, but I am most anxious to get to work. It was a long ride here and I know you have much to be done so I want to get started right away. I'm a bit concerned about this being so far away from the city and Walter having to pick me up in the mornings and take me back at night. That's a big burden so I want to get started right away. You're most kind and I need the work, so by your leave, I'll get started if you tell me where to start."

She tilted her head back, laughing heartily at his assertiveness.

"Walter, please get Mr. Blair started on his day's work. We don't want to discourage this kind of enthusiasm." She was still chuckling as the two left the room.

♥♥♥

Robert was soon dragging fallen limbs off the grounds of the estate to the back, into a large pit created for just this purpose. He looked at the trees as he lifted and dragged the limbs, noting that many of the trees would need pruning soon. Some of the limbs were hanging much too low and smaller branches were robbing the trees of their shape. He knew very little about it but felt certain if he were conservative, he would do no damage to the trees.

"When you get a few more limbs in the pit, just set it on fire," Walter instructed. He was struck by the look of shock and surprise in Robert's eyes but was uncertain about the reason for his reaction.

"Is there something wrong?" he inquired.

"Uh, no, that's fine." He was in disbelief regarding the waste of burning this ample supply of fuel but was embarrassed to make any comment.

The waning morning quickly passed as Robert worked diligently. In what seemed like a few minutes, Walter appeared, calling him to lunch.

Robert, reluctant to stop work, replied, "Oh, that's okay. I had breakfast this morning and Ellen packed me a sandwich so I'll just eat it as I work. I want to get as much of this done today as I can."

"Nonsense," Walter retorted, "come on in and have some hot soup. Miss Molly insists on feeding her staff, and besides, you need to rest. You've been struggling like a horse. You have until 4:00 before I take you back to the city."

"4:00?" Robert exclaimed in disbelief. "I won't even be started good by then!"

"You don't have to get it all done in one day. I'll pick you up in the morning and you can get back at it."

Robert reluctantly left his work and was soon chatting warmly with Miss Molly. She was a delightful lady, very easy to talk to and obviously interested in the welfare of her employees. She was particularly interested in hearing about Ellen and Stephen.

However, as soon as Robert finished his ample lunch of potato soup and the sandwich Ellen had packed him, he excused himself to return to work.

♥♥♥

It was dark by the time the two men arrived back in the city. Robert's uneasiness increased as the sun set. He just couldn't see Walter continuing to make that long drive twice a day just so Robert could perform approximately six hours of work.

Walter handed him an envelope as they arrived at their destination.

"This is your pay for today, Robert. Miss Fulton pays her staff daily that don't live on the premises. I'll see you in the morning at 7:00. Have a good night."

"Thank you, Walter, I'll be ready. Good night to you too. And be careful driving back."

As Walter drove away, he noticed Robert picking up scraps of cardboard lying near the curb. He was curious as to what he would do with it when it suddenly dawned on him. It was for burning. He remembered the look in Robert's eyes as he instructed him to burn the limbs in the pit.

Of course, he thought, *how thoughtless of me! We should have brought some of the wood he picked up today. Why didn't he say something?*

He knew the answer to that question as soon as it crossed his mind. Robert did, after all, have pride and dignity. Walter made a mental note to load some wood into the trunk of the limousine tomorrow morning before returning to the city.

The Blair home was filled that evening with excited descriptions of the Fulton estate and all the work that needed to be done, as well as Cletus' day at the food market.

Robert tossed restlessly for most of the night, fearful that Walter wouldn't be there in the morning. Perhaps that was why he was paid. The $3.00 was much appreciated and seemed like a small fortune for just a few hours work, but it wouldn't go far if he only had one day's work.

♥♥♥

But Walter did return the next day, promptly at 7:00. Robert released a deep breath for what felt like the first time since arriving home last night. As he ran down the steps to the car, Walter moved to the trunk and opened it. Robert stopped in curiosity as he took a bundle wrapped in canvas out of the back of the car.

"Take this upstairs to your family before we leave," he directed as he handed the bundle to the surprised Robert. "Bring the canvas back and we'll load it up again tonight before leaving Miss Fulton's."

Robert stared speechlessly at this benevolent and perceptive gentleman. His gratitude and emotions showed on his face as he turned to hurry upstairs with the firewood.

♥♥♥

The sunrise that day was even more colorful than the day before.

"Wow," breathed Robert, "it's spectacular! If that sailor's adage is correct, we're in for a super storm."

"Yes, it really is quite breathtaking, isn't it?" Walter agreed. "No matter how hard man tries, we can never create anything even remotely as lovely as just one of God's sunrises or sunsets. Kind of puts us in our places, doesn't it?"

♥♥♥

The day sped by, and Robert finished carrying all of the fallen branches and limbs into the backyard near the burning pit, but he didn't get them all cut up. He loaded up a tidy bundle of the small pieces into the canvas for transport back to the city as Walter had directed him earlier. He was certain neither Miss Fulton nor Walter could comprehend how much they were doing for his family.

♥♥♥

As the two men traveled from the city to the country on the third day of Robert's new career, the heavens were heavy with thick, gray clouds. They seemed to be sinking closer to the earth as they traveled, their weight too much for the skies to hold. Robert peered anxiously into the sky.

"Looks like we might get some of that weather the sunrises have been promising," he remarked, trying unsuccessfully to hide his concern.

"Yes, I think you're right. But don't worry. If it starts snowing, I'll bring you back home right away. I know you don't want your family being alone. And get some extra wood before we leave. If it snows, the pit will be covered and it'll be difficult to get it out."

Robert worked even faster than usual throughout the morning. There was an urgency in the air as the skies grew grayer and the clouds became heavier, laden with moisture. Both men knew it would probably be moisture in the form of snow.

Sure enough, it began to lightly snow around 2:00 so Walter immediately called Robert inside in preparation for their return to the city. The massive bundle of firewood was loaded into the trunk, extra coal was brought to the fireplaces in Miss Molly's bedroom, the bathroom and the kitchen since Walter may be gone longer than normal and wouldn't be there to feed the huge furnace in the basement, and Miss Molly cautioned them to take care as they left.

The nearer they got to the city, the faster and thicker the snow fell. The firewood in the trunk became a boon, keeping them from sliding off the roads into the ditches.

What'll I do if Walter can't get out of the city? Robert agonized. *I can't expect him to stay with us. But I can't let him sleep in the car either. He'll freeze to death. Lord, what'll I do?*

By the time they arrived in the city, the snow was to the bottom of the front bumper. Both men knew there was no way that Walter could get back to the country in this blizzard, especially after taking the wood out of the trunk. Walter made the decision Robert was dreading before any words or offers escaped Robert's lips.

"Looks like you're going to have company tonight, Robert. I hope your wife doesn't mind uninvited guests."

"Oh, no, not at all." Robert hesitated only briefly. "We'll be honored and proud to have you, but I must warn you that it's not much. Certainly not what you're used to. Of course, it beats being out in the cold."

Walter recognized that his friend was embarrassed and apologizing for his home. He was touched but wisely made no comment. No matter how bad it was, he was determined not to further embarrass Robert or his family. He would graciously accept their hospitality in the spirit in which it was given. He felt certain that the Blairs would give the very best that they had to everyone, no matter how little that was.

"I need to stop somewhere and call Miss Molly so she doesn't worry. Is there a phone somewhere close?"

"Yes, down at the market where we get our groceries. Cletus, our neighbor and friend, works there so I'm certain it'll be okay to use it."

"Good, I'll pick up some groceries too. We might be stuck for a couple of days."

♥♥♥

Robert explained to Cletus what was happening as Walter spoke to Miss Fulton on the phone. Walter began gathering up groceries quickly as they prepared to leave. The stack of wares accumulating on the counter amazed the two friends. There was a whole ham, a large bag of potatoes, onions, two dozen eggs, three pounds of sliced bacon from the meat counter, a pound of real coffee, butter, milk, cabbage, carrots, cheese, three loaves of bread, a pack of rolls and enough pork chops to feed half the block! In addition, he placed two large bags of coal at the counter along with a fresh pound cake, ice cream and chocolate sauce.

"Can you think of anything else we might need, Robert?"

"No, sir, I think you've pretty well covered everything. There might not be room for all of us in the apartment with all this food!"

"How about candles? Do you have candles? The power may go off."

"No, we don't."

Soon the bill was added up and it came to $12.74. Robert and Cletus were stunned. Robert attempted to give money to Walter, but he refused. They had never
known anyone to spend that much at one time at the grocery store. Even in the good days.

Walter paid for the groceries and they struggled to get them to the car. Mr. Schmidt came downstairs as they were leaving.

"We'd better close up early, Cletus. You go on home before it gets any worse. If anybody needs anything and can get here, I'll hear them knocking and can come down. Do you need to take anything else with you?"

"No, sir, thank you very much. I have a bag already so we'll be fine." He didn't mention in front of Walter that it was discards and nearly spoiled food that filled his bag. He, too, had his pride.

"Come on and get in the car with us, Cletus," Walter offered. "We may all have to push if we don't soon get started."

♥♥♥

Robert agonized for the few blocks to the apartment building. He couldn't help but be anxious about the situation in which Walter was walking. Their flat was clean (or as clean as it could be made given its condition) but to say it was humble was an understatement. Actually, it was uninhabitable if the truth be told, but it was somewhat better than the night shelter and considerably more positive than living on the street. He attempted to comfort himself with that logic as they stopped in front. Walter was, after all, a fair and kind man who seemed non-judgmental and unpretentious, so, hopefully, he would have compassion for the plight of the family. Surely he wouldn't be afraid to stay with them! His anxiety and nervousness increased as *that* thought entered his mind!

Robert ran ahead to forewarn Ellen while Walter and Cletus unloaded some of the groceries. He rushed to their door without his customary whistling from the third floor, alarming both his family and the Dantons, as he knocked hurriedly.

"What's wrong?" Ellen asked with alarm as she opened the door.

"I'm sorry, Ellen, but we have a guest. Walter can't get back to the country tonight and must stay with us. I know it's a terrible imposition to drop this on you but I really had no choice. He's been so good to me and we can't expect him to sleep in his car." Robert threw out his hands in a gesture of helpless resignation.

Ellen smiled warmly at her husband, understanding immediately his concern. He was incredibly sensitive to the fact that he was unable to provide adequately for his family, even though he knew logically that there was nothing else which would improve their circumstances. Common sense and logic also assured him that their lot was not unique, and they were, in many ways, among the more fortunate within their society. They did, after all, have a roof, such as it was, over their heads, he had a job, they were together, and they had their health.

"It's fine, Robert," she soothed her husband gently. "We're proud to have him, and we'll make him as comfortable as possible. And how like you to be so kind as to invite him in out of the cold!"

He loved her so.

Soon all the groceries, Walter and Cletus were safely inside. Walter was grateful that everyone was concentrating on the bags of food and coal as they entered so that the look of shock he was certain crossed his face was not detected. He quickly regained his composure, determined not to betray his distress and concern for the adversity these young families were enduring.

Robert introduced Walter to the adults and then the children. Ellen reached out both her hands, warmly welcoming him into their home. The children gathered around eagerly, happy and glad to meet this wonderful man who brought in so much bounty.

"Welcome to our home, Walter, and we are *so* proud to have you here! Robert speaks so highly of you and this is indeed an honor." Ellen greeted him graciously.

Any misgivings he had upon entry into the squalor of their surroundings disappeared in the presence of this elegant lady. He was among friends.

Soon the small fire was blazing merrily, voraciously consuming the gift of coal, and the women quickly prepared what promised to be a banquet. They combined a portion of the food which Walter had presented with some that Cletus had provided. They were soon dining on fresh salad, delicious pork chops, creamed potatoes with real butter, steamed cabbage, hot rolls, coffee and cold, sweet milk for the children. The pound cake with vanilla ice cream and chocolate sauce provided a welcomed dessert.

After the huge meal, the families were completely satisfied, and lay on the floor around the stove, basking in the discomfort of overeating.

"Now I know how a hog feels," observed Cletus.

"Cletus!" Birdie glanced at Walter, blushing as she did, embarrassed by Cletus' crude analogy.

Walter laughed loudly, putting Birdie at ease. "Yep, so do I, Cletus. So do I. Ladies, that was indeed a magnificent meal. My compliments to both of you. You're certainly excellent cooks."

The children dozed as the women cleaned up the dishes and the men discussed current events.

"I don't reckon we can solve the world's problems here tonight, gents," Cletus observed, "but I want to thank you for your fellowship, the warm fire and the great food. I s'pose things could be a might worse than they are, 'specially since all our blessings after the holidays. Robert, you and Ellen and little Stephen have certainly been a blessing to me and my family, and I feel twice blessed to now count Walter as yet another friend. And my new job! My cup runneth over for sure."

They all basked in the added warmth of companionship and gratitude for several minutes.

"We really need to get over to our place, Birdie." Cletus broke the spell. "Everyone is tired and we need to get the hot plate fired up. We can't thank you folks enough for this great night."

"Be here in the morning for breakfast." Robert invited. "That hot plate can't be very warm."

"Oh, we're fine, really, we are," Birdie assured him, "but we are most thankful for the invitation."

"Be here at 7:00. We'll be up," Ellen insisted.

"Walter, you sleep on our bed and we'll stay here in the front room and take care of the fire," Robert said.

"No, no, I won't hear of taking your bed and putting you on the hard floor."

"Well, we don't want you on the hard floor either."

They all looked at each other for a moment, not sure how to solve this problem.

Suddenly Walter's face lit up. "I know!" he exclaimed. "The car has a huge back seat which comes out quite easily and the trunk is filled with warm blankets. Miss Molly has never trusted a motor coach (that's what she calls it) and insists on having plenty of cover stowed away in case there's a breakdown 'in the middle of Egypt', as she says." He chuckled as he thought of his employer.

In a few minutes, the large back seat was tucked in cozily beside Stephen's cot and blankets were distributed.

"Take these four over to the Dantons if you don't mind, Robert. We don't need all of these with the warm fire."

Fearless Heart

Robert leaped to comply with the generous request, and soon both families were fast asleep, warm and well fed for the first time since Christmas.

Gail Cauble Gurley

Chapter 6
Snowed In

Breakfast was particularly delicious the next morning. The lights flickered several times during their meal, so after a brief discussion, it was decided that everyone should take a bath and the laundry should be done just in case the power went off.

"I'm going down to the store and pick up a few more groceries and call Miss Molly to let her know the situation here. There's no way we can get back to the country today and probably not tomorrow either. She'll worry if I don't keep her advised."

"I'll go with you." Cletus offered. "Mr. Schmidt may not have the store open and there's no need to bother him by knocking on the door. I'll just unlock and let us in and I'll run upstairs to let him know we're there."

"Here, take some money." Robert moved toward their savings.

"No, your money is no good, Robert. The least I can do to repay you for your hospitality is buy the food. Besides, Miss Molly would be outdone with me if I did anything less. We'll be back as soon as possible. It'll take a while since we're walking so don't worry."

♥♥♥

The women and children went down to the bath after they left. Robert waited by the fire, his thoughts on their current situation. He was worried about not being able to work. His insecurity regarding the welfare of his family prevented any ability to relax. It seemed that his days were one long anxiety filled study in fear, and struggling with his enemy, Time, was becoming increasingly bitter. He wanted his family safe and secure now.

The children rushed back into the room, scurrying to the heater, shivering and dancing up and down. He hurried to them, drying their hair with fresh towels and slipping warm shirts over their still damp bodies. He brushed their hair, fluffing it through his fingers over the stove so as to dry it more quickly. Soon they were settled on the floor on one of Walter's wonderful wool blankets, playing with marbles and jacks and crayons.

The women soon returned, echoing the shivers and exclamations of their children after crossing from the bath down the long, cold hall. They huddled around the heater, drying their hair. Small sputters erupted as droplets of water struck the hot surface of the heater.

Robert went to the bath, dreading what he was certain would be, at best, a lukewarm shower. The hot water heater wasn't topnotch and much water had been pulled out of it over the past hour. Sure enough, his concerns were confirmed, and soon he too stood over the heater, lips blue, shoulders trembling, drying his hair. He hoped the water heater would have recovered sufficiently by the time Walter and Cletus returned so as to allow them a comfortable shower.

The two returned about an hour later, finding the children playing on the floor, and the women and Robert busily doing laundry. They entered with two more bags of coal which were deposited in the corner near the stove with the remaining coal purchased the day before. The three bags of groceries were handed to the women. Walter was touched by the response from the families to these goods. He felt like Santa Claus.

Walter and Cletus found the water in the bath to be almost comfortable by that time. Walter, however, was deeply distressed by the fact that these good people were forced to endure such primitive conditions. He suddenly found himself angry with the landlord, a man he did not even know. Surely he could provide better services than what Walter observed. He held his tongue, not wanting to further the stress and anxiety the Blairs and Dantons were suffering. Instead, he decided to do something constructive and began assisting the others with the laundry. Soon the room was crisscrossed with clean clothes, the air moistened by rising steam and perfumed by the smell of soap. The adults proudly stepped back, observing the fruits of their labor and basking in the sense of accomplishment it gave them.

"Well," Birdie remarked, "I guess cleanliness really is next to godliness. It sure smells good anyway."

The children were getting restless so Birdie and Cletus bundled all three of them up to take them downstairs for awhile. It was agreed that the snow was too deep to venture across the streets to the park but they could build a snowman on the sidewalk.

The Blairs decided not to join their friends as Ellen wanted to keep an eye on the clothes and take down the dry ones so as to hang more wet ones. Also, there was the ever-present fear of fire so they would not leave the room unoccupied as long as there were any clothes hanging up.

After a noisy descent down the stairs by the Dantons and the children, Robert, Ellen and Walter settled down for conversation.

♥♥♥

"Where are you from, Walter?" inquired Robert.

"I'm from Issaqua Harbor, the village near Miss Fulton's estate. I don't know why they call it Harbor as so far as anyone has ever been able to determine, there's never been a harbor there. It's an Indian name and it just stuck. They may have had a harbor at one time but when the white man settled it, there was no sign of one. That's one of those details which will probably forever be lost to history."

They settled back to listen to what they perceived to be an interesting and fascinating story from their friend Walter.

"My parents worked for Mr. Fulton, Miss Molly's father, from the time my father was fourteen years old. When he married my mother four years later, she went to work in the kitchen, and they lived in the small cottage behind the big house. That's the place I was born, in that small cottage. I still call it home but I live in the big house now so I can be close to Miss Fulton in case she needs anything. The cottage is in disrepair anyway but we're hoping Robert can help get that fixed this summer." He glanced over at Robert as he spoke. "Of course, you'll have to have some help but we'll go into the village and find somebody as soon as spring arrives.

"Anyway, after I was born, my mama would take me to the big house with her and place me in a cradle there in the kitchen. I literally grew up on the hearth of that kitchen. Mr. Fulton was a hard and bitter man, and Miss Molly wasn't allowed to be with him and his wife at mealtime so she took her meals with us. She was a strikingly beautiful young woman and was very kind to me and my mama. I can remember her playing hide and seek and peek-a-boo with me in the pantry. She taught me to count and say my ABCs and saw to it that I got to school in the village when I was old enough. She's a fine lady."

"Why wouldn't her father let her eat with them?" Ellen wondered.

Walter made no direct response to her inquiry and continued his story.

"She wasn't allowed to any of the big dinners they gave for their friends and stayed in the kitchen with us. People would ask about her but Mr. Fulton would just glare at them and make no response. They finally stopped asking and then stopped coming to the parties all together.

"Mr. Fulton had all his money in the stock market. He had most of it in his business and made a great deal of money. I can remember hearing Mrs. Fulton pleading with him one time to take their money out of the stock market but he refused. Shortly after that, Mr. Fulton had a bad stroke and wasn't able to talk or walk anymore. Mrs. Fulton allowed Miss Molly into his room one night to try and make peace between them.

"Mama was in the room and she said Miss Molly was on her knees by his bed, holding his hand and crying. She said, 'I love you, Papa. Please...' But he just turned away. Miss Molly left the room, still crying. Later that night, Mr. Fulton died. He died alone as my mother had gone downstairs to get him some fresh water, and while she was gone, he died."

"Oh, how sad," whispered Ellen.

"Yes, he was a most stubborn man. Well, after he died, Mrs. Fulton sold all of his stocks. His attorney came in and we could hear him shouting from all over the house about how she didn't have the right to sell his stock. But she stood her ground. I guess she had had so many years of difficulty in dealing with Mr. Fulton that an attorney who had no legal hold on her wasn't going to scare her off.

"She put the money in several banks in New York City. I can remember riding in the car with her and my father while he drove her to the city once a month to conduct her business at the banks. She wanted Miss Molly to take dinner with her in the dining room after that, but Miss Molly liked being in the kitchen so Mrs. Fulton began taking her meals in the kitchen with us too. We all had a grand time!

"After supper, Miss Molly would help me with my homework, and Mrs. Fulton would sit by the fire, talking to my mother or embroidering. My mother taught them both to crochet and Mrs. Fulton loved to do that. There are still some lace doilies in the house that she made. She took to it really well.

"When I was sixteen, Mrs. Fulton died and Miss Molly got the estate. Right after, she and my father drove into the city and came back hours later with several big bags of money. Miss Molly had closed all the bank accounts and put everything in a large safe in the house. She didn't trust banks and she didn't trust the stock market. Seems like she did a wise thing since both have since failed and she would have lost everything.

"I can remember another attorney coming here to talk to her after her mother died. We didn't hear him shouting but when he came out of the library, his face was white as a sheet and his lips were drawn tightly together in a straight line. We could tell he was angry. I guess it was a bitter pill for these men of power to have to concede to a female. I'm certain if there had been anyway to do it, Mrs. Fulton and Miss Molly would probably have both been committed to mental institutions."

They sat there, digesting what Walter had said, chilled by the truth in his words concerning the danger generated by the independence and self reliance demonstrated by these two strong ladies.

"After my parents died," Walter continued, "I stayed on with Miss Molly as her driver and friend. I can't imagine ever living anywhere else. She's always been like a second mother to me and still treats me like family. Actually, I'm the only family she has."

♥♥♥

Robert was remarkably soothed by Walter's story. He knew instinctively that Miss Molly was a kind and generous person but knowing that she had suffered adversity made her somehow more approachable and easier to accept. He realized that he had placed her on a plain of class high above his own, someone with whom he could relate only from a distance. How foolish. He felt like a snob. The weight of his earlier uncertainty and anxiety lifted. These were genuinely kind, caring people he was associating with. There was no class distinction, no need to fear. They would be fair and just and honest to both the Blairs and the Dantons.

Soon the Dantons returned with the children and mayhem ensued as the children took their wet, cold gloves off and shared stories of a snowball fight.

"I won!" Julie declared.

"Huh uh," Carson objected. "You did not. You cheated. You didn't throw it; you stuffed it down my shirt. That's not fair!"

Cletus interrupted as the children argued. "I don't believe anybody won, if the truth be known. Besides it wasn't a battle or a contest. It was just fun."

"Yes," Birdie agreed. "Cold, wet fun. And I brought some snow up so we can make some snow ice cream."

The children all cheered, their argument forgotten, as the women busied themselves making the sweet treat.

♥♥♥

Walter returned home from his daily telephone reporting to Molly the next day around 4:00 and took his shower before other residents would begin to use the facilities. The clothes had been neatly folded, with the women lamenting the fact that they had no iron with which to smooth them further. They shared another delicious and filling meal and talked and visited until time for the children to retire for the evening.

"If the power goes out tonight, all of you come back over here. I don't care what time it is, you come back over here. You cannot stay in that apartment with no heat at all. Do you understand?" Ellen directed.

"Okay," they laughed, "we will."

"Promise?"

"Promise!"

Ellen settled Stephen down into their bed and returned to where the men sat, taking one of the chairs near the stove.

"I want to talk to you both," Walter began. "I had a conversation with Miss Molly yesterday, and we discussed it again this afternoon, so we want to make you a proposition."

A few days ago, Robert would have been alarmed by this announcement, thinking that he was about to be fired, but after learning more about the person Miss Molly was, he no longer felt threatened. Just curious.

"Robert, you know how Miss Sophie is about ready to retire as Miss Molly's housekeeper. Her husband is getting worse and her health isn't so good anymore either. She's almost seventy now and in addition to having trouble walking, her eyesight is quickly failing. Miss Molly wants to give her a pension and Miss Sophie's daughter has agreed to look after her parents. She lives near them and they aren't ready to leave their home yet to live with her but she can look after them from her house.

"Miss Molly is very pleased with your work and your sense of responsibility, Robert. She would like for you to be her groundskeeper and hire some more help in the spring so that the estate can maybe be brought back up to its former glory."

He turned to Ellen. "She needs a new house manager, Ellen, and would like for you to consider taking the position. There's a small apartment upstairs, opposite from her quarters and over the kitchen, and you and your family can live there. She really needs someone who can be there all the time now. I'm there but she needs a woman. You would hire somebody to do the cooking and cleaning and make certain everything is taken care of as far as noting any repairs needed and keeping the house stocked with food, cleaning items, that sort of thing. She can explain more to you if you're interested."

Robert and Ellen stared at each other, their eyes wide, their mouths open, unable to speak. They were overwhelmed by the offer.

"I think you'll like the apartment," Walter continued. "It's two bedrooms with just a very small kitchen as you'll take your meals downstairs. It has a living room with a fireplace and a private bath. It's heated with the same central system as the rest of the house. What are your thoughts?"

"We don't know what to say." Ellen stuttered, "This is just too wonderful."

"Yes!" Robert exclaimed. "We say yes. Yes, yes. And thank you! Thank you, thank you, so much."

They talked until nearly 10:00 and were preparing for bed when the power went off.

"Huh oh," Robert observed.

"The Dantons. Go get the Dantons, dear. We'll make room for them."

Soon the small family from across the hall was huddled in with the Blairs and Walter, sheltered against the cold darkness by friendship and generosity. They did not yet know the news destined to change their lives as well as the lives of their protectors.

The prayers of Ellen and Robert that night were filled with praise and thanksgiving for this wonderful gift of opportunity which had been bestowed upon them. They lay awake for several hours, too excited to sleep, whispering about this wondrous blessing and wondering about what would happen to their friends from across the hall. They came up with a plan that they would present in the morning. Then they drifted off into deep, peaceful sleep.

♥♥♥

Ellen awakened early, the rooms still gripped by darkness. There was no light seeping through the window from the streetlights below, so she knew that the power must still be off. She crept quietly to the window in order to peer out. There was a weak brightness to the east so she deduced that it must be about 6:00. She heard Robert stirring, and soon, Birdie and Cletus were also moving around.

The candles Walter had provided were located, and soon their small circles of warmth pierced the darkness, casting flickering shadows against the walls. Ellen and Robert dressed and moved into the front room.

The whole group was soon awake, lighting candles, feeding the fire and getting dressed in the dark bedroom vacated by Robert and Ellen.

Carson and Julie were completely confused when they sat up, not remembering their trip across the hall in the middle of the night.

"What happened?" Carson inquired.

"The power went off and Mr. Blair came after us so we wouldn't get cold. Wasn't that kind of him?" his mother explained.

"Yeah, but how'd I get here?"

"You walked, son," his father laughed.

They were amused by his confusion but he quickly forgot all about it. He was just happy to be with friends, and to be warm.

The room was soon filled with the odor of bacon and eggs and ham and fresh coffee as breakfast bubbled on the heater. They gathered around, held hands and blessed the food before consuming the goodness. As they ate, Robert advised the Dantons of their offer from Walter.

"That's wonderful! Absolutely wonderful! We're so happy for you!" Birdie cried.

"Yes," Cletus glowed with delight for his friends' good fortune, "it really is wonderful! It couldn't have happened to anyone more deserving. What a great blessing! And bless you, Walter, for such a gift to these good people."

"When do you think you'll get to leave?" inquired Birdie.

They all looked to Walter.

"Well, it's hard to say. I don't think we can leave today but Robert and I can go out and try to dig the car out so that as soon as things melt a little, we can get on the road. I have chains in the trunk and we'll put chains on all four wheels. Believe it or not, it'll probably be a little easier traveling after we get out of the city since there won't have been much traffic on the roads outside. And the chains will help us over any ice we encounter. It's really imperative that we get back to Miss Molly's estate as soon as possible as there's no one to keep the furnace going. The constable from the village checked on her yesterday and brought more coal in. Her food supply is fine but while the constable was there, he took Miss Sophie home so she could help her daughter take care of Mr. Dempsey, Miss Sophie's husband. So I'm really anxious to get back. If we can get the car dug out today, we'll plan on leaving tomorrow."

"I'll help too if Mr. Schmidt closes the store early today. Guess it depends on whether people can get out or not. We sure are gonna miss you good people," Cletus lamented.

"Yes, yes, we will," agreed his wife, reaching over and clutching Ellen's arm warmly.

Robert cleared his throat. "Well, we'll miss you too. Very much. As a matter of fact, Ellen and I discussed it last night and we were thinking that maybe your family could just move into this apartment. At least there's a heater here and the fire escape isn't broken like the one in your apartment. And we can leave you our old hotplate for cooking when you don't have a fire. With yours, it'll be twice as easy to cook, especially in the summer. Also, we'll have no use for these chairs and the mattress and Stephen's cot, so if you don't mind, we'll just leave them. We'll take our dishes as we have a kitchen in the apartment and may need them."

"You can take them if you like, Robert," Walter interrupted, "but you won't need them. The kitchen's fully equipped and all you'll need are your clothes. You won't even need to take your towels."

"Well, then, it's settled. You can have it all if you would like."

"Oh, Robert, that's wonderful," Birdie breathed happily. "Life will be so much easier here than at our place."

Her face suddenly clouded and she stated anxiously, "I hope Mr. Minson won't mind," as her thoughts turned to their unpleasant landlord.

"Don't worry about that. I'll tell him this morning that we'll be leaving before our rent is due again and that you will be living in our apartment. I doubt that he knows where any of us live anyway. I know he's never darkened *our* door." Robert assured her.

"And, one more thing," he continued as he turned to Cletus. "Our pact remains the same. We will all continue to stay in contact with each other and make certain all needs are being met."

♥♥♥

Soon Cletus left for work and Robert and Walter checked the car to see what needed to be done to free the grip of winter holding it captive on the curb. They began to shovel the deep snow, depositing it against the curb well above and behind the vehicle so as not to simply re-arrange the prison. As they worked, they noticed Mr. Minson peeking from behind the closed curtains of his first floor apartment. It caused Robert to feel uneasy, but Walter felt his own anger rising. It would be the decent thing to offer assistance or at least to make his presence known by speaking to the two men struggling on the street. To stand behind the curtains like a common spy was not very hospitable.

They worked for nearly two hours when Walter suggested they return upstairs to warm up and dry out so as not to get sick.

"Good idea," Robert agreed, "and I'll stop by Mr. Minson's place on our way up and let him know our plans. He's been very interested in our activities all morning."

"I noticed!" Walter snorted.

♥♥♥

After two taps on the landlord's door, it finally opened a crack and a voice snarled, "Yeah, whaddya want?"

The two men standing in the hall exchanged a quick glance before Robert gulped and explained, "Mr. Minson, I'm Robert Blair from Apartment 4A. I wanted to let you know that we'll be moving in the next day or so before our rent is due. I've found a job outside the city." He couldn't hide the pride in his voice as he shared this wonderful news.

"So, just make sure you're gone before the first." The door closed abruptly.

Walter stepped forward, pounding determinedly on the door, his anger rising.

"Mr. Minson," he spoke loudly, "we aren't through yet!"

"What!?" The door opened slightly wider this time.

"Uh, we wanted to let you know that the Dantons who live in Apartment 4B will be moving into our apartment. They don't have a heater in theirs and with two children, they'll be much more comfortable in 4A." Robert was also feeling anger at this rude man.

The door opened widely and Mr. Minson stood in the opening. They were stunned by the warmth and brightness of the room behind him. Even though the power was still off, there were numerous oil lamps and candles lighting the area and a large fire roared in the fireplace. A heater that looked much like an oil heater sat in the corner near the front window.

"Whaddya mean, you have a heater? How much rent do you pay a month? If you have something extra, the rent should be more!"

"That heater was there when we moved in, Mr. Minson, and I'm certain it was left by former tenants, especially since there's not one in any other apartment that we've ever seen. I don't understand how anybody is able to survive since the heat doesn't work in this building. When we rented, it was with the understanding that water and heat were provided and that has not been the case. So I don't see any reason for the Dantons to have their rent raised for something they've never gotten in their apartment and will have to pay to maintain in our apartment. That is, unless you're going to provide coal or wood for them to burn."

Robert's anger was obvious and Mr. Minson quickly backed down. He was a bully but was unwilling to argue with this angry man. He turned his attention to Walter.

"And who are you? And is that your car that's been parked on the street for the last three days?"

Walter had hesitated to interfere in Robert's business, especially since he was handling it so well, but he welcomed this opportunity to confront this unpleasant person.

"My name is Walter Monroe. I'm a guest of the Blairs and I am responsible for the vehicle parked out front."

"Well, it needs to be moved. It's in the way."

"Of what?" Walter retorted.

"Well, it just doesn't need to be parked on my street in front of my building." Mr. Minson was becoming quite flustered.

"*Your* street? I was under the impression that this street belongs to the city of New York. But if it's your street, I must insist that you clear the snow off so that I can move my vehicle from in front of *your* building. And if this is your building, I have some concerns about the condition of it. I was wondering who to hold responsible for the obvious repairs needed to this building. Maybe you and I could go down to city hall and discuss it with the officials down there."

Minson's face paled and he was momentarily silenced.

"Just do what you want!" he hissed. "Just be out of there before the first or have the $8.00 rent!" He stepped inside and slammed the door, bolting it against the two men standing in the hall.

Walter muttered under his breath, his anger and disgust obvious.

"I don't think he'll bother the Dantons," Robert observed. "Looks like you hit a nerve with the city hall threat."

"That wasn't a threat. I'd love to take him before some officials to have him answer for the condition of this building. *His apartment doesn't seem to be lacking any comforts.*"

♥♥♥

As their anger subsided, they were aware of a baby's cry coming from above. They climbed the stairs, and it became louder as they reached the second floor. The urgent cries were emanating from the third floor. They both stopped, glancing at the door behind which the screams escaped. Robert moved toward the sounds and Walter followed.

A gentle tap on the door brought a small slit as the door opened slightly, the face of a young woman, streaked and swollen by tears, peering out at them. The source of the loud vocalization struggled in her arms as she held him close, wrapped in numerous blankets.

"Who is it?" she asked shakily, her voice uneven.

"Ma'am, my name is Robert Blair and this is my friend Walter Monroe. My family and I live up on the fourth floor. Is everything okay with you and the baby? We couldn't help but hear his cries."

"I'm sorry if he bothered you. He's cold and hungry." The young woman began to sob uncontrollably as she pushed the door shut. They could hear her sobbing helplessly behind it.

"Ma'am, my wife will be down in just a minute to see if she can help. Her name is Ellen. Please let her in, we mean you no harm. We just want to help."

There was no response but in just a couple of minutes, Ellen and Birdie tapped at the door hiding the young woman and her infant.

"Hello!" Ellen called through the barricade. "My name is Ellen Blair and this is my friend Birdie Danton. Will you please let us in? We're your neighbors and we'd like to help you and your child."

The door slowly opened and she peered out cautiously, her child nearly hysterical by now. They both appeared to be near exhaustion.

"Please," she invited, "come in. I'm sorry for being so rude to your husbands. I was frightened."

After a brief explanation as to everyone's identity upstairs, the women quickly surveyed the scene and determined the seriousness of the situation.

The apartment was neat and nearly fully furnished which was an indication that the young woman was new to poverty. She had not yet been forced to sell her worldly possessions for the sake of survival. It was, however, quite cold and the small coal heater sat empty and silent at the side of the room, no heat radiating from within.

"Where is your husband?" Birdie inquired kindly.

"He's at work. He found a job with the city's street department last week, and when the snows came, he had to go and I don't know when he'll be able to come back. It was so sudden, we didn't have time to prepare. I have money for the rent but I'm afraid to buy milk for the baby because he may not get back before the first and I know that we'll be out on the street. I don't know what to do or where to turn." She started sobbing anew as she finished her story.

Ellen moved to her side, placed her arm around her shoulders, and directed quietly, "Leave a note for your husband and tell him you're upstairs with friends in Apartment 4A. It's the door to the left at the top of the stairs on the fourth floor. We're crowded but it's warm and there's plenty of milk for the baby and food for you."

"Oh, thank you so much!" Her relief was immediate and touching. "We'll pay you back, I promise."

"Don't worry about that right now; we just need to get you two upstairs out of this cold place."

♥♥♥

Soon the young woman and her child were warm, their hunger satiated, and the child was snoozing contentedly in his mother's arms. Only after the urgency of their hunger was appeased was she able to tell them her story.

"My name is Josie Carroll and my husband is Phillip. This is our son Travis. He's six months old and I can't tell you how grateful I am to you for helping us. He hadn't eaten all day and I was frantic." Her tears began again as she recalled her terror at their recent state.

"Anyway," she continued, "Phillip lost his job three months ago. We moved here just as a temporary solution until he could find another job and we could do better. We didn't have a whole lot of savings since we had just had the baby a couple of months earlier, and he wasn't expecting to lose his job. Well, he was getting really scared and we didn't have the money to get back to Ohio to my folks so we were kind of stuck. We were so happy and relieved when he found this job last week. He promised that we'd be just fine and he'd have us a better place to live right away.

"And then this snow came along and he had to leave when his boss came to our door after dark to get him. We had planned to go to the store the next day since he would be paid before the first and we could replace the $8.00 rent money. But things didn't work out and I ran out of groceries day before yesterday and milk yesterday. I also ran out of coal for the stove early yesterday morning.

"I didn't know which way to turn or who to turn to so when you knocked on my door, it was an answer to a prayer. I usually don't open the door like that but I had no choice this time. Thank you, thank you so much." Her tears started anew.

"I assure you, Josie, you're safe here," Robert promised.

♥♥♥

The evening passed quickly as the ever-growing group talked and shared. Birdie

and Josie became fast friends, and Ellen was so grateful since she knew that they would be leaving in the morning if at all possible. She found it hateful to leave her good friend without an ally in this place. Josie promised to be that ally. She continued to be amazed at the grace and benevolence being showered upon them all by a loving and merciful God.

They crowded into the small rooms that night for sleep, each heart filled with love and gratitude for the blessings they were, and would be, receiving.

♥♥♥

Early the next morning as the Blair family prepared to load their few belongings into the massive trunk of the limousine with confidence that they could exit the city, Phillip Carroll bounded up the stairs, his face contorted with anxiety and concern. He clung desperately to his family, his thankfulness to the strangers who saved them extremely touching.

Walter had walked to Schmidt's store after breakfast to call Molly Fulton and let her know that they were coming home so that she would expect them. He cautioned her not to worry as it would probably take much longer than usual due to the snow and his plan to drive much slower than normal.

She gave him a list of needed food items for the manor along with a maternal caution.

"Just be careful. I've waited for this day for a long time, and I'm just a bit anxious about the safety of all of you."

As soon as everything settled down somewhat from Phillip's arrival, the massive back seat/bed Walter had used while a guest of the Blairs was tucked snugly into the car, and they prepared to leave the city. The friends bade a painful farewell, bittersweet in its circumstance but heartening in its pursuit.

"You have our number, Cletus," Walter reminded his friend. "Be sure to keep in touch. We want to know how you are and if you need anything. And remember what I told you about your move."

"Oh, yes, sir, I'll be sure to call if there's any trouble from the landlord. And we'll let you know how we are. Just have a good life." He directed his last remark to the Blairs, struggling to control his emotions.

"We'll talk soon," Robert promised. "Take care."

The two small families huddled on the sidewalk, waving tearfully, until the dark limousine was out of sight.

Chapter 7
Fulton Manor

Their melancholy over leaving their friends soon evaporated in the excitement of the great adventure they were embarking upon, and the comfort of knowing that the Dantons had new friends in Josie and Phillip and their baby son. It was good not to be alone.

Stephen bounced over the back seat, from window to window, unable to contain his exuberance at the wondrous sights he had never before observed. He was awestruck by the miles of tall buildings rising before him and couldn't decide which side of the car to take. He was afraid of missing something so he attempted to see everything, until his mother finally directed him firmly but gently to quit running around the back and stepping on her feet. He then began to hang over the front seat between Walter and his father, eagerly gazing out the front windshield in an attempt to observe both sides of the street at the same time.

By the time they left the city, however, he was so exhausted by the excitement and stimulation of the move that he retreated to the consolation of the massively comfortable seat beside his mother, and was soon fast asleep.

The men carefully scrutinized the road in front, closely following the few ruts laid down by earlier traffic, most of which appeared to be farm wagons. The ditches were still filled with snow and apart from a slight indentation, were difficult to discern. Fortunately, the chains kept them from sliding off course, so they knew that as long as they could see the roadway, they should be fine. Ellen remained silent, not wanting to distract their attention or interrupt their concentration. She said a silent prayer of relief that little Stephen had fallen asleep. Of course, she wasn't surprised, as none of them had slept much the night before. There was just too much excitement for the upcoming adventure.

Soon she too was deep in sleep, confident in the ability of the men to steer them to their destination safely.

Fortunately, even though the trip to the manor was slow, it was uneventful. They met no oncoming traffic and the clunking of the chains on the tires assured them of their safety. Walter quickly unlocked the large gate at the entrance to the manor so that they could enter. The trip up the driveway proved to be no easy task, however, as the tall trees lining the passage kept any of the snow from melting. Faint tracks left by a truck from the city making deliveries a day earlier helped somewhat but they had mostly disappeared, buried under snow falling from the trees lining the drive.

"Maybe I'd better get out and move ahead with a stick or something to make certain we don't get off the drive," Robert offered.

"Yeah, I'm afraid so, if you don't mind. We sure don't want to get off in a ditch when we're this close. Of course, if we do, we can certainly walk the rest of the way but it's still not a pleasant situation to try and get this car unstuck. We'd probably have to leave it until the spring thaw, and we'll need to get out to the village before then."

Robert found a branch that had been broken loose by the heavy snowfall and soon had it pulled off the tree for use as a guide through the drifts. He was wrapped in Walter's heavy coat and scarf, wearing Walter's fur lined boots and gloves, as well as Walter's wool hat with the earmuffs pulled down. He resembled a large bear lumbering through the white deposits.

He swept from side to side with the pole, making a wide sweep to mark the ditches. It took almost a half hour to reach the manor, but they managed to avoid falling into the trenches.

Robert was greatly relieved to retreat into the warmth of the car as they approached their destination.

Ellen had awakened and was happy to have her husband back in the safety of the vehicle. Her relief, however, did not diminish her wonder at the grandeur of the manor as it came into view. Robert's explanation and description of the home had been precise, and, it appeared, accurate, but nothing had prepared her for the sight before her.

It will take an army to keep this place running, she thought to herself with anxiety.

She made no comment to the men and attempted to awaken Stephen. He sat up groggily, surveying the scenery.

"Wow!" he shouted, immediately alert. "It's a castle!"

"That's a very accurate description, son!" his father laughed.

♥♥♥

They hurried inside, Walter most anxious to reach his employer. Ellen had no time to really digest the beauty of the interior as Walter rushed them down the hall toward the kitchen where he knew Molly Fulton would have retreated. The glory of the walls, ceilings and floors, however, did not escape her eyes. She felt a sense of reverence and also a strange feeling of security and welcome, as if this was a very hospitable and loving home for her family. She began to relax as they entered the kitchen to meet Molly Fulton.

♥♥♥

Molly sat by the stove, her crocheting in her lap. She looked up when the door swung open, relief and joy flooding her face. She jumped to her feet, spilling her work on the floor, and clapped her hands in delight.

"Hello!" she sang out joyfully. "I'm so glad to see all of you! I've been just a bit lonely here all by myself. And you are Ellen and little Stephen."

She rushed to greet them, as quickly as she could with her cane, and clasped her arms around Ellen warmly. She knelt on the floor in front of Stephen, not wanting to frighten him by touching him, but obviously glad to see him.

"I've been waiting for you too, young man. I am so glad that you're here. You and I are going to have a grand time livening up these old halls!"

Ellen and Robert were somewhat overcome by the exuberance of her greeting, but were warmed by it. Obviously, she had been quite lonely. They both felt a pang of compassion and tenderness for this dignified lady, and Ellen knew at once that they would be great friends. Robert felt a touch of guilt as he remembered how she had tried to talk to him when he first came here. He had rejected her efforts in his eagerness to begin his work and his callousness toward her loneliness dismayed him. Ellen and Stephen were going to be well loved and cared for here, he was certain.

Walter and Robert scurried about, bringing in coal and building a fire in the fireplace as well as feeding the fire in the cook stove where Molly had been sitting. They then went to the basement and soon had a fire blazing in the cold furnace. Blessed warmth crept through the house, pushing out the icy coldness gripping the rooms.

"As soon as it's warm enough, I'll show you to your apartment so you can get settled," Molly explained, "but first let's start a dinner. You poor things must be nearly starved! We'll make some sandwiches to hold you over. We'll use the bread Walter brought from the city. Do you know how to make bread, Ellen?"

She smiled at Molly's excitement, touched by her enthusiasm.

"I think I can probably make bread if there's a good recipe. I haven't made any in several years and I've almost forgotten how," Ellen responded.

"Oh, my dear, Sophie has a wonderful recipe. Actually, it's more directions than a recipe but I think we can figure it out together. We'll get started as soon as everyone is fed. Maybe we'll have fresh bread for dinner! I took a goose out of the freezer when Walter called so we'll get him in the oven right away."

Soon the goose was slipped into the large oven, and ham was sliced for sandwiches. Coffee was perking on the stove and

Stephen was eagerly munching on his sandwich, washing it down with a glass of cold milk. It was a very cozy, homey, almost pastoral scene, and Molly Fulton basked in it as she happily watched the scene in her usually empty and lonely kitchen.

♥♥♥

The men ate their sandwiches after returning from their fire building and then brought the Blairs' belongings into the house. Molly led them up the stairs off the kitchen to the apartment on the second floor.

She opened the door and announced proudly, "Welcome home. I can't tell you how glad I am that you're here."

Ellen gasped in admiration. "It's lovely," she breathed, "and so big!"

Stephen raced around, excitedly exploring everything. "It's the best house we ever had! Come quick, Mommy, and look at my room! It has cowboys on the bedspread and a cowboy hat and a cowboy gun and a holster! I can't believe it! Hurry! Come look!"

"I hope you don't mind that I took the liberty of getting those things for Stephen," Molly apologized. "I had them brought in from Carver's Mercantile the day I found out you'd be coming to live with us. I hope you'll allow me to buy him some boots later, but I didn't know what size he wears."

"Oh, Miss Molly, you're doing too much! We don't know what to say and we certainly didn't expect this." Ellen was slightly distraught by her employer's generosity.

"Please, my dear, I mean no harm. It's just that I have no family and will receive such joy in having someone to care for. I have no grandchildren and hope you will allow me to spoil your son. If it bothers you in any way, please let me know."

Ellen moved to Molly, placed her arms around her and hugged her warmly. She wiped away her tears as she remembered her own dear mother so far away.

"Thank you, Miss Molly. Thank you so much. We really do appreciate everything."

"Let me show you around," Molly offered, changing the subject.

The living room was small but spacious with comfortable furniture gathered around the ample fireplace. There was a sofa covered with a sturdy, navy blue fabric. A large chair in matching fabric set nearby and looked comfortable enough to sleep in. A wooden rocking chair, coffee table, two end tables and two electric lamps completed the furnishings. Two windows at the end of the room stood guard. Covered with thick, cream colored draperies to ward off the cold, they held the promise of admitting cool summer breezes when hot weather arrived.

The kitchen to the side of the living room was open and separated from the area by a wide counter with bar stools tucked under so as to be utilized as an eating surface. Upper and lower cabinets lined the back wall with the lower cabinets interrupted by a large sink holding both hot and cold water faucets. The walls of the rooms were painted a warm gold and reflected cozily into the shining wooden floors. A Persian rug of gold, navy and burgundy settled in front of the fireplace.

The larger bedroom was completely furnished with a double bed, dresser, armoire and a large wardrobe for storing clothes. In addition, there was a walk-in closet which was a luxury neither Ellen nor Robert had ever known. There was even a dressing stool in front of the dresser mirror for Ellen to sit and brush her hair, using the elegant silver brush and comb set provided for her.

The walls were white, and the two windows were covered by light blue draperies. A Persian rug of blue, yellow and cream covered the pine floors.

Between their room and Stephen's was the longed for bathroom, which contained a claw-footed bathtub with a shower attached. There were two pedestal sinks, each crowned by a large, oval mirror. A mahogany chest with two drawers and two doors opening to shelves set between the sinks and the commode. A small window at the end of the room was filled by a stained glass scene of mountains, trees and a bunch of blue grapes in the foreground. Ceramic tiles of blue and yellow embraced the walls and floors.

"Wow!" murmured Stephen. "How many people use this bathroom?"

"Just three, son," Molly laughed. Walter had explained about the community facilities in the apartment building.

"Just us? Is that true, Mommy?"

"Stephen!" she admonished with embarrassment.

"That's okay, Ellen." Her employer continued to laugh at Stephen's joy. It was refreshing to see what she had taken for granted for so long through the eyes of a child obviously pleased beyond explanation at this practical necessity. He recognized it as a luxury while she had not even thought about it. It was good for her to experience his enthusiasm. Sort of made her think about her life in a different perspective.

♥♥♥

After a delicious dinner of goose, canned green beans from the pantry, baked sweet potatoes smothered in butter, cinnamon and sugar, fried squash from Schmidt's grocery store, and fresh homemade bread created by Molly and Ellen, the small family was led on a tour of the grand manor by Walter and the mistress. Ellen's doubts regarding her ability to care for this huge mansion increased as she entered each room. She said nothing but her silence became deeper and more profound with the opening of each door.

They returned to the kitchen, which would quickly become the favorite meeting place of the Blairs, as it was for Molly.

"Are you all right, my dear?" Molly addressed Ellen with concern in her voice. "Are you ill?"

"Oh, no, ma'am, I'm fine. Just feeling a bit overwhelmed." Ellen instinctively knew that she could voice her honest concerns without fear of retribution.

"About what?"

"The size of this magnificent house, Miss Molly. As we entered each room, in addition to seeing the beautiful draperies and rugs and tapestries and furniture, I saw surfaces to dust and clean and scrub. It's an incredibly big job and I'd be dishonest if I told you I'm certain I can handle it all alone. I want to do a good job for you but..."

"Oh, my goodness, is that what's bothering you?" Molly laughed with understanding. "Don't give it a second thought. You certainly aren't expected to keep all of this clean. I want you to manage the household, which means as soon as the weather is fit, we'll find someone to do the cooking and cleaning. We also need someone to help with the yard work. Robert can't do all that by himself and Walter has his hands full taking care of running my errands and helping all he can with what's left of the family business.

"I'm afraid things have gotten a bit out of hand over the past couple of years. I was concerned about Sophie after she became ill, she's been such an important part of my life for all of my life, and I was afraid if I offered to get someone else in here to do the work, she'd misunderstand and be hurt. You and Robert and little Stephen have been a Godsend and it'll take a couple more years to get everything on track.

"You remind me of Robert the first day he came to work. He couldn't get at it quick enough. I appreciate your concern and obvious efficiency, but I assure you, I'm no ruthless taskmaster. I just want things to be brought back to as nearly original condition as possible but we have no timetable. We'll just take it a day at a time. It certainly didn't get in this condition overnight and it can't be fixed overnight."

"Thank you, Miss Molly. I really mean that." Ellen was obviously relieved.

♥♥♥

She arose early the next morning and went into the kitchen to prepare breakfast for her family and her employer. Soon Walter and Molly arrived and they all enjoyed a breakfast warmed by friendship and love and family.

Ellen wasn't certain how to handle Stephen while she worked as he was not used to sharing her with other duties and other adults for long periods of time. She had no need to worry.

Molly soon commandeered Stephen and they disappeared into the front of the house. As Ellen moved through the hall with a dust mop, she heard their voices coming from the library. She had toured it briefly the night before so she knew where it was located. She quickly checked on her son to make certain he was not bothering anything or misbehaving for Miss Molly.

She stood there at the door watching for a few minutes, enjoying the scene of her small boy playing with Molly Fulton. Molly was hiding behind the large sofa and would crawl out of his sight as he rounded the end, searching for her. She would pop up when she reached the front and shout "Boo!" He would squeal with delight and rush around to cling to her. She would then hide her face behind one of the many accent pillows on the furniture and count to 10 while he hid.

He was scurrying around, desperately seeking a hiding place, when he spied his mother. She placed her finger over her lips and then guided him behind the heavy drapery covering one of the windows.

As Miss Molly reached 10, she stood up and announced, "Here I come, ready or not!"

She likewise saw Ellen and waved gaily at her. She turned toward the drapery as a stifled giggle escaped from behind the folds.

"Why, hello, Ellen. Do you know where Stephen has gone? I don't see him anywhere."

"Noooo, I don't see him either," she responded as another giggle danced across the room.

"He's not behind the chair and he's not under the table. Let's see, maybe he's hiding between the books on the bookshelf. No, on second thought, he's much too big to hide in there. Oh, dear, wherever could he be?"

Stephen could stand it no longer and burst from behind the drapery, flailing the fabric excitedly.

"Here I am! Here I am!"

He danced around Miss Molly and his mother, delighted with his triumph of fooling Miss Molly.

Ellen left the two of them together in the library, certain that they would entertain each other with no problem.

♥♥♥

By dinner, Stephen could count to 10 and was bubbling with accounts of the fun he and Miss Molly had during the day.

"I hope you didn't wear her out, son," his father cautioned.

"Oh, pshaw, he did no such thing. We had great fun today. And tomorrow we're going to find a book in the library to read. Stephen will have a surprise for you tomorrow night at dinner."

They giggled as they whispered together, delighting in sharing a secret from the others. Ellen, Robert and Walter enjoyed seeing them so happy. They were like two children and had become fast friends.

After cleaning up the dishes, they all sat beside the fireplace in the kitchen. Molly had brought a story bible into the room from the library, and Stephen sat on his mother's lap as she read the story of Noah and the flood.

"I'll bet Noah had a birdhouse like mine on the ark too, don't you, Mommy?"

"I'm not certain, dear, but he probably did because he had birds."

"Do you think it was blessed like ours?"

"If it was on the ark, it was blessed, son, because the whole ark and everyone and everything on it were blessed. That's how God delivered them from the flood."

"That's right." Stephen agreed wisely.

As he was tucked into bed later, he gave a sincere and grateful prayer.

"Thank you, God, for this home and for my new friend, Miss Molly. And thank you that Mommy and Daddy have Miss Molly for a friend too."

Chapter 8
Illness

Stephen was unusually quiet the next day. Ellen was busily removing dust and cobwebs and was grateful for Miss Molly's attention to him. She knew they were reading so she was not concerned.

The day quickly passed and soon it was dinnertime. They gathered around the table in the kitchen and Molly and Stephen whispered together as they prepared to eat.

"After we eat, I'll give you my surprise." Stephen promised, his cheeks flushed with eagerness.

He barely touched his meal and Ellen decided it was due to his being so excited. As soon as dinner was completed, he ran to a cabinet on the sidewall of the kitchen. He reached behind the cabinet and rescued a large piece of paper, rolled into a cone. He ran to his mother and thrust it into her hands, climbing expectantly into her lap.

"What's this?" she inquired.

"A surprise! Hurry and open it. It's for you, and Daddy too."

She unrolled the paper and spread it on the table. A large scene of colored stick figures and trees and clouds and birds emerged as the paper flattened out. Stephen had drawn a picture for them.

He excitedly explained what everything was.

"This is you, Mommy. This is a new red dress and this is your hair." He accurately captured her shoulder length blond hair pulled to the right side of her face.

"And here's Daddy."

"What's he holding?"

Walter and Robert moved around behind Ellen as Stephen interpreted the figures.

"He's holding the birdhouse, Mommy." He was surprised that she didn't recognize this treasured item.

They all exclaimed warmly over his creation, and he was enjoying the flattery immensely. He rested his head against his mother's shoulder and she kissed him gently on the forehead.

Suddenly she reached her hand up and rested it on his forehead. "You feel warm, Stephen."

Concern crossed every face in the room as they fell silent, focusing entirely on the young boy's physical condition. Perhaps his silence and flushed appearance were more serious than they had first assumed.

♥♥♥

He was soon settled into his bed, surrounded by his parents, and Molly and Walter.

"He's really hot." Ellen observed. "Robert, I'm frightened."

He slipped his arm around her in an attempt to comfort her but his own feelings of helplessness felt suffocating.

"Walter, please go into the village and get John Sheffield," Molly requested. "He's our doctor," she explained to the Blairs. She didn't like the looks of this at all and didn't want to take any chances.

The chains remained on the car just in case it became necessary to leave the compound so it wasn't long before Walter was moving down the drive toward Issaqua Harbor.

The others stood anxiously by, washing Stephen's face with cool water, waiting with concern for the doctor's arrival as he drifted into an uneasy and restless sleep.

After nearly an hour, Dr. Sheffield arrived. Molly met him at the door and whispered apprehensively before he entered.

He was a tall, distinguished looking man in his mid-fifties. His shoulders were straight and strong and his white hair was full and thick. He had a soft, kind voice and his dark brown eyes were filled with the concern, wisdom and resignation of many years spent treating the ill. He was a third generation physician, following both his grandfather and father in the calling of healing. His family had cared for the Fultons for as long as either had been in the area, so he felt a bond with Molly Fulton.

He spoke briefly to the parents, shaking hands warmly with Robert and nodding kindly to Ellen, and learned that Stephen had not been ill long at all. He had been fine yesterday and although a little quiet this morning, showed no signs of illness. He checked him thoroughly, listening with deep concern to his lungs. He looked up at Molly, his eyes meeting hers. The look on his face caused her to place her hand over her mouth to stifle her cry.

"I'm sorry, Mr. and Mrs. Blair, but Stephen has pneumonia."

They both cried out in terror and grief at his pronouncement.

He hurried on in an attempt to reassure them. "I'll give him every medicine that we have and he's young and strong and obviously healthy. We'll do everything that we can and hopefully, he'll recover but it'll be a long battle. I'll send nurses from the village to help and will get the medicine here at once.

"Molly, where's the nearest phone?" They both hurried from the room as she led him to the front parlor.

Ellen and Robert clung together, Ellen sobbing quietly. They both knew that pneumonia was tantamount to a death declaration, as they knew no one who had survived it.

♥♥♥

Molly and Dr. Sheffield returned from making the call.

"The medicine will be here shortly. I've ordered it from the pharmacy and

Mr. Gordon, the pharmacist, will bring it out."

Molly stood there for a minute and then had a look of inspiration on her face.

"John," she turned to the doctor, "call Benjamin back and ask him to bring Hattie Mae with him. Maybe she can help."

Ellen and Stephen looked up hopefully, aware that something important had just occurred.

"Well, it can't hurt," the doctor responded. "I've seen her do some wonderful things." He rushed out of the room back to the phone.

"What's happening?" Ellen inquired.

"Hattie Mae Phipps is our local healer. She knows just about everything about herbs and old-fashioned cures. She's been an institution in this community for years. With her, along with the doctor's medicine, Stephen will have even more of a chance to get well. If anybody can do anything, she can. I hope you don't mind."

"No, no, of course not." Robert assured her. "We're grateful for anything that anyone can do."

Before long, the medicine and Hattie Mae arrived. Dr. Sheffield administered the medication and then stepped aside to let her examine his charge.

She was a stout woman, ageless in her appearance. She could have been 30 or 60. Her long hair, streaked with bits of gray, was pulled back into a casual bun at the nape of her neck. She wore a long, black skirt covered by layers of loose fitting blouses, vests and sweaters. Her face was lineless but small crow's feet nestled at the edges of her green eyes. Her fingers were short, her hands smooth and white. Her fingernails were neat and clean.

She acknowledged Robert and Ellen briefly as she moved to the sink to wash her hands. She pushed her many sleeves up and scrubbed to her elbows, using plenty of soap and hot water.

She moved to Stephen's side, looking down on him with kind concern and deep resolve. She listened intently to his chest, laboring to pull in oxygen.

"We need to get that congestion broken up," she observed. "I need lots of onions and some bandages. A sheet will do fine. I also need a pot of hot water and a rubber tarpaulin. And a bucket."

She soon had everyone scurrying around, filling her orders. A pot of water was placed on the stove in the Blairs' kitchen, and the burner turned up on high beneath it. As soon as Walter entered with the onions, Hattie Mae directed Robert to slice them all and place them in the pot of hot water to boil. She tore the sheet into squares, placing them on Stephen's chest to make certain they were the right size. She slipped the rubber tarp beneath Stephen as Ellen and Molly lifted him tenderly.

"I'm going to make a poultice of onions to put on his chest," she explained. "That should break up the congestion. It's not going to be pretty, that's why I need the bucket but don't be scared when he starts throwing up. Do you have a hot plate?"

"No, I'm afraid not," Molly stated. "But we can send for one."

"No time now." Hattie Mae stood there thoughtfully for a moment. "Let's get his bed into the kitchen and put another pot of water on. Put these eucalyptus leaves in there and let's get some of those fumes and steam into him right away."

The men soon had the small bed setting near the kitchen stove and another pot of water containing eucalyptus leaves sat poised to boil.

The pot of onions was poured into a strainer and cooled slightly. The cloths on Stephen's chest were formed into a sort of nest and the transparent onions were placed in. The escaping steam and odor entered Stephen's nose and assisted in breaking up the congestion. Bandages were wrapped snuggly around the onions in an effort to channel the fumes directly into his lungs through his skin.

Soon Stephen began to cough.

"It's working! Hand me the bucket and stand back!" Hattie Mae directed.

Long ropes of bloody mucous poured into the bucket, causing Ellen to cry out in alarm.

"No, no, this is good! It's coming out!" Hattie Mae assured them.

"Amazing." Dr. Sheffield breathed in awe.

After the wave of illness passed, Hattie Mae reached into her bag and pulled out a jar of some sort of grease.

"Please, someone, skim a couple tablespoons of eucalyptus leaves from the water and put it in a teacup."

Robert hurried to comply with her instructions and soon she opened the jar of grease, reaching inside with her fingers and pulling a generous amount out. She placed it in the teacup with the eucalyptus leaves and stirred it briskly.

"Phew! What is that stuff?" Molly held her nose, crinkling her face in displeasure.

"It's bear grease. Smells bad but it works really well in breaking up any leftover congestion, especially when mixed with the eucalyptus. It would be better if the leaves were fresh but I don't have any this time of year so the dried ones will do just fine."

She spread the concoction on Stephen's chest and wrapped him in more pieces of torn up sheet, not only to keep the effects inside, but to also protect everyone and everything from the mess and the grease and the smell.

♥♥♥

The doctor and Hattie Mae would stay the night, keeping a vigilant watch over their young charge. The adults stood by, unable to rest, watching and praying throughout the long night. At 3:00 AM, Stephen stirred and moaned slightly.

"Thirsty," he muttered.

They all rushed to his side, careful not to get in the doctor's way.

"The fever has broken," he announced as he looked up from his examination. "I think he's going to be fine."

The room was filled with relief, and happy tears, as everyone hugged each other.

"Dr. Sheffield, Miss Phipps, we can't thank you enough," Robert stated. "We are so very grateful. Thank you both so much."

"I'm afraid you'll have to thank God and Hattie Mae for this miracle," Dr. Sheffield admitted. "I had very little to do with it. Just give him plenty of liquids, especially fruit juice if you have it, and make sure he rests for at least a week. Keep giving him the medicine I brought and if there is any change, give me a call at once. It's going to take him awhile to get over it. He'll be weak for probably at least a month so just keep him as quiet as you can. He'll begin to become active as he feels like it.

"And, Hattie Mae, I'm beholden to you." He turned to his colleague. "I'm very grateful you were here and were able to help. Thank you from me as well as these good people."

"Oh, well, I'm just glad I was able to help. We got him early, that was the main thing and he's young and strong so that helped too. It just wasn't his time. God has other plans for this one, that's for certain."

♥♥♥

Walter settled the two healers into the guest rooms for the remainder of the night. Soon the household was deep in exhausted and relieved sleep, with Ellen sleeping in a chair by Stephen's bed in case he awakened. She stirred several times, to give him water and just to reach out and touch him in order to assure herself that he was indeed fine.

Everyone slept late the next morning. Walter entered the kitchen first and made a large pot of strong coffee. He fed the ever-hungry coal furnace, reminding himself once again that there would be a new, oil-fired furnace installed this summer, so it would no longer be necessary to feed the basement monster. He would not miss this huge piece of ravenous equipment.

♥♥♥

Ellen sat up with a start, not certain what had awakened her. She looked around, momentarily confused by her location and the loss of sleep over events of the previous evening. She soon realized that she had been aroused by the smell of fresh coffee coming up the stairs from the kitchen. She quickly checked on Stephen. He was cool and sleeping peacefully.

Robert was soon up and dressed, running downstairs to the kitchen. He and Walter discussed the previous evening's emergency, and Walter was relieved to know that little Stephen seemed to be resting comfortably.

They prepared a breakfast of lumpy oatmeal and toast. Walter squeezed fresh orange juice and as they prepared trays to deliver to the Blair apartment and Miss Molly, the mistress of the manor appeared in the kitchen with Dr. Sheffield and Hattie Mae close behind.

Hattie Mae tossed out the oatmeal and started over. Soon bacon and eggs were ready for everyone except Stephen. He would eat smooth oatmeal and plenty of juice. Molly asked Robert if they could all eat upstairs so they could be with Stephen, and he welcomed the suggestion.

He carried the trays holding their breakfasts upstairs to alert Ellen and soon everyone was crowded cozily into the small apartment. Stephen was propped up on pillows, loving the extra attention he was receiving. He consumed his oatmeal hungrily, making no complaints about the bacon and eggs everyone else was having. His oatmeal and orange juice suited him just fine.

Walter returned the doctor and Hattie Mae to town while Robert busied himself with bringing in coal and shoveling snow off the pathways near the house. Ellen and Molly stayed beside Stephen, with Molly reading Aesop's fables. She delighted him as she acted out parts of the stories, leaping and jumping around his bed. Her cane had disappeared shortly after the Blair family arrived at Fulton Manor, an apparatus she no longer needed. Stephen was soon fast asleep, exhausted and weak from the previous evening's events.

While he slept, Ellen washed clothes in the laundry room off the downstairs kitchen and hung them on the line stretched across the room, grateful for this convenience. She prayed almost constantly as she worked, thanking God for sparing Stephen, for sending them to Molly Fulton, for the healers who were sent to help, and for the many blessings bestowed on them since Christmas.

PART III

TRIUMPH

Gail Cauble Gurley

Chapter 9
Spring at Last

The gray, cold days of February dragged relentlessly on. The adults did all possible to keep Stephen's spirits up and to hasten his recovery. It was slow but steady, his strength increasing gradually. His color was still absent but each day a patch of pink spread further across his cheeks, and his eyes regained their brightness and luster. His laughter became stronger and was soon ringing through the long halls of Fulton Manor. Only then did the household begin to relax.

February finally disappeared and March burst forth with gusty winds and frequent downpours, washing away the remaining January snows. Stephen enjoyed sitting at the large window in the library, watching the wind blow the raindrops across the lawn and down the windowpanes. He never tired of examining the heavy, dark clouds scurrying across the sky, changing shapes as the wind whipped them to and fro.

"Look, Miss Molly. There's a ship. Huh oh! One of the sails just broke off."

"And over there's a dragon, Stephen. Do you see him? He has wings and a really long nose. Maybe it isn't a dragon but a flying elephant."

They laughed together at the fantasy shapes, changing moment to moment. It was particularly exciting when a stray sunbeam managed to slice through the menagerie of heavy clouds, tossing a golden shaft across the dreary world.

"It's a promise of spring, Stephen," Molly assured him. "It will be here soon. Those tall stick trees will be filled with thick, green leaves. The grass will be a deep, dark green, even darker than the leaves. If you look very closely, you can see little sprouts sticking out of the ground over there near the hedge. Do you see them?"

Stephen studied intently the spot she was describing. He leaned closer to the window, squinting seriously. Suddenly, his eyes popped wide open, as did his mouth, in wonder.

"I see them! There they are! What are they? There's millions of them!"

"They're jonquils. Or I like to call them buttercups. They're beautiful yellow flowers that bloom very early in the spring. They smell wonderful and when they open, we'll bring bouquets of them into the house. They brighten up every room. And we'll hold one under your chin to see if you like butter."

"How can you tell that?" he wondered.

"The buttercup will tell us. You'll see."

"Wow, I can't wait to see that. Let's not forget."

"We won't forget, Stephen." She smiled tenderly down at the small head pressed against the window, eager to absorb the wonders of the world, as she gently stroked his head.

♥♥♥

He had frequently explored the room and wondered about the pictures hanging on the walls, especially the angry looking, scowling man assigned to the back of the room.

"Who's that man?" He pointed to the large portrait.

She followed his eyes, her gaze stopping on the source of his curiosity.

"That was Myron Thaddeus Fulton, Stephen. My father."

"Where is he now?"

"He's passed on, dear." She saw the confusion on his small face. "He's dead," she clarified.

"Oh. How did he die?"

"He had a stroke. That's an illness in the brain."

"Why was he so angry?"

"He wasn't always angry, I'm certain, dear. He had a great deal on him."

"Like what?"

"Things you wouldn't understand right now. You'll understand more later."

"I'm too young now?" He had heard that explanation many times in his nearly five years.

"Yes, dear," she laughed, hugging him warmly. "You're very smart but there are some things you just don't understand yet. But you will as you grow up."

"I hope I grow up soon."

"It'll be soon enough, Stephen, it'll be soon enough." She smiled pensively at his eagerness to mature.

♥♥♥

April was well upon them when the first jonquils burst open. Stephen was enchanted and couldn't wait to rush into the yard to test Miss Molly's theory about liking butter. The first bloom was barely cut when he demanded, "Do I like butter? Do I? Do I?"

"Whoa, wait a minute." Molly laughed. "Let's get the flowers inside to a vase first."

He stood beside the library table, dancing with excitement, as she placed the first bouquet of spring into a crystal vase. She immediately removed a long yellow cup from the center of the bunch.

"Let's see," she said thoughtfully as she tilted his chin back with her fingers. She slipped the yellow orb beneath his chin.

"Yep, you like butter. Buttercups always know."

"I wanta see, I wanta see! What's it doing?"

She stood him up on a chair so that he could see his reflection in the large mirror hanging on the buffet.

"Wow-w-w." he whispered in awe. "My chin is yellow. It really knows! Let's see if you like butter."

He turned, thrusting the flower under her chin, studying it carefully.

"Yay! You like butter too. See? Your chin is yellow just like mine."

♥♥♥

On another visit to the library, his attention turned to the portraits once again, his curiosity ever present regarding Miss Molly's family.

"Who are these other people? Besides your daddy."

"Well, that's Marie Jane Bowman Fulton, my mother."

"Wow, she's pretty. Is she still alive?"

"No, I'm afraid not."

They moved on down the wall.

"That's Marvin Harley Bowman, my mother's father; Thelma Joyce Bowman, her mother; and Calvin Miller Fulton, my grandfather who was also my father's father. We don't have a picture of his wife. Her name was Ethel Louise Fulton."

"Where are they now?" Stephen inquired.

"They're all dead, dear."

"You sure know a lot of dead people," he stated matter-of-factly. "Who's the little girl?"

"That's Molly Elizabeth Fulton. Me."

"You were pretty then too." He said it with the honesty of a child with no thoughts of impressing or flattering. It was just the sincere observation of an innocent. Had she looked otherwise, he would certainly have stated so, having no concept or intention of hurting her.

♥♥♥

Each day the promise of spring was more evident. The limbs and branches stretching from the tree trunks in the front yard turned a soft yellow, then chartreuse, and finally a pale green as the leaves pushed their way out of the buds into the increasingly strong sun and warm air.

"I think it's time we go to town and find some help," Walter announced to Robert at the dinner table one night.

"Yes, I agree, the weather is getting warmer everyday. I've pruned huge clumps of small branches off most of the trees in the front, but there are many more needing it. Also, I'd feel considerably more comfortable if we found someone who knew a little more about what they were doing than I do."

"Can I go to town with you? Please?" begged Stephen. He was almost 100% recovered from the pneumonia and was now gripped by an annual affliction which attacked so many in late April. He had Spring Fever.

Ellen and Robert glanced at each other across the table.

"What do you think?" he asked her as their eyes met.

"Well-l-l-l-l. I think it'll be okay. He seems to be fine and his color is good. His cough is gone and he's been eating well. What do you think, Miss Molly?" She turned to Stephen's chief advocate and playmate for her opinion.

"I think you're right, Ellen. I can't imagine his being anymore fit than he is. My grandfather used to say, 'Fit as a fiddle and ready to sing.' I think Stephen fits into that category."

Stephen shouted with glee and ran around the table, thanking everyone individually with a hearty hug.

"What am I going to sing?" he questioned as the room erupted in laughter.

Molly looked to Ellen for approval as she whispered quietly, "Will it be okay to get him the boots now?"

Ellen smiled, nodding her agreement and gratitude to their benevolent hostess.

"Since you're going to town, young man," she addressed Stephen, "now's a good time to get those cowboy boots I promised you."

Another round of happy shouts erupted and reverberated off the walls and ceiling.

"Mercy!" his mother noted, placing her hands over her ears in mock disapproval.

"By the way, Robert, how are the Dantons doing?" Molly inquired.

Robert called them each weekend to make certain they were well.

"They're doing fine. Josie and Phillip Carroll moved from the building two weeks ago and I think Birdie is a little lonely. Carson and Julie miss little Travis too, but Cletus is still working at the grocery store for Mr. Schmidt. They've been really worried about Stephen but I've assured them he's recovered nicely."

"Do you think they'd be receptive to moving out here to the country with us to help?"

Ellen's heart raced with anticipation at this suggestion and she turned eagerly to her husband.

"Well," he stuttered, overcome by the generosity of her suggestion, "I will certainly call them and ask. That's very kind of you, Miss Molly."

"Not at all." She shrugged off his comment. "They may not be able to come but we can certainly make the offer. Why not call them right now? Do you think Cletus is still at the store?"

♥♥♥

Soon Robert had Cletus on the phone. They chatted a few minutes, exchanging greetings and updating each other on all the family members. Ellen stood anxiously in the background, wringing her hands and holding her breath in eager anticipation.

"I'm glad everyone is doing so well there, Cletus. Please give Birdie and the children our regards, but one of the reasons I called was to make you a proposal. Miss Molly has suggested that I call and see if you and your family would like to move here to the manor and help out. This is a huge place and Ellen and I can't possibly get everything done that needs doing. Do you think that's something you could do?"

He stood silently for a few minutes, listening, interjecting an occasional "uh huh" and "yes, I understand."

Finally, he stated, "Of course, we understand, Cletus. It sounds like things are getting better and better for your family and that's our main concern. I appreciate your loyalty to Mr. Schmidt and if anything happens or it doesn't work out, I want you to give me a call right away. We'll talk every week anyway but just keep me advised."

He turned to a disappointed Ellen and explained, "Mrs. Schmidt took a bad fall this past week and Mr. Schmidt has asked Cletus and his family to move in with them. There's a small room at the back of the store they're fixing up for them. Birdie will help

Merrywether Lodge
Malevolent Spirit
Book 2

"A spine chilling thriller that will keep you on the edge of your seat"

Merryweather Lodge
Ancient Revenge
Book 1

"Chilling tale of love, passion, sorcery and sacrifice"

...erryweather Lodge, ...rd-Winning Author Pauline Holyoak

...n experiences at a remote little cottage near Stonehenge ...ith fantasy, colorful characters and haunting ...ie screen"

...w.whiskeycreekpress.com www.amazon.com www.amazon.co.uk

Mrs. Schmidt and take care of their home for them, cooking and cleaning and doing the laundry. They have free room and board, and as much as Cletus appreciated the offer from Miss Molly, he said he couldn't turn Mr. Schmidt down, not after all he's done for them. I agree with him and am very proud of his stand on this."

"Oh, dear." Ellen sighed. "Well, I'm proud of them too and I certainly support their decision but I'm understandably disappointed."

"Should anything go wrong or change, the offer stands, Robert, so please enforce that to him the next time you talk."

"Thanks, Miss Molly, I certainly will. And thank you once again for the thought."

♥♥♥

Early the next morning, the men and Stephen left for the short trip to Issaqua Harbor. It was an unseasonably cool late April day so Stephen was wrapped up warmly. He stared excitedly out the back window, not wanting to miss a thing, but impatient to get into town where his promised cowboy boots awaited him.

"Over there is Carver's Mercantile," Walter explained as he pulled over to the curb across the street to park. "We'll go there first as most of the men in town who aren't working will be there."

They exited the car and started across the street. As they approached the store, a

large dog suddenly came crashing through the front plate glass window, followed closely by a man tumbling through the opening and onto the gravel walk in front of the store.   Two more men burst through the front door, stuck there side by side, neither of them able to exit as the opening was not large enough to accommodate both of them at the same time.

"What in the world?" exclaimed Walter.

Robert reached out and pulled Stephen behind him as protection against any potential danger.

The two men stuck in the doorway finally exploded through and stampeded down the street, away from the building, without a backward glance.

Two other men came to the doorway and were laughing uncontrollably at the theatrics. They were slapping their knees, holding their sides and leaning against the doorframe for support as their glee filled the street.

"Claude Carver, what in the name of notion is going on?" Walter inquired. "What have you and Dooble been up to this time?"

Claude Carver stood there in a white apron, which matched his white hair. He was a thin, wiry man with a face wrinkled by time and working in the sun, his hands knotted by hard work and arthritis. One had the impression, however, that the wrinkles filling his face were mainly caused by laughter.

Dooble Howell was a short man, probably no more than 22 or 23 years old. His right leg was several inches shorter than his left, causing his right shoulder to bulge out into a slight hump. His eyes were clear and intelligent with no bitterness or anger at his plight in life. His clothes were ill-fitting and dirty. His hair, although combed, looked as if it had not been washed in quite some time. There was dirt under his fingernails, evidence of hard labor working in the barns around the city as well as any warehouse where he could find work.

"Come on in, Walter," the owner of the store managed to gasp between peels of laughter. "You ain't gonna believe what just happened."

Robert looked over at Walter in wide-eyed wonder, and Walter shook his head, rolling his eyes back into his head in mock exasperation.

"Those two can be a menace when you put them together but they're really quite harmless," he chuckled to Robert.

Robert relaxed somewhat at the reassurance from his friend, but he allowed Walter to enter the store first. The two revelers were still laughing and slapping each other on the back as they entered.

Mr. Carver attempted to regain control as he saw the strangers with Walter.

"I'm sorry, Walter. Didn't realize you had brought guests. How do, my name is Claude Carver and this here is Dooble Howell. Sorry about the display but we was just having some fun." He succumbed once again to uncontrollable laughter. After he finally regained some composure, Walter introduced Robert and Stephen to the two.

"Now, for heaven's sakes, can you tell me what went on in here?" Walter wondered.

"Well, seeing as how it's been so cool today, I had a fire in the stove." He pointed to the large, pot-bellied stove centered in the building. There were several chairs around it, two of which were turned over.

"That's how all this happened. You know how unmerciful and downright mean the Howard boys can be, especially when they're together."

"That was the men you saw exit the building so abruptly when we got here. They're brothers. Really harmless but they can be a bit mischievous when all three of them are together," Walter explained to Robert and Stephen.

"Anyhow, they've been teasing Dooble something awful. Got downright nasty about his being short and all," Calvin continued. "Well, yesterday, Winton Howard asked Dooble what part of West Virginia he was from."

"I told him I'm not from West Virginia, I'm from right here." Dooble took up the story. "Then he said, 'You must be a ridge runner from West Virginia. Otherwise, how come one leg's shorter than the other?' Then Roy called me hunchback because of this hump on my shoulder. They thought that was real funny."

"Yeah, and after they left, me and Dooble put our heads together and come up with a plan to get 'em back. I was glad it was so cool today so they wouldn't be suspicious about a fire in the stove so I had a pretty good one going when they got here. They brought their old dog with 'em too. Anyway, they were sitting around the stove, all leaned back in their chairs. I think William was even snoozing. About that time, Dooble arrived. 'Here comes old Limpy,' Roy told the others. William looked up and then put his head back down and Winton said 'Morning, Shorty.' They all kinda laughed." Claude erupted into another fit of laughter so Dooble took over once more.

"I didn't say nothing to them. I just walked over to the stove and stood there warming my hands. 'You fellows doing okay?' I finally says. They all looked up. I guess they were a little curious about my being so nice to them. Anyway, when they looked up, I reached in my coat pocket and pulled out three sticks of dynamite. They weren't really dynamite, they were empty, but the Howards didn't know that. When they saw those sticks, they all perked up and the chairs all settled back on the floor. 'What you gonna do with that?' Roy wanted to know. I didn't say a word, just reached down, opened up the stove door and threw those three pieces of dynamite into the fire."

All the men were laughing now. Stephen wasn't sure what dynamite was, but he figured it was something that frightened the Howard brothers.

"When Dooble threw those sticks in that fire, you never saw such scrambling and scratching in all your life!" Claude continued. "They were so fired up, it got their old dog excited, and he busted right through the front window with William right behind him. Roy and Winton threw chairs every which way, and they got stuck in the door trying to get out. I'm telling you that was plumb funny! I ain't laughed this hard in a long time. Feels good too. Especially seeing as how they deserved it."

"I'm really sorry about your window, Claude," Dooble apologized.

"No need to be," Claude waved his hand in dismissal. "It was absolutely worth it. I've got a spare one in the back and I'll get it put in."

"I'll help you. I guess it's the least I can do."

♥♥♥

While the two worked to clean up the broken glass and bring the new window from the back, Stephen began trying on cowboy boots. Walter worked at filling the list Molly had given him, and Robert helped Stephen.

As Stephen was deciding on his boots, Robert looked around and his eyes rested on women's dresses hanging on a rack. He was glad he had brought money with him.

Stephen found the boots he liked and Robert suggested, "Let's find your mother a new dress."

"Okay, that's a great idea. A red one! She looks pretty in red."

"I'm not sure that's a good choice, but we'll see what we can find."

Stephen found a lovely red dress, simple and elegant in design. It had a princess waistline and slightly scooped neck. It was short sleeved with a flared skirt and was reduced to $2.00. Robert found one made of blue gingham. It was a shirtwaist dress with a belt and roll-up sleeves and cost $1.00.

"This will look good with her blue eyes, son."

"Yes, but this will look good with her blonde hair." Stephen was clutching the red dress hopefully.

"I tell you what – she's such a good mom and a good wife, we'll get both of them for her. She hasn't had a new dress in a long, long time."

"Yay!" Stephen cheered.

"Daddy, can we get Miss Molly something?"

"Of course, son, and I think that's a wonderful idea. What did you have in mind?"

"Something pretty because she's so pretty," Stephen responded.

They looked around and found some vases but that didn't suit Stephen. He looked at some brooches and handkerchiefs, a hatpin and white gloves. Finally his eyes rested on a silver music box. He picked it up, turning it over gently in his hands. It was shaped like a birdhouse and when he lifted the roof, a tiny bluebird inside spun around as the music box played a haunting melody.

"What's the name of this song?"

"It's called 'Always,'" his father answered.

"Can we get this, Daddy? Please? Then Miss Molly will have her own birdhouse. It's not as big as mine but it plays music and she'll know that I'll love her always. We can put my boots back. I don't need them. I really want to get this for Miss Molly."

Robert checked the price and saw that it was $1.00. He was relieved that it wasn't a priceless treasure because he would have hated to disappoint his son. His devotion to Miss Molly was quite touching.

"I think that's a lovely gift for Miss Molly, son, and I'm sure she's going to love it. You're a very thoughtful young man and Miss Molly is the one buying your boots so we don't dare go back without them. She'd be really disappointed." His pride in Stephen was evident.

♥♥♥

They waited patiently for Claude and Dooble to finish installing the glass, helping all they could. As they prepared to pay, Stephen saw a pair of black slippers. They were flat and were ballet style.

"Look, Daddy, these shoes would be beautiful on Mommy's feet. Can we afford these too?"

Robert quickly added them to their growing stack. Walter handed the boots to Stephen after he paid for them and Stephen put them on at once.

Walter turned to Dooble. "Dooble, are you interested in working for Miss Molly out at the manor? Robert is going to need plenty of help in the yard and doing repairs this spring and summer."

"Why, sure, I'd be beholden." Dooble was genuinely surprised at the offer. It was difficult for him to find work because even though he was very capable of doing most anything, people were reluctant to hire him due to his disability. He depended on yard work and sweeping out buildings, usually for food. The town blacksmith let him sleep in his barn, and Claude let him use the shower off the back porch at his home when the water pipes weren't frozen. There was no hot water so Dooble hadn't been able to take a shower since before Christmas.

"You can stay in the cook's quarters behind the kitchen until we can repair the cottage behind the house. It needs a lot of work but the roof doesn't leak. I was just in there last week, and the chimney looks okay, but there's a few loose bricks on top. We'll need to check it all the way down. There's a wood stove in the basement of the manor, and we'll put that in there before next fall. A couple of windows need to be replaced. They're boarded up now so the cold and the rain won't come in but neither will the light. It needs a lot of painting and the roof is looking a little shabby so we'll see about getting that fixed before next winter. And we'll get you some work clothes and boots that fit before we leave here. Miss Molly insists that her employees be safe while they work."

"Thank you, Mr. Monroe. Thank you kindly." He shook Walter's hand vigorously. They were touched by his gratitude.

♥♥♥

Soon they all climbed into the limousine for the trip back to the manor. Dooble had his few worldly possessions wrapped in a towel and tied with a shoestring. The only shoes he owned were on his feet.

"Is that all you have?" little Stephen inquired.

"Yep, little man, this is it! I travel light."

They soon left the village and moved through the countryside. Stephen kept glancing over at his traveling partner seated on the other end of the back seat. He began to squirm a little, turned his head and watched the view going by. Finally, he turned toward Dooble.

"You smell bad, Mr. Dooble."

"Stephen!" His father was aghast.

"That's okay, Mr. Blair," Dooble laughed. "He's right, of course, and he didn't mean no harm. I apologize, little man, and I'll try to do something about that as soon as I can."

Stephen settled down and made no further comments.

Gail Cauble Gurley

Chapter 10
Welcome, Dooble and Patches

The group arrived with Dooble and the trunk filled with gifts. It was difficult to determine who was more excited, Ellen or Molly, as they accepted their surprise gifts from Stephen and Robert.

"This music box is the most special gift I have ever received, Stephen, and I'll treasure it always." Molly exclaimed.

"That's the name of the song it plays," Stephen observed.

"I love these dresses!" his mother said. "I can't believe my two loves were so thoughtful as to bring me two dresses and a pair of beautiful shoes as well. I feel like a princess. It's just too much. Just look at this red one! I can't wait to wear it to church. And the blue one is perfect too!"

"I picked out the red one," Stephen proclaimed proudly.

Walter settled Dooble into the cook's quarters off the kitchen while the women celebrated their gifts. Dooble was as excited as they were as he toured his palatial new quarters. There was a twin bed with a real mattress, sheets, a pillow, blanket and even a bedspread. The armoire seemed large enough to live in and he knew he'd never have enough clothes to put into it.

He was especially thrilled by the small bathroom which adjoined his room. There was a bathtub, a pedestal sink with a medicine cabinet and a commode. There was even hot water.

"This is your package, Dooble. We wanted to make sure you had good work clothes and safety shoes while working. Miss Molly doesn't want anyone hurt." He laid the large bundle on the bed and turned to leave.

"Thank you, Mr. Walter, I'm much obliged. I want to pay Miss Molly back, however, for this."

"No need to. She wouldn't accept it anyway. I'll leave you to get unpacked and settled in. We eat dinner at 6:00 so we'll call you. If you get through before then, please come out and join us. We almost always stay in the kitchen when we're in the house, especially when it's cold. If you need anything, just call." He pulled the door shut as he left the room.

Dooble was dumbfounded by the day's events, and stood there in mute shock for several seconds. He shook his head to clear it, wondering if he was dreaming. He was filled with joy as he realized that he was not, and this was indeed happening to him – Dooble Howell, of all people.

He tore eagerly into his package, pulling out all the treasures inside. There were three pairs of work pants, three blue work shirts with short sleeves, two long sleeved flannel shirts, new underwear and socks and a new pair of high top boots with steel toes. He was amazed, and his hands trembled with excitement as he gently touched each piece.

He hurried into the bathroom and took a hot, soaking bath. He found a razor and shaving cream in the medicine cabinet and was soon clean, head to toe. He slipped into his new clothes, rolled the right leg up to compensate for his defect, and pulled on his new boots. They slipped on easily and felt wonderfully comfortable on his feet.

He cleaned up his room, taking his dirty clothes to the door and standing there for a minute, building up the courage to exit. Soon he slowly opened the door and stepped out shyly. He stood there, blushing, uncertain, holding his dirty laundry and waiting for guidance as to his next move.

The room filled with appreciative sounds of approval and acceptance.

"You look good, Dooble!" little Stephen announced.

"Yeah, I guess I do clean up okay, thank you, Little Man."

"Just drop your laundry in the basket inside the laundry room, Dooble. I'll do the laundry probably tomorrow," Ellen instructed.

"Thank you, ma'am, but if you don't mind, I'd like to just throw them away. They're really pretty wore out and they were too big anyhow." He would have been mortified to have her wash these dirty rags so he would rather just throw them away than subject himself to that embarrassment.

"Okay, Dooble, whatever you say."

"And Miss Molly, I thank you so kindly for these new clothes. These are the finest ones I've ever owned. My room is like a castle and I'm just so proud to be here. I assure you I'll do a real good job for you, whatever you need done."

"Well, we're proud to have you, Dooble, I assure you. And I hope you're comfortable in your room. If you need anything, please just ask." She was touched by his gratitude over the tiniest room in the house. She felt humbled by his obvious pleasure over his new clothes, room and job.

♥♥♥

The dinner set before Dooble was magnificent by his standards. There was fried chicken, potato salad, green beans, homemade bread and a custard pie. His coffee cup was bottomless, and he had never had so much coffee at one time in his life. He was afraid he was making a pig of himself but no one seemed to notice.

As they sat there talking and digesting their food after the meal, Stephen turned to Dooble who was sitting across the table from him.

"You smell better, Mr. Dooble."

"Stephen!" his mother gasped, nearly falling out of her chair.

Stephen turned to look at his mother, a look of shock and confusion on his face.

"Oh, that's okay, Miss Ellen," Dooble laughed. "We already had this conversation in the car on the way here and Little Man don't mean no harm."

"Oh, no, you don't mean...Oh, Dooble, I'm so-o-o-o sorry. Stephen, honey, you mustn't ever say things like that. It hurts people."

"I'm sorry, Mommy, I didn't mean to." Stephen was in distress and his eyes filled with tears.

"He has the beautiful honesty of a child, Ellen, and had no idea that it wasn't socially correct," Molly interjected. "It's a shame we can't all be that way and there's no harm done, I'm certain."

"He said nothing out of meanness, ma'am, I assure you. I know the difference, believe me." Dooble reached across the table and playfully punched Stephen on the shoulder. Soon the whole unpleasant incident was forgotten as they all pitched in to clean up the dishes.

Dooble returned to his room early, eager to try out his new bed. He was exhausted by the excitement of the day coupled with the heavy meal he had enjoyed. He turned down the covers and gasped out loud. *Sheets!* he thought to himself. *I don't remember ever sleeping on sheets before!*

♥♥♥

Dooble and Robert worked in the front yard the next morning, cutting limbs and hauling them to the back.

"We'll work on the cottage after lunch when it gets warmer." Robert stated.

Dooble was a tireless worker and made no complaints about struggling with the awkward limbs and branches.

♥♥♥

The men completed the work in the front yard within two days.

"We'll take some more off next fall but I think that's good for now. We don't want to damage the trees since the sap is up and the leaves are out," Robert observed.

They turned their attention to the cottage. Dooble was enchanted by the structure. It was covered in red bricks, some of which had moss attached. Two windows had been broken out, probably by the settling walls, but the other windows had twelve individual panes of glass and opened by swinging out on hinges. A large brick chimney stood at one end of the house and served as the main heating source. The front entrance was extended out from the rest of the house, and was covered with the same stone that covered the manor. The front door was a Dutch door, which was designed to allow the top to be opened in hot weather and the bottom closed to keep errant children in or stray animals and chickens out.

The interior was one large room with the kitchen area against the back wall. A new faucet had replaced the hand water pump some years earlier but the original pine cabinets remained. The floors were wide pine boards and were covered with the warm, glowing patina of time and former good care.

A bathroom had been added to the back during the 1920s, and the bedroom was in a loft area overhead. It opened into the downstairs area and was guarded by rough hewn railings. This openness allowed heat to enter the room during cold weather. The room was A-shaped under the steep roof, and it was necessary to walk leaned over when approaching the sides of the room. The bed, consequently, set in the middle of the room, facing the guardrail. A large window behind the bed could be opened to admit cool breezes in hot weather.

The two men worked tirelessly for a day, repairing brickwork on the chimney, replacing the broken windows, painting the windows of the manor, replacing damaged steps and repairing the roof on the cottage. The manor needed some roof work but Robert was afraid to let Dooble crawl up there so he decided to try and do it himself.

"I almost hate to suggest this, Mr. Robert, but the Howard brothers are roofers. You might want to contact them and see if they can do it."

Robert laughed at the irony but decided he might as well contact them. He would keep an eye on them and surely, they wouldn't do anything in retaliation while they were working for the trick Dooble had played on them at Carver's Mercantile. Besides, maybe they had learned their lesson after the dynamite in the stove incident.

♥♥♥

The very next day, the whole family traveled to town. Ellen had not yet been and she was as excited as Stephen. She was enthralled with Carver's Mercantile, and she and Molly looked at all the merchandise the store had to offer. It seemed to Robert that they touched most of it too.

The Howard brothers entered the store, stopping in surprise when they saw Dooble. They stood for a minute, unsure of whether to enter or leave.

"Morning, fellows, good to see you again." Dooble greeted them. "Come on in. No need to worry. I got no dynamite today."

Claude Carver laughed aloud. "Yeah, come on in, fellows." he invited.

Introductions were made, and soon an agreement was reached that the Howard brothers would repair the roof on the manor and replace the one on the cottage. They would be at the manor the next morning. Robert felt certain they held no grudges for the joke that had been played upon them as they seemed quite mellow and meek. Perhaps it had been good for them to be the brunt of a practical joke. They seemed to have grown up a little as a result of it.

The family spent the day in the village, going into all the shops and exploring the small park. Stephen fed the ducks, and they had a lunch of sandwiches on the park bench.

They bought some groceries and supplies for the manor and Dooble bought some new clothes.

"I'm beginning to feel like a clothes hog," he admitted. "I've never had so many clothes before in my life but I wanted something really nice to wear to church. My work clothes will kind of stand out when we're there."

As they exited Carver's in preparation to leave the village, they saw Mr. Carver standing on the side of his building, feeding a dog.

"Is that your dog, Mr. Carver?" Stephen inquired.

"Nope, I don't know who she belongs to. She just showed up one day and was hungry so I fed her. Looks like she's in the family way too. I don't know what I'm going to do with her. I sure can't have a litter of pups underfoot. She's a real nice dog and don't bark none but I figure somebody just put her out 'cause they didn't want to bother with her no more."

"That's mean!" Stephen cried. "Mommy, can we please have her? Please? I'll take care of her."

Ellen was flabbergasted. She stood in confusion, not knowing how to respond.

Once again, Molly came to Stephen's rescue.

"I think that's a wonderful idea, Stephen. We could use a dog at the manor. She'll help keep the raccoons and squirrels at bay. And when the puppies arrive, I'm certain some of the other folks in the country around us would like to have one. A dog can be a real asset out in the country. We once had one that woke us up one night with very loud barking, and when we went to check, we found that the barn was on fire so he saved all of our horses for us that night."

"Oh, thank you, Miss Molly. Thank you, thank you, thank you. And I'll take care of her, I promise."

Ellen smiled her thanks to her employer and friend, but Molly really was spoiling Stephen. However, the young mother was grateful that she cared so much for him.

So it was that when they returned to the manor, there was one more occupant in the car. She was a white dog with pointed ears and a shaggy tail. There was hair growing on her legs, much resembling feathers.

"Shew!" Stephen exclaimed. "She stinks!"

"Stephen," his mother scolded, "we've discussed before about your saying ugly things."

"But she's a dog, Mommy; she doesn't understand what I'm saying."

"We don't know that for sure, Stephen, and besides, it's not nice to say anything unkind about any of God's creatures. Even if it's true!" She raised her hand to stop his next comment because she knew it was coming, and to cover her nose against the offensive odor from the dog.

"Okay," he stated sheepishly. "What are we going to name her?" he wondered, his momentary shame forgotten.

"What would you like to name her?"

"How about Snowball? She's white. Or Whitey. Or we could call her Rescue because that's what we did."

They all laughed as he continued to stroke her.

"She needs to be brushed," Stephen observed. "Her hair is tangled in patches."

His face suddenly lit up. "That's it. We'll call her Patches."

The dog looked up at the young boy and wagged her tail.

"She likes it. Look, Mommy, she likes it. Hey, Patches, girl. You're my new friend and we're going home."

♥♥♥

Ellen absolutely drew the line at letting Patches sleep inside the house.

"She can come inside during the day, but she needs to stay somewhere else until her puppies get here."

So Patches was confined to the carriage house during the nights to await the arrival of her puppies. Stephen, true to his word, took very good care of his dog, feeding and brushing her daily as well as getting her clean water each day. Dooble helped him give her a bath, as she was too large for Stephen to handle alone. They filled a large tub with warm water and washed her with lots of soap. Stephen squealed with pleasure as she sprayed them by shaking water out of her hair when they removed her from the tub. They dried her off with towels and Stephen brushed her vigorously to remove the excess water.

He took her into the house to show off her new bath and Ellen greeted them at the kitchen door.

"Well, hello, you two. I thought Patches was getting a bath, why is Stephen so wet?"

"Oh, Mommy!"

"She looks really good, son. You and Dooble did a fine job."

"Yeah, and she smells better too."

"Stephen." his mother warned.

"Well, she does."

She shook her head in resignation.

The Howard brothers worked for several days completing the repairs to the manor roof and replacing the cottage roof. They did really good work and were there each and every day, right on time and working the entire day.

On the day they completed their work, they all approached Dooble. Robert was standing inside the carriage house and watched the scene play out.

As they approached, Roy, who was the oldest, removed his hat and held it in front as he spoke to Dooble.

"Dooble, uh, we just want to say how sorry we are for all the mean things we've said to you in the past. You're a good person and we meant no harm. We're much impressed by the way you work. You could work circles around anybody, even somebody with two straight legs. We hope you don't hold no grudge against us." He extended his hand as he finished his awkward speech.

"No hard feelings, Roy. And thanks to all of you. There was no damage done so let's just forget about it." He shook each hand as it was extended to him, and the brothers turned to leave, much more tolerant than when they arrived several days earlier.

♥♥♥

It rained the next day so Patches was left in the carriage house. Dooble took food out to her after breakfast and made certain she had water. Stephen worried about her all day and kept pacing the floor and staring out the window. Even Molly had difficulty distracting him.

Before dinner, Stephen and his parents were in the library where Robert was working on plans for the flower garden. Molly had retired to her room to take a rest before dinner and Ellen and

Stephen were letting everyone know that dinner was ready when the front door opened. They looked up as Dooble entered the room with a cardboard box.

"We have puppies," he announced.

Pandemonium ruled as they all rushed to the box. Stephen was nearly beside himself with excitement.

"How's Patches?" he inquired.

"She's doing great. She's tired right now and really anxious because I took her babies away but I'll take them back in a minute."

"How many are there?" Robert asked.

"There's six. Three males and three females. I'm afraid I'm going to have to destroy one of the males though. He's crippled."

"What do you mean destroy? What does that mean, Mommy?"

"Honey, that means that the puppy is suffering and Dooble will have to make sure he doesn't suffer anymore."

"Does that mean he's going to kill him?"

The adults looked at each other and made no comment.

"No!" Stephen screamed. "You can't do that! I won't let you!"

"Little Man, I'm sorry but this pup was born with very short front legs. He won't be able to walk around and he'll be better off if I destroy him."

"No! You weren't destroyed when your leg got shorter!" Stephen was crying hysterically.

They stood in stunned silence at Stephen's comment.

"The puppy stays." They all turned to see Molly standing in the doorway. Stephen ran to her, clinging to her as he sobbed uncontrollably.

"It's okay, sweetheart. Nobody's going to hurt your puppy. We'll do everything we can for him and if he dies, it'll be God's will, not ours."

♥♥♥

And so it was that six new puppies joined the residents of Fulton Manor. It was agreed that Stephen would keep the one born with short front legs and the others would be given away to neighbors as soon as they were old enough. Patches would also remain.

Stephen spent most of his day in the carriage house with Patches and her babies. Molly and Ellen visited each day also to make certain all was well. To everyone's surprise, the small one with the deformed front legs thrived.

"I'm sure Stephen's determined will and love are making him stronger," Molly observed.

"I think you're right." His mother agreed.

After several days, they decided it was time to name them. They had waited to see their developed personalities, which would determine a proper name.

The solid white male who looked most like his mother was quite passive and was more interested in sleeping than developing a personality.

"Let's call him Boo," Stephen suggested, "because he's white like a ghost. Maybe if we call him Boo, it'll wake him up."

The solid black male was constantly jumping at the sides of his box, trying to escape, so they named him Bouncer. The black female was named Pepper.

There was another black female with tiny white spots sprinkled across her back. She looked like someone had sprinkled salt on her so they named her Freckles. The white female with black paws had a bushy tail like her mother's and would violently wag it anytime someone entered her domain.

"Let's call her Sweep," Molly suggested, "since she seems to be sweeping the floor with her tail every time we come in."

And so they were all named except for Stephen's little special needs male.

"Whatever are we going to name him?" Robert wondered.

"Let's call him Gimpy," Stephen offered.

"Son, do you know what that means?" his father inquired uneasily.

"No, but Dooble said one time that the Howard brothers called him that one time so I figure it must have something to do with his legs."

They all laughed, shaking their heads in amazement at the innocent perception of this young child.

"Okay, Gimpy it is," his father agreed. "But understand that he's named with love and this is no insult."

Chapter 11
The Announcement

April passed with a late frost that blanketed the fresh, green lawn with silver sheets. May dawned with a bright sun, determined to penetrate and shatter winter's grip. The crocus, jonquils and hyacinths around the manor and the cottage were so thick that they seemed to be shoving and pushing each other as they searched for a caress from the sun. Stephen loved to walk to the edge of the beds and gaze at the lushness, reaching out frequently to touch a particularly bright bloom or bury his nose into the depths of fragrance.

"Be careful, Stephen, there are bees in those flowers," Molly warned.

He jumped back as a honeybee zoomed by his face, barely missing his nose. He turned to Molly with a look of fearful surprise in his eyes. She laughed as he turned to her.

"You have pollen on your nose."

"What's pollen?"

"That's the yellow powder in the flowers that the honey bees gather. They use it to make honey."

"Can I see? Where do they make the honey?"

"We have some bee hives behind the cottage. I'll let you see them but you stay away from them. They can sting you very badly. And Gimpy too. They get agitated very easily in the early spring. This is their busy season gathering pollen and making honey. This is also when the queen bee lays her eggs for the next generation of honey makers."

"Come on, Gimpy, let's go see."

The small dog was Stephen's constant companion, seldom leaving his side. He slept in a box beside Stephen's bed, and Ellen had caught him in Stephen's bed several times. She had warned him against putting the small dog in the bed with him.

"You may roll over on him, Stephen, and dogs don't belong in the bed."

"But, he's my friend, Mommy. And he gets cold."

"He doesn't get cold in your warm bedroom, Stephen. Leave him in his box please."

"Okay." Stephen reluctantly agreed.

The little creature had learned to maneuver quite aptly with his front legs. He bounced along joyfully, just happy to be with Stephen. If they encountered particularly uneven or treacherous terrain such as gravel piled beside the drive, he would just roll over and over or stand and wait for Stephen to pick him up. He had become quite self-reliant and was even able to ascend steps. He was slow but managed quite well. Stephen taught him to turn around and back down steps using his hind legs so there were few places that he could not go.

Robert and Dooble watched with gentle humor as the three came down the drive toward the cottage. Gimpy was bouncing happily along; Molly was walking slowly so as not to leave Stephen and Gimpy behind, and Stephen was skipping and hopping from one side of the drive to the other, chattering like the squirrels playing in the trees.

"Where are you three going?" Robert stuck his head out of the door and called to them.

"We're going to see the bee hives." Stephen announced happily.

"Don't get too close and don't bother them. They're pretty busy these days."

"Okay, we won't bother them."

They moved away and Robert studied them as they moved along.

"Dooble, do you think we could build some kind of little carriage or skate for Gimpy to push around on? It looks very painful, the way he bounces along."

"Most possible," Dooble replied.

♥♥♥

The trio rounded the cottage, and Molly pointed out three white boxes setting at the edge of the trees at the back of the cottage yard. Several small honey bees zoomed past them as they stood there looking in the direction of the boxes.

"There they are. In those boxes."

They sat on a stone wall, watching the steady line of bees going back and forth from the hive, by the cottage, to the front yard and to the manor's front yard, where they gathered their bounty. Gimpy sat quietly beside his small master, not noticing the bees at all. Stephen was altogether enchanted by the process and enjoyed the afternoon immensely.

They returned to the front of the manor later and sat in the chairs on the front porch. Dooble had wiped the winter dust and dirt off, so they settled into them comfortably, watching the bees and viewing the flowers. Stephen and Gimpy would frequently grow tired of simply sitting so they would jump off the porch and race around the yard to the drive and back, then to the flowers and back.

"We need a walkway." Molly observed.

Stephen looked around and decided that was probably a good idea. The grass was wet and his mother got upset when he came in with wet feet.

"You'll get sick again, Stephen." she had cautioned.

"Where will it go?" he asked.

"I don't know. We'll let Dooble decide. Remind me to ask him at dinner tonight."

♥♥♥

Molly made the request of Dooble at the dinner table that night.

"Dooble, can you put a walkway from the front porch to the drive and flowers for us? It's a little difficult for Stephen and Gimpy to get through the grass, especially this time of year with it being so thick and wet."

"Yes'm, I'll take care of that," he promised.

"How are the repairs to the cottage coming?"

"Oh, they're coming right along. We'll be through in a couple of days. We've got just a little bit more painting and cleaning to do. And the Howard boys did a real good job on the roof. It didn't leak but it was sure worn out and would soon have started leaking."

The family sat quietly together, moving into the warm night to gather on the front porch. Stephen, Gimpy and Patches played off the porch, running around the trees and across the drive. Dooble watched them as they played. He seemed to be studying their movements.

"Time to come in, Stephen," his mother called. "It's getting too dark and damp out here."

"Okay, Mommy. Come on, Gimpy, let's go in. Good night, Patches. We'll see you in the morning."

♥♥♥

Stephen's fifth birthday was on May 12 and it was a gala affair. The yard was filled with balloons and there was even a pony from the farm down the road for Stephen and his friends from Sunday school. All the children were fascinated by Gimpy, and by the end of the party, the little dog was only too happy to see them leave. He attempted to escape beneath a chair but tiny hands soon dragged him out. He was very glad to reach his box sanctuary beside Stephen's bed that night. And Stephen was glad to get in bed too. He had had a busy and wonderful day.

"He's growing up," Robert whispered as they stood beside his bed, watching their son sleeping peacefully.

"Yes, he is. And doing it beautifully." Ellen could not hide her pride.

They moved into their living room and sat quietly side by side on the sofa, reliving the excitement of the day.

"Miss Molly is such a blessing to us, Robert. There's no way that we can ever repay her or show her how much we love and care for her."

"I don't think we need to worry about that, dear. She seems to receive great joy from loving and caring for us, especially Stephen. I know she has no obligation but it's a miracle, the way she loves us. She makes no demands on us and seems to thrive on giving."

"Well, she is concerned about one thing. She asked Dooble more than a week ago to put a walkway down from the front porch to the drive and the flowerbeds. He hasn't done it yet, and I think it bothers her somewhat. You have finished with the cottage, haven't you? Is there anyway that you two can get that walkway done?"

"I'm sorry, dear, I forgot about it. I do remember her mentioning it to Dooble and I'll be sure to remind him in the morning. We finished the cottage and we have plenty to do but there's no excuse for this not being done. Thanks for reminding me."

"I'm sure you will, darling. If you don't mind, I'm going to bed. I'm not feeling well."

"What's wrong?" he was instantly concerned.

"Oh, nothing, I'm just tired. I guess I have spring fever. I'll be fine so don't worry."

♥♥♥

After breakfast the next morning, the men began their work on the compound.

"Dooble, Ellen reminded me last night that Miss Molly had asked over a week ago that we put a walkway down from the front porch to the drive and flowerbeds. I had forgotten about it, quite frankly, but we need to get it done. I'm sure you forgot it too."

"Nope, I remember."

Robert was surprised and a little irritated at Dooble's confession.

"I don't understand." He waited for an explanation. He had never heard Dooble admit to not doing something he was asked to do, and he was interested in hearing what he had to say to justify it.

"No need to put one down 'til we know where to put it. I been studying them to see where they like to walk. I feel that people should decide where walks go instead of walks deciding where people should go. I checked it last night and I think we can put it down now. If you look, you'll see where the grass is matted down in a real plain pattern from the porch to the drive and flowers. That's the way they want to walk so that's where we'll put the walkway."

"I apologize, Dooble." Robert was ashamed for doubting his friend. "I should have known you had a good reason."

"No need to apologize. You had no way of knowing what I had in mind. I'd explained it had I known it was bothering anybody."

Robert laughed. "Guess I learned a valuable lesson. I'll be a bit more patient in the future and have more faith in your dependability."

"Nope, don't have no faith in me. You'll put your faith in the wrong place. Put your faith in the Lord. He's the only one who won't let us down."

♥♥♥

The two men spent the day digging up the matted down grass so that the new concrete walkway could be poured. It swept gently out into the yard and back in the opposite direction toward the drive. It approached a birdbath setting in the yard and then moved by a fishpond before reaching its destination. It branched off from the birdbath, wandered between two large oak trees, and up to and beyond a stone bench near the flowers before ending at the edge of the irises.

Robert stepped back and looked at the route of the path.

"You were right, Dooble. It follows the path they have chosen in order to most enjoy the lawn. I would have run it straight to the destinations without curving it around as Stephen, Miss Molly and Gimpy have done."

"And look what we would have missed," he pointed out.

"Yep, you're right once again. I had hardly noticed the birdbath, and quite frankly, didn't even know the bench was there. It's quite a beautiful walkway."

"It becomes more of a walk to travel down it than a way," Dooble pointed out. "Each trip down this path will be an adventure. We'll see the birds taking a bath, stop and watch the fish, watch the squirrels in those big old oak trees and sit on the stone bench before finally seeing the flowers or reaching the drive."

"This sounds more like a sermon than digging a walk," Robert observed.

"I ain't no preacher, Mr. Robert," Dooble pointed out.

Robert was impressed by the depth of his companion's sensitivity. He felt humbled in the presence of this caring, philosophical man.

♥♥♥

The family was thrilled at the dinner table that night about the new walkway. It was the main topic of discussion, and they all went out to the front to investigate it more closely. Gimpy was unable to bounce on it yet due to the roughness of the gravel base, but Stephen held him up as he moved his tiny back legs across the surface.

"We'll have the cement poured soon, son, and Gimpy can walk on it a little better. And Dooble and I have decided to try and build some sort of skate with wheels to tie around Gimpy so he can move a little better over most surfaces."

♥♥♥

Robert awakened early and moved quietly downstairs so as not to bother Ellen and Stephen. He made a pot of coffee and made the day's plans in his head.

He was still studying when Ellen and Stephen, carrying Gimpy, came down.

"Good morning, my two loves, how are you both?"

Stephen leaped on his father's lap, and asked eagerly, "Are you going to build the skate for Gimpy today, Daddy?"

"Probably. We'll at least try to get started on it, but we want to pour cement in the walkway too. We won't get all of that done either, but we'll start near the house."

Molly arrived in the kitchen after the men had left to begin their chores.

"Good morning, everybody. Where are the men?"

"Robert and Dooble have already gone out to start work on the walkway and Walter was going to your company to take care of some business."

Molly moved a little closer to Ellen, concern on her face.

"What's the matter, Ellen? You look ghastly."

"Oh, I'm okay."

"How long have you been sick?"

"Several weeks, I guess."

"Oh, my dear, that won't do. We're getting you to the doctor today. Why haven't you told someone?"

"There really wasn't any need to. I'm only sick in the mornings."

"You mean...?" Molly's eyes were huge.

"Yes, ma'am, I'm afraid so."

"Oh, my heavens, this is absolutely marvelous! I couldn't be happier! This is the best news this house has ever heard! Does Robert know?"

"No, ma'am, I was not sure how to tell him. I didn't know what this would mean to our being here. I mean, I wasn't sure how you'd feel..."

"Heavens, my dearest Ellen, I'm beside myself with joy. This is joyous and wonderful news, and I assure you I couldn't be happier." She actually clapped her hands in her excitement.

Ellen began to weep with relief as she accepted Molly's hugs and adulations.

"What's going on?" Stephen asked, somewhat alarmed by his mother's tears.

"It's okay, son, and Mommy is fine, I assure you. I wanted to tell your father first but the way things have worked out, I guess he'll be the last to know. How would you like to have a baby brother or baby sister?"

"Yayyyyyy! Are you sure? When, Mommy?"

"Yes, I'm sure and I'm thinking probably right after Christmas."

"Oh, boy, I can't believe it. Can we go tell Daddy right now?"

"I think that would be a great idea, honey."

"While you two do that, I'm going to call Dr. Sheffield and make an appointment for you to go see him right away. And when you get outside, ask Dooble to come in here so you can have a minute to yourselves."

♥♥♥

Ellen and Stephen found the two men outside the carriage house, sorting through scraps of lumber, looking for a base for Gimpy's skate. Several small wheels lay in a pile nearby. They had also pulled long pieces of lumber out so as to build a frame around the walkway to hold the cement. It would be labor intensive since it was so curved so they were careful to choose pieces which were flexible yet strong enough not to split when they were molded around the curves.

Robert looked up in surprise as his family approached.

"Is anything wrong?' he inquired.

"No, everything's fine, but, Dooble, Miss Molly asked that you come in for a minute please. Would you like to go with him, Stephen?"

"Yeah." he welcomed the chance to walk with Dooble. Dooble's steps were nearly as small and slow as his own, so he did not have to struggle to keep up.

"What's wrong, Ellen?" Robert was quite anxious by now.

"Nothing, sweetheart, I assure you. I just wanted to tell you that you're going to be a father again."

Dooble and Stephen stopped and turned around as they heard a shout of joy and laughter escaping from Robert. It echoed off the walls and through the trees. He was jumping up and down, and pulled Ellen into his arms, dancing gleefully around the yard.

"What in the world?" Dooble uttered.

"I'm going to have a new baby brother or sister," Stephen announced proudly.

"That's wonderful, Little Man. No wonder your daddy is excited. That's quite a bit of exciting news."

♥♥♥

The simple structure of a skate for Gimpy was completed only after Robert had settled down somewhat from the unexpected and welcomed news. They were even able to pour the first section of the walkway, but Dooble swore at the dinner table that Robert's feet never touched the ground all day.

"Dr. Sheffield said he'll see you tomorrow, Ellen, and I think Robert should go with you. You can take the car in. I don't think Walter will be using it tomorrow and I'll look after Stephen and little Gimpy."

"Thank you, Miss Molly, we appreciate it," Ellen smiled at her friend.

"Oh, by the way, Gimpy, we have that skate for you. Let's see how it works."

The skate was fastened around Gimpy's small body. They took him to the front yard to see if it would work in the grass. He stood there, looking confused, for a few minutes and finally moved his back legs as Stephen called him. He stopped in obvious surprise when he moved forward without bouncing, but soon was running around easily.

"Look!" Stephen shouted. "The cement is still wet enough for us to write in. Come here, Gimpy, let's put your wheel prints in the cement."

The adults laughed as the tiny dog's back feet and front wheels were pressed into the cement. He snarled his objections and was quite comical trying to lick his back feet. He pranced gingerly across the grass, attempting to clean it off. Ellen rescued him and gently wiped the residue from between his toes.

Stephen placed his handprints beside those of his small dog, and Molly inscribed their names.

"Now," she chimed, "the walkway has been properly dedicated and is now the official property of Stephen Blair and Gimpy."

♥♥♥

Dr. Sheffield gave Ellen a clean bill of health the next day. He started her on some vitamins and told her there wasn't anything special that she should do.

"Just do what you normally do, Ellen, but if you have any problems at all, call me at once."

He called Robert in to reassure him concerning his wife's condition, as he had been impatiently pacing in the waiting room. They all sat and chatted for a few minutes, the doctor getting updated on the manor and Molly.

As they started to leave, Robert shook his hand and then mentioned, "Doctor, you know that Dooble works at Fulton Manor and I've been worried about his back since he has one leg shorter than the other. Do you have any ideas of how we might be able to help him?"

"Your concern is admirable, Robert, but I don't know what to do to make it better. I'll look through some of my literature and make some calls to see what I can come up with. I don't have a great deal of experience with braces and such, and Dooble's the only patient I've ever had who has one leg shorter than the other. But I'll sure try to find some information for you."

"Thank you, doctor, I appreciate it so much. And thank you for taking care of Ellen."

"I'm very happy for you nice young people. There's no reason why she won't have a fine, healthy baby."

Gail Cauble Gurley

Chapter 12
Back to the City

The family arrived at St. Christopher's Episcopal Church in the village the next Sunday morning. Within a few minutes, everyone in the church knew that Ellen Blair was with child. In small towns and villages around the world, this blessed news seems to float on the air like static electricity and very few announcements are necessary.

Ellen looked radiant in her red dress and black slippers. Robert stood close beside her, his arm linked protectively through hers. Stephen was likewise extra attentive, and Molly watched them proudly, smiling slightly. Walter held the heavy church door open for all of them to enter, and he and Dooble fell in behind the group. Dooble looked especially gallant in his new clothes. He was wearing a navy blue suit with a white shirt and a bright red tie.

"Is my tie too bold?" he asked Ellen uneasily.

"No, Dooble, I think it looks quite handsome. You see, it matches my dress."

He relaxed and moved forward with confidence and self assurance after her encouragement. He held his head high as he walked fearlessly into the church with his new family.

They were greeted with smiles as they took their seats in the third pew on the left, their customary spot. A young woman in the third pew on the right side of the church glanced shyly in their direction, peering demurely at Dooble's new clothes.

Father Branson greeted them at the door as they were leaving after the service.

"It's good to see you, Miss Molly – all of you. Good morning to you all. And Ellen, you look quite lovely today in your red dress. There's a glow about you this morning."

"Why, thank you, Father," Ellen said.

"I'm going to have a new baby brother or sister," Stephen blurted out proudly.

"Oh, that is good news, my children," the rector stated. "I'll pray for a safe and happy wait for this blessed event.

"You have that beautiful glow that only an expectant mother possesses, Ellen. We're very happy for you, and I will pray for you and the baby, and your whole family."

"Thank you, Father."

He turned his attention to Molly. "You're looking quite fit these days, Molly. Not that you haven't always been lovely but I haven't seen you use your cane in quite awhile."

"I'm happy, Father. Happier than I've been in many, many years, and I have my new family to thank." She pointed to the group standing behind her.

"Walter has always been like a brother and a true blessing but Ellen, Robert, Stephen and Dooble have brought laughter and happiness into the house. It's a home now and I find that I don't even need my cane. Besides, I couldn't keep up with Stephen and Gimpy and Patches if I had a cane.

"But we are going to have to have some more help very soon. We've been looking anyway but now with Ellen in her delicate condition, we need to find someone right away. Do you happen to have any ideas, Father?"

"As a matter of fact, yes, I think I may. Pattie Darby is a member of our church who has no family and she's been taking care of Mr. Paul Ramey. He wasn't a member of our church but a fine gentleman. She lived in his house and cared for him until his death last week. She's still staying at the house but will have to leave by the end of next week. I would be more than happy to arrange a meeting for you to meet her and talk to her."

"I think I know who she is. She's a quiet young woman, isn't she? She sits on the right side of the church. Has a mark on her face?"

"Yes, that's her. And that's a birthmark. That's one thing that makes her so shy."

"Well, we certainly don't object to that. I would love to talk to her, and if Ellen thinks she'll be satisfactory, it's fine with me. Ellen is my house manager now." She smiled fondly at her young friend standing at her elbow. "Would you like to meet her, Ellen?"

"Oh, yes, ma'am, I certainly would. Can we meet her today or should we schedule a time for her to come out to the manor? Whatever you think, Father."

"There's no time like the present." He looked around but was unsuccessful in locating her. "Looks like she's already left. I tell you what, I'll go up to Mr. Ramey's place and find her. I'll just bring her on out to the manor after lunch."

"Why not just come on out for lunch? We'd be pleased to have you both," Molly invited.

♥♥♥

In less than an hour, the rector's horse drawn carriage pulled up in front of the manor. Patches ran out to inspect the large, gray horse standing in the drive. She made no aggressive moves or sounds, but was quite curious about this large beast which smelled so strange. The horse was nervous and stamped his foot uneasily, keeping a close eye on this small, potential attacker. He had no need to fear, however, as Patches soon lost interest and focused her attention on the occupants in the carriage.

She approached Pattie, tail wagging and tongue hanging out.

"She looks like she's smiling," Father Branson noticed.

Pattie bent down and patted her head. "Hello, girl, how are you?"

"Her tail is wagging from the eyes back," the father laughed. "I think you have a new friend, Pattie."

"There will be no complaints from me. I like dogs and she seems like a nice one."

They walked across the large front porch, and just as they arrived at the front door, Walter opened the door, inviting them inside. Pattie was stunned into silence by the opulence of the manor. She gazed at the interior in disbelief, tiptoeing softly, as if she were in a great cathedral.

"Are you all right?" The rector turned to her, concerned by her sudden silence, as they followed Walter toward the kitchen. She was a quiet woman anyway, but this silence was nearly profound in its depth.

"Yes, Father, I'm fine," she whispered.

He smiled as he realized that she was intimidated by her surroundings, and he reached out, kindly taking her arm to gently guide her down the long hallway. He remembered very well having similar feelings the first time he entered these halls.

The kitchen was light and cheerful with laughter and conversation echoing off the tall ceiling. Everyone glanced up as their guests entered, and Robert and Dooble stood.

"Welcome to Fulton Manor, Pattie and Father. It's good to see you both. Please, come on in and have a seat. Lunch is ready," Molly greeted her guests warmly.

Stephen sat between Molly and his mother, and he stared curiously and intently, but not unkindly, as introductions and greetings were exchanged. His mother tensed as she carefully observed her son, ready to head off any innocent yet potentially hurtful remarks he may make to Pattie regarding the large, blue birthmark on her face.

As Pattie was introduced to Stephen and Ellen, Stephen prepared to speak.

"Wh..."

She quickly placed her hand on her son's shoulder, stopping his comment in midair. She began to exchange pleasantries with Pattie, interrupting him. He looked up in surprise and confusion at his mother and understood from the look on her face that he had better be silent for a minute.

Dooble stood quietly, watching the newcomers. Gimpy bounced from under the table at Stephen's feet, anxious to greet them also, and Father Branson exclaimed, "Who do we have here?"

Ellen's hand slipped off her son's shoulder, and he quickly explained, "That's my dog, Gimpy. He bounces like that because he has short front legs. He was born that way, but he gets around just fine, and he's my best friend. Daddy and Dooble built him a skate with wheels and we tie that around him sometimes when we're outside, but it's not on him now."

Gimpy bounced over to Pattie and stood at her feet, wagging his tail violently.

"He likes you," Stephen observed.

Pattie's face lit up with a truly beautiful smile as she leaned over and gently rubbed his ears.

"May I pick him up?" she requested meekly.

"Sure. He won't bite." Stephen watched them closely, making certain Gimpy was safe. She snuggled him tenderly under her chin, and he licked her face eagerly. She talked to the little dog as he squirmed in her hands. Stephen relaxed as he understood that his little friend was in good hands.

"You have a pretty smile," he remarked. He looked up quickly at his mother, uncertain that what he said had been the right thing. Her smile reassured him that he had indeed not said anything hurtful.

"Thank you, Stephen, and you have a wonderful little dog."

"This is the second dog that's fallen in love with Pattie since we arrived," the rector said. "There was one in the driveway when we pulled in, and she was wagging all over when Pattie talked to her."

"That would be Patches," Robert stated.

"Well, it looks like she's been accepted by your animals."

♥♥♥

They enjoyed a delicious lunch of pot roast, potatoes, carrots and onions all baked together. Tender asparagus with cheese sauce, and freshly baked bread accompanied the hearty roast and vegetables. A chocolate cake was a welcomed and delicious dessert, invoking many ohhhs and ahhhhs as the large pieces fell onto the dessert plates.

Pattie began to help clear the dishes as soon as everyone was finished, and they soon had the kitchen tidied and in order. The men retired to the front porch and the women sat in the parlor to discuss Pattie's duties.

There was no question that she would become a part of the manor staff. Everyone liked her instantly, including Patches and Gimpy. It was decided she would return the next day with her belongings. Walter would drive into the village and pick her up, and Dooble would move into the cottage. He was ready to move anyway, and they were just waiting until repairs on the long fence running behind the estate were completed before he took the time to relocate.

"Are you sure?" Pattie inquired. "I don't want to cause anyone to lose their room."

"Oh, yes, dear, we're sure," Molly comforted her. "It was the original plan that he live in the cottage so he can be near the grounds. He takes care of those. And your being right off the kitchen is perfect so that you can be near the kitchen and laundry. I would like for you to take on most of the responsibilities of caring for the house since Ellen is in the family way so having you in the quarters off the kitchen is necessary. And Dooble understands that he isn't being misplaced. He'll probably be much more comfortable out there anyway."

"Yes, ma'am, if you're sure. I am so grateful for this opportunity and will do a good job for you."

"I'm certain you will, my dear." She smiled as she remembered that Dooble had used almost the identical words when he was hired. She felt most fortunate to have such an efficient and caring staff.

They moved outside with the men and gave them the news that Pattie would be living with them now. Stephen was thrilled, and welcomed her warmly. The two dogs had no concept of what was transpiring, but they danced fervently around her just the same. Their immediate devotion to her was touching, and even after Gimpy left her side to return to his young master, Patches stayed close by her.

They talked well into the afternoon before the two visitors left to return to the village. They thanked their hostess graciously and moved to the carriage. Dooble assisted Pattie into her seat and stood there silently as the horse turned around and moved back toward the gate to the road. Patches cried as her new friend left, and she had to be restrained to prevent her running after them.

"She'll be back, girl," Stephen promised. "Tomorrow."

♥♥♥

They sat on the porch, discussing their luck in finding Pattie, the coming baby, the next day's duties and the Dantons in New York.

"Do they know about the baby, Robert?" Ellen inquired.

"No, I haven't called them yet. I'll have to do that tomorrow for sure. The store should open by 8:00 so I'll call first thing. I'm certain they'll be thrilled for us."

"I think it would be a good idea for us all to plan a trip to the city very soon," Molly announced. "Walter and I need to go talk to the banker with some business about the company, and I think it would be a great time for us to spend some time with the Dantons and have a picnic in the park you speak of so often. Maybe we can even meet Mona Dorsett."

"That would be wonderful, Miss Molly." Ellen and Robert were thrilled, as was Stephen. He loved Miss Molly and the dogs but he missed his young playmates.

"Maybe Miss Mona will have some more birdhouses." he speculated.

The evening quickly approached, and they sat in the comfortable rockers on the porch, enjoying the dusk and the rasping sounds of the cicadas singing in the trees. Suddenly, Stephen sat straight up, his eyes wide and his muscles tensed.

"What's that?" he gasped.

They looked toward his gaze, and spied the tiny specks of light fluttering about, flashing on and off.

"We called them lightning bugs when I was growing up," Molly recalled.

"The Indians used to call them grass stars," Dooble explained, "but we call them fireflies."

"Are they on fire? Do they need help?"

"No, they're not really on fire," Dooble chuckled. "That's just the name we give them. They live in the grass during the day and fly out at night to light up the darkness. Have you never seen one before?"

"No, I haven't. Can we catch them?"

"We can catch a few and put them in a jar with holes punched in the lid if you'd like but you'll have to turn them loose before we go inside for the night. They don't like being confined and they may die if we leave them in there."

"I don't want them to die. Maybe we just better leave them alone. Will they hurt you?"

"No, not at all. Come on, we'll catch a few and turn them loose."

Soon Stephen was clutching one gently inside his cupped fists, careful not to injure it. He giggled as it crawled along his palm. Suddenly, the tiny bug wiggled out between two of its captor's fingers and flew away, his tail flashing warmly. Stephen ran around the yard, chasing them joyfully. He stopped beneath one of the large oaks guarding the front yard and peered up into the darkness of the thick leaves.

"What's that noise?"

"It's a cicada," Molly explained. "It's an insect that makes that noise by rubbing his back legs against his wings. If we look around carefully, we can probably find one of his shells. As they grow, they get too big for their skin so it splits open and they fly out with a brand new skin."

"Ewwww! Does it hurt when it splits open?"

"No, it doesn't hurt."

Soon a transparent, feather light insect shell rested in Stephen's palm, where just a few minutes ago the fireflies had crawled. He was utterly enchanted and kept the shell with him as they returned to their apartment. He placed it gently on the roof of his birdhouse and pondered the magic he had seen this day.

♥♥♥

Robert delayed his going out to begin working the next morning so he could call the Dantons at 8:00 and give them their good news. Ellen was standing beside her husband and could hear Cletus shouting with pleasure. He called to Birdie and soon she and Ellen were on the phone, laughing and crying.

"We're coming to the city for a visit soon," Ellen promised. "We'll let you know exactly when."

"That's wonderful!" Ellen exclaimed. "We can't wait to see you, and I hate to spoil the mood by being the bearer of bad news after this wonderful announcement, but we had a tragedy here in the city of couple of nights ago. Cletus was going to call Robert today and let you know. Here, I'll let Cletus tell you."

"Wait, let me put Robert on." She handed the phone to her husband, a frown of concern on her brow.

"What's the matter?" Robert wondered.

"Some kind of tragedy in the city a couple of nights ago. Cletus will tell you."

She stood uneasily by as her husband listened to Cletus.

"Oh, no!" he cried. "How bad?"

"Oh, no.

"Uh huh… Yeah… I see.

"Uh huh… Thank heavens you and your family are okay. It's a blessing you were able to move when you did.

"Uh huh… Okay, Cletus, thanks for letting us know. And we'll let you know as soon as we have a definite date to come to the city.

"Yeah, we're looking forward to it too. Can't wait to see all of you. And I'm really sorry about the fire. That is just so bad.

"Yeah, you too. 'Bye."

He turned to his wife, his face stricken with concern and disbelief, as she waited anxiously for an explanation.

"The apartment building burned down this past Friday night."

"Oh, no," she gasped, her hand over her mouth. "Was anyone hurt?"

"Yes, three. They're all dead."

She cried out in shock and pain. "What happened, do they know?"

"They're not sure but it seems that there's going to be a full fledged investigation of our former landlord. Officials have been talking to some of the tenants about the conditions there, and they're looking for the owners of the building now. Seems they live somewhere in New Jersey, and Minson was the one who was supposed to take care of the place. The fire department and the city people are reportedly concerned about the lack of heat and the poor electrical wiring in the building.

"The really scary thing is that the fire actually started in Cletus's and Birdie's old apartment. That's where the three men died. There was no fire escape in there, if you remember."

"Yes, I do remember. That was one of the reasons we suggested they move to our apartment."

"The inspectors at the fire department are very upset about that, according to what the newspaper reported this morning. I feel so bad about those poor people living there. I can't help but worry about what will happen to them now. I know they didn't have much but they lost what little they did have. Cletus said the paper stated that the Salvation Army is helping all they can with relocating the residents."

"Thank God for that organization," Ellen remarked. "They seem to always be there, willing to pitch right in."

Walter returned from the village with Pattie just as Robert was beginning his work. Ellen got her settled into Dooble's old room and started her on dusting the walls. Pattie soon came out of the front parlor with a heavy load of draperies and lugged them outside where Patches waited and trotted behind her as she worked. She stretched them across several clotheslines standing side by side, and pounded the dust and cobwebs out of them with a broom handle.

Ellen noticed what she was doing and thought to herself that they were correct in their choice, but was so deep in her own thoughts, that she made no comment to Pattie.

♥♥♥

Ellen and Robert were both pensive for the remainder of the day, the news of the tragic events heavy on their minds. The others shared their sorrow at the dinner table that night and Molly decided it was time to set a day to travel into the city. She felt the Blairs needed closure by visiting the site of the tragedy, and also needed to visit their friends there.

"I'm sorry I wasn't very good company today, Pattie," Ellen apologized, "but this news has been on my mind all day. By the way, you really did a beautiful job, especially with the draperies, and this dinner was wonderful. Thank you so much."

"Yes, thank you, dear," Molly added, "we're very glad to have you here."

Pattie blushed with pleasure and smiled her gratitude. Dooble watched her from across the table and helped her carry the dishes from the table into the kitchen sink.

Ellen and Molly exchanged glances and Molly winked at Ellen. Robert caught their exchange but was completely mystified as to what was going on. He decided to wait until later to inquire of Ellen. Women had these secret signals which went way beyond his realm of comprehension.

"How about next Friday?" Molly offered. "I'll call Mr. Freedle, the banker who handles the company affairs, and make certain that's okay with him. I'll do that first thing in the morning, and then you can let the Dantons know. And Robert, I'd like very much for you to accompany Walter and me to visit with Mr. Freedle. I hope that you will be interested in becoming involved in the workings of the business. Thanks to you and Dooble, the work outside is going quite well, and I believe Dooble can take care of most of it. Walter really needs some help with the factory, so we immediately thought of you. Is that something you think you might be interested in?"

"Why, Miss Molly, I hardly know what to say. Of course I'm interested in doing anything I can to help but what kind of business is it?"

"Of course. How silly of me. We've never explained that to you, have we? My grandfather started the business of producing engines for steamships and some trains. My father was in the process of switching over to gasoline engines at the time of his death, and we've been struggling with it ever since. I'm afraid I know nothing about it as Father never included me in the workings of the business, and Walter knows very little about it either. He's very good with the business and financial doings but not the mechanical. We thought if you are interested in coming in with it, maybe the two of you can figure out what to do. And I want you to learn about the rest of the business too from Walter – the financial and all. I'm even receptive to selling it at this point if we can find a buyer."

"I'd really like to give it a try, Miss Molly. I worked on gas engines at the steel mill before Ellen and I were married so I know a little about them. Of course, it was different motors but the concept is basically the same."

"That's wonderful, Robert. Thank you so much. I'd really hate to have to sell the company since my family started it, but if it isn't going to be able to produce, there's no reason in keeping it open. Maybe if I sell it, the people who work there will have an opportunity to work with new owners. We made our living in that company and our money is intact, thanks to our removing it from the stock market and the banks, but I still don't want to have to close it if we can make it work."

♥♥♥

Early the next Friday morning, Walter pulled the limousine around to the front of the house and Molly, Robert, Ellen and Stephen crawled inside for the trip to the city. Stephen was beside himself with excitement, both at the trip and the prospect of seeing his friends, Julie and Carson.

"Now, you're sure you'll be okay here all day by yourself?" Molly asked Pattie.

"Yes, ma'am, I'll be fine. I'm going to polish the main staircase and the paneling in the foyer today, and I'll have dinner on the table at 6:00."

"Yes, that's fine. I'm certain we'll be no later than 5:00, and if you have any problems while we're gone, just call for Dooble."

"He'll be working on the windows at the side of the house, Pattie, so he won't be far away," Robert advised. "Just be careful if you climb up on a ladder and don't take any chances."

"Yes, sir, I won't. And thank you."

As the limousine pulled out of the drive, Ellen and Molly exchanged another mysterious glance.

"What's going on?" Robert asked from the front seat. "That's the second time I've seen that look pass between you two."

"We think Dooble is sweet on Pattie," Ellen confided.

"Really?"

"Yes."

"And just what makes you think so?"

"Just a feeling we have."

Robert and Walter laughed.

"Do you two approve in case it's true?" Walter wondered.

"Of course!" Molly said. "We think it would be wonderful."

"I wonder if Dooble has any idea about this," Robert asked.

"If not, he probably will have before long," Walter predicted.

"Oh, shush, you two. You make us sound like two busybodies. We just think they're two very nice people, and we hope it's true," Molly scolded kindly.

Stephen sat at the window, peering out into the countryside, completely oblivious to the conversation taking place around him. Ellen was thankful for his inattention as she was almost certain her son would mention their thoughts to Pattie and Dooble if he knew.

♥♥♥

They arrived in the city and parked across the street from the apartment building. They wanted to make this their first stop and were shocked by the appearance. A burned out, empty brick shell stood with most of the two top floors completely gone and the rest lying crumbled inside the basement. A rope was wrapped around the building and across the sidewalk with a Keep Off sign posted.

Stephen was quite concerned about the building and its occupants.

"Where is everybody who lived there?"

"The nice people at the Salvation Army helped them, son, so we're certain they're fine," his mother reassured him.

They walked back to the park toward Mona Dorsett's usual worksite. They were relieved to see her there as they approached her cardboard boxes filled with flowers and vegetables.

Stephen broke into a run and shouted to her, "Hey, Miss Mona, hey!"

She looked up and stared, not recognizing the child running toward her. She saw the group behind him and finally recognized Robert and Ellen. She stood up from her wooden box and waved a warm welcome.

"Hey, what in the world are you good folks doing here? It's so good to see you! Are you moving back? Who's that with you?"

A flurry of laughter and explanations and greetings and introductions passed for several minutes before the conversation settled down. Mona was disappointed for herself that the family wasn't moving back to the city but glad for them.

"Where are you staying now, Miss Mona?" Stephen asked.

"Still here and there, Sonny, but ole Mona's doing just fine. I appreciate your concern but don't worry none."

"He treasures his birdhouse, Miss Mona. He keeps it with him all the time and receives a great deal of comfort from its presence." Ellen felt good as she shared this news with Mona and saw the joy it brought her.

"Why, thank you, Miss Ellen, for sharing that with me, and Stephen, I'm really glad that you like the birdhouse. It's a very special gift filled with love and hope."

Molly bought a bag of tomatoes to accompany the picnic lunch stored in the trunk, and had a thought as she paid for them.

"Miss Mona, we plan to have a picnic later here in the park with the Dantons. We would really like for you to join us if you can."

The others quickly agreed and Mona smiled her thanks.

"Why, thank you, ma'am, I'd be honored. Just let me know and I'll close down my shop and meet you."

"We'll come over and get you," Robert offered, "and we'll set up at those two benches over there." He pointed in the direction of the benches several hundred feet away.

"Okay, that's fine. I'll keep an eye on them and make certain nobody else gets them," Mona promised.

As they left to go to Schmidt's store, Robert observed, "I'd sure hate to be the poor soul who tries to use those benches before we get back."

♥♥♥

They pulled up in front of Schmidt's Grocery Store within a few minutes, and Stephen was finding it hard to control his excitement over seeing his friends. Soon the two families were hugging and laughing and talking, the children running around in ecstasy.

The Dantons greeted Molly and Walter warmly, very glad to meet the people who were so important to their good friends. Mr. Schmidt came out onto the sidewalk to greet everyone and invite them inside.

"I'm sorry my wife isn't here but she's not doing too good these days. We sure are grateful for Cletus and Birdie. They've been angels for the two of us. And I'm so proud to see their friends. Any friends of theirs are friends of ours."

They asked Mr. Schmidt and his wife to have lunch with them but he reluctantly declined.

"I'm afraid she isn't able to make it, but we thank you kindly for the invitation. It wouldn't be no problem closing the store for a while, but I can't expect her to come down those steps just now. You nice folks just have a good lunch and enjoy each other's company. Cletus, take your time. We aren't busy right now so it'll be fine and just have a good time."

♥♥♥

Cletus, Birdie, Ellen and the children went to the park while the others tended to their business at the bank. The children played on swings and a seesaw by the lake, and the adults sat talking. They did not realize how much they had missed each other so the time sped by as they caught up on everything that had happened to them all. The biggest and best news, of course, was the expected arrival of the new baby after Christmas.

In what seemed like a very short time, Molly and the men returned, and they seemed to be satisfied with the outcome of their meeting. Ellen asked no questions but she could tell from their demeanor that all seemed well.

"Is anybody hungry?" Ellen inquired.

"Yayyyyy!" the children came running immediately.

They soon arrived at the two still-empty park benches designated earlier as their picnic spot, and Robert brought Mona over to join them. After a brief blessing of the food, they ate heartily of the picnic before them, and were soon deep in sharing conversation, stories and fellowship.

Pattie worked for several hours applying a brilliant shine to the mahogany railings embracing the staircase. She began to feel hungry so stopped to make a sandwich. She decided to make one for Dooble since she hadn't seen him all morning and was certain he was probably hungry too.

"Dooble!" she called as she stepped out onto the front porch with a large sandwich and a Mason jar of cold tea.

"Yo!" he answered from around the corner of the house.

"I have your lunch!"

"Thank you, I'll be right there!"

He came to the porch, wiping his hands on his pants, and staring at the floor. He reached out and took the sandwich from her.

"Won't you join me?"

"Well," she hesitated briefly. "I don't have my sandwich made yet but if you don't mind waiting, I'll be proud to join you."

He would have waited all day.

When she returned several minutes later, he had picked three large peonies and presented them to her.

"I thought these would look nice on the table," he pointed to the small round table setting at the back of the porch.

They sat at the table, Patches and Gimpy at Pattie's feet, and ate their food in silence, glancing at each other occasionally, and sharing a shy smile.

Dooble finished his meal, stood, and said, "Thank you kindly, Miss Pattie. That was most delicious."

"You're welcome."

He stood there awkwardly for a few seconds, not knowing what to do, and then stepped off the porch and returned to his work.

Pattie picked up the flowers and dirty dishes, returned to the kitchen and placed the peonies in a crystal vase in the center of the kitchen table. She smiled at them, rubbed Gimpy's ears happily, and returned to her work in the foyer.

♥♥♥

The family returned home at 5:15, exhausted but rejuvenated by the trip and visiting with friends. Stephen burst into the kitchen, looking for Gimpy and Pattie.

"Gimpy, come here, boy! Hey, Miss Pattie."

She turned from the stove, greeting the young boy as he rolled on the floor with his beloved Gimpy.

The others made a more dignified entrance but greeted her just as warmly.

"Ooooo, the flowers are lovely. Did you pick them?" Molly asked.

"No, Dooble did."

Molly and Ellen exchanged a knowing glance while Robert rolled his eyes and Walter shook his head incredulously.

♥♥♥

Pattie and Dooble took their lunch together each day. Robert left them alone so that they could talk, but they seldom verbalized. They were both painfully shy, possibly due to their disabilities and thoughtless criticism from strangers during their lives, and the consequential withdrawal from social contact. Neither of them had been taught how to reach out to others so it became a standoff.

Molly stood at the kitchen window one noon watching the two as they ate their lunch, the ever-present Patches at their feet.

"Ellen, we need to do something to get those two talking."

"What we need to do is leave them alone," Robert interjected.

"Of course, you're right, Robert," Molly sighed, "but it makes me sad to see two people who care so much for each other, yet they don't know how to reach out." She stood, watching sadly, for a few minutes before turning back to the table.

"By the way, Robert, I almost forgot to mention it but Pattie said Dr. Sheffield called yesterday. He said you had asked him about something for Dooble and he has some information for you."

"Oh, great, thank you. I'm trying to find some kind of apparatus for his leg that will help him walk straighter. Walter and I will stop by his office on the way to the plant this morning."

"Seems I'm not the only one concerned about others," she chided.

"That's different," he retorted.

♥♥♥

"Good morning, gentlemen," Dr. Sheffield greeted the two as they waited in his office.

"Good morning," they both replied.

"I understand you called about our conversation regarding Dooble, Doc, and I wanted to see what you found out," Robert ventured.

"Fine, Robert. Come on into my private office, both of you."

They sat opposite his large desk, waiting to learn what he had discovered.

"It seems they've developed a shoe down at Johns Hopkins in Baltimore that's built up and better than similar ones in the past. It was developed for just the problem that Dooble has. They've had it for a while but I've never had reason to use one so I wasn't aware of it. The sole is actually the same thickness as the leg is short so that the short leg is the same length of the longer leg, if that makes sense."

"Yes." Robert exclaimed. "I see. That's ingenuous. What do we have to do to get one?"

"He'll have to be fitted but they're sending me all the information of what to do so I can do it here in my office. Basically, I'll have to make accurate measurements of both his legs from the hip joint down taking into account any bone malformations or dislocations, get his exact shoe size and they'll have one built for him. They send several soles which can be strapped to his current shoe to see if any of their standard ones will work."

Robert was thrilled. "That'll be so much better for him. I can't wait. How soon can you do this?"

"Well, I'll have to wait for the information to arrive from Johns Hopkins. They're mailing it so that'll take at least a week but I can get on it as soon as it arrives. Of course, you know, Robert, that it's going to be expensive."

"How expensive?"

"Probably between $50 and $75, depending on how complex the measurements are. When the bones are bowed out on the shorter leg, it's my understanding that one side of the shoe has to be built up higher for stability and then the thick sole added. Just in observing Dooble, I haven't noticed any bowing. I'm certain his spine is curved, however, but just wearing the shoe will help correct that.

"Do you think he can afford it? I won't charge him anything, of course, but Johns Hopkins will have to have their money up front."

"I don't know," Robert said thoughtfully. "I'll be certain to ask him. He doesn't have any expenses but I never ask him what he does with his earnings. I know he bought some new clothes. Ellen and I can help some too."

"Yes, I was getting ready to say that I'll be happy to help," Walter interrupted.

"Sounds like it may work out. That is, if it's what Dooble wants."

"I hadn't thought about that," Robert admitted. "Guess it would be a good idea to get his thoughts. I didn't want to raise his hopes so I didn't mention that I had asked you anything about it. I'll ask him tonight."

"Okay and I'll call you just as soon as the information arrives from Johns Hopkins. By the way, how are things going down at the plant?"

"Pretty good, pretty good." Robert was immediately enthusiastic.

"Yes, Robert is having some great ideas of what can be done to better increase production, so hopefully, it's going to take off soon. We just need a way to get our new gasoline engines marketed."

"My wife's father knew the family quite well that developed the Morgan farm tractor. She grew up with the children in that family and stays in contact with at least one of the girls. I'll ask her if you'd like."

"Great! We'd really appreciate it, Doctor. If we can just get into a place to show how it works, I'm certain it would be well accepted."

"Okay, I'll ask her this evening and let you two know if I find out anything."

Their spirits were high as they arrived at the factory, already buzzing with activity. It was moving much more efficiently since Robert had set up an assembly line. When he first arrived, workstations were scattered everywhere with no organization at all. If someone needed a part at one station, he may have had to walk across the whole building to retrieve it. At Robert's suggestion, he and Walter quickly set them up in sequence as to how the parts would be assembled and in close proximity to each other.

They had no mechanically moving line yet but were attempting to locate one through the automobile industry in Detroit. Robert had hopes that all these problems would soon be ironed out and even the workers seemed more eager. Robert was going to be good for the company.

Gail Cauble Gurley

Chapter 13
A Proposal

The summer sped by with the Fulton Engine Company progressing nicely. It was hopeful they would soon have a lucrative contract with the tractor factory, and Dooble's new elevated shoe gave him much more agility and ease in moving. Molly, Stephen and Gimpy spent countless happy hours on the front porch and in the front yard. Patches seldom joined them as she was nearly always with Dooble. She was really more devoted to Pattie but wasn't allowed into the house, so she was happiest when midday arrived and her friend joined Dooble for lunch.

Patches sat by the back door at dinner, waiting for Dooble to exit. On most nights, he would walk with her around the house to join the others on the front porch. He wanted to be certain she wasn't left waiting in vain for his appearance, and evenings on the front porch were the happiest part of the day for them all.

They were sitting there silently one evening, just enjoying each other's company and listening to the cicadas and tree frogs. The "grass stars," as Stephen preferred to call them, began to drift slowly about. He, Gimpy and Patches were all so tired and stuffed by the delicious dinner that they made no move off the porch to chase them. They merely lay quietly and watched their bodies twinkle on and off.

Stephen was resting on his stomach, his chin propped into his hands. He turned to Pattie who was sitting in a rocking chair pushed close to Dooble's.

"Miss Pattie, where are you from?" he asked curiously.

"I'm from here in the village, Stephen."

"Oh." He watched the fireflies for a few minutes and then broke the silence once more.

"Are your parents still here?"

"No, my mother died when I was born, and my father was killed in an accident when I was two years old. He was cutting down trees and one fell on him. I lived with my grandmother after that. She was my mother's mother and I loved her dearly. I was almost twenty when she died and I still miss her."

"What was she like?"

Pattie smiled gently, her eyes misting over as she reached back into the past beyond the veil of forget, through her memories.

"She was a wonderful woman, Stephen, very kind and gentle. We didn't have much but I was never hungry and I was truly loved. She had a vegetable garden, and I would help her pick beans and shuck corn."

"What's shuck corn?" he asked.

"That's taking the husks off the outside so you can get to the ear of corn growing inside."

Stephen was satisfied with her explanation and fell silent as she continued.

"She canned dozens of jars of vegetables, and we would eat those all winter. We ate the fresh vegetables in the summer. She had green beans, limas, corn which she cut off the cob to can, pickles of all sorts, sauerkraut she made from the cabbage she raised, and tomatoes which she used to make hot, thick soup. That was *really* good on a cold winter's day.

"She also had lots of different fruit trees. There was a pear, peach, cherry, two different kinds of apple trees, a fig bush and even a grapevine. Actually, there were two grapevines. One was purple and she called the other white. I always wondered why she called them white because to me they were pink. Anyway, she would make wonderfully delicious jams and jellies and preserves from all the fruits each year. It seems the woodstove in the pantry off the kitchen was burning all summer long. But she never complained about the heat.

"She had chickens too so we always had eggs. She would trade eggs and vegetables to a neighbor for milk and butter. And when one of the chickens would quit laying eggs, we'd have fried chicken or chicken and dumplings for supper.

"I can remember each fall when it got really cold, she would kill a hog that she raised. My aunts and uncles and the neighbors would come before daylight and cook meat all day. They made sausage and liver pudding, and country hams which my uncles hung in the smokehouse. The fresh meat was put in the springhouse where it froze, and I can't remember any of it ever spoiling. Of course, I never ate a bite of it."

"Why not?" Stephen wondered.

"Because I always made a pet out of the hog while she was raising it. I'd go with her to feed him, and I'd stand and talk to him. I would always hide behind the heater in the kitchen while they worked, not wanting to see any part of what was going on."

"What did you feed him?" Stephen was very interested in her story and was fascinated by the activities she was describing.

"Grandmother would buy bags of feed at Carver's and she mixed all the peelings and scraps from her canning in with it. She added water and would mix it all up and pour it in a trough through a slot in his wooden pen. The pen had a roof on it and he never wallowed in the mud, so he was clean, but the food she gave him looked and smelled pretty gruesome. He loved it though and would make all sorts of grunting noises while he ate."

Stephen laughed out loud. "What was her name?"

"Minnie Frick," Pattie explained.

"That's a funny name," Stephen giggled.

"Stephen!" His mother spoke sternly.

"Sorry, Miss Pattie," he apologized meekly

"That's okay, Stephen. It was an old name. I think she was named after a school teacher named Minnie who taught out west in the early 1800s. There was a blizzard out there one day during school and the teacher tried to lead all the children to safety. The children all survived but she died, and she became a national hero, so I think my grandmother was named after her."

Stephen remained quiet as she continued her story.

"Grandmother would save the empty feed bags and make dresses for me out of them. They were really pretty fabrics, but tended to be a little scratchy. I wouldn't fuss much though because she was doing the best she could, and I realized that. They would be better after she washed them a few times. She'd make lye soap in a big black pot in the backyard and after a few washings with that, the material softened up."

"What's lye soap?"

"She made it out of hog fat and lye somehow. I never did know exactly how she did it because the lye was poison so she made me stay away from it. She'd cook it up and pour it into square wooden boxes. When it set up, she would dump it out and cut it into small squares with a large knife. She wrapped it in waxed paper and stored it in the shed behind the house. She locked it in a metal trunk to keep the vermin out."

"What are vermin?"

"Mice and bugs and 'possums. That sort of thing. Anyway, that lye soap would make everything bright and white and very clean. She was quite proud of her laundry when she hung it on the line to dry."

"Sounds like you had a happy childhood, Pattie," Molly spoke kindly.

"Yes, ma'am, I really did. It was hard work but it was a good life. Grandmother used to make the best fried apple pies I ever tasted. She would dry the apples by slicing them, then spreading them out on boards in the sun and covering them with cheesecloth. I'd stand there all day with a rag tied to a long pole and keep the flies shooed away. I didn't mind a bit, though, because I loved those pies so much. I've tried to duplicate them but have never been successful. I think it must have been the kind of apples she used."

"What does it mean to dry apples?" Stephen inquired.

"That takes all the juice out of them and leaves the sweetness. They get real small and shriveled up. They turn brown and feel somewhat like leather, though not as tough. You can eat them dry but they're better when cooked with water and put into pastry for frying."

"I'd like to try some of those, Pattie," Ellen said.

"Walter and I will bring some apples home tomorrow," Robert offered. "I think we'd all like to try them. We'll get you set up with boards if you'd like."

"Oh, yes, sir, that would be great. I'd love to try but as I said, I've never had any to turn out as good as my grandmother's."

"Do you have any of those dresses left she made you out of feed sacks?" Stephen continued to be enchanted by her accounts of her life as a child.

"No," she laughed, "but I do still have a few quilts she made for me. As a matter of fact, I have one on my bed right now, and I could probably find some of the fabrics from my dresses in them. She would take them as I grew out of them and cut them into blocks to be added to her quilt tops."

"Can I see? Please?" Stephen pleaded.

"Sure. I'll be proud to show you." She left to retrieve the treasured quilt from her room.

After she left, Stephen rolled over on one elbow and looked up at Dooble.

"She's a nice lady," he remarked. "Now I understand why you're sweet on her."

"Stephen!" Ellen and Molly both gasped in horror.

Walter and Robert laughed heartily.

"But you said…" the child cried.

They did not notice in the early dusk that Dooble was grinning from ear to ear.

Ellen and Molly made a hasty retreat into the house after briefly admiring Pattie's quilt. They were sorely embarrassed by Stephen's innocent betrayal of their gossip. They had been wrong to think that he had not heard their every word in the car that day.

Robert and Walter soon followed, still chuckling.

Stephen was enchanted by the quilt that Pattie shared with him. She pointed out the different squares made from her feed-sack dresses. Stephen looked up as his father came to the door.

"Come on in, son. It's getting late," his father directed.

"Why were they laughing?" Pattie asked as they left.

"Oh, nothing important. Just something Stephen said," Dooble answered.

They sat silently for a few minutes.

"I like your quilt, Pattie. And I enjoyed your story."

"Thank you, Dooble."

She sat there, not knowing what to do, and finally stood to go inside. He stood as she did, and turned to her. He stood close enough to make out her features in the early darkness, and walked deeply into her eyes, getting lost in their depths. He reached out a trembling hand, gently brushing a sprig of hair off her forehead. She watched him, afraid to breathe for fear of breaking this delicious spell.

He leaned forward and gently kissed her waiting lips. He turned and stepped off the porch, Patches behind him. By the time she was able to open her eyes, he was gone.

♥♥♥

The summer waned and the New York autumn arrived in all its glory. The cicadas, tree frogs and fireflies disappeared for another year. A kaleidoscope of brilliance burst across the yard, spilling through the woods and reaching over the road's edge. Red, burgundy, gold, yellow and orange decorated the trees, and soon, the yard. Raking leaves became a dawn to dusk task for Dooble with Walter and Robert helping when they returned home from work each day. Stephen and the dogs spent hours each day diving into the large piles of bright crispness, hiding from each other. The sharp odor of burning leaves permeated the air as huge mounds of leaves were stuffed into the burning pit near the cottage.

Pattie cut branches of color and placed them into crystal vases throughout the house. She also taught Stephen how to place individual leaves between two pieces of waxed paper, and iron them to be placed in heavy books for pressing.

"This is the most use these old books have had in a long, long time," Molly observed.

"I want to make some leaves for Miss Birdie, Miss Mona and Julie too," he advised his mother.

"I think that's a wonderful idea, Stephen, and very thoughtful of you. But it'll have to be soon as it will snow before long, and we don't want to get snowbound somewhere other than here at home," his mother cautioned.

Ellen was heavy with child now that October was fast approaching. She knew if she was to go to the city, it would have to be within a few weeks. So it was that a visit to the Dantons was planned for the following Saturday.

"Your timing is perfect, buddy," Cletus remarked to Robert over the phone. "The investigation into the fire has been completed and a full report will be in the newspaper this weekend. According to what's been already reported, it looks like Mr. Minson's probably going to jail. Or at least to court."

"Wow! That's amazing but I'm not surprised. I always felt that something wasn't quite right about that whole setup. He was such a nasty man, that I wouldn't be surprised at his doing something illegal. I just hope and pray that he did nothing to cause the death of those poor people.

"By the way, Stephen has a small gift for Miss Mona and we're all anxious to see her. How is she?"

"Oh, no, I keep forgetting to mention it to you when we talk that she fell last month and broke her hip. We thought for sure she'd die but she rallied. But when she was ready to leave the hospital, a social worker put her in a nursing home."

"That's terrible. I'm so sorry to hear that and I'm sure everyone else will be too. Do you know where she is?"

"Yeah, Birdie and Julie went to see her just two days ago. She's in the bed, and we were worried about the kind of treatment she'll get at one of those places. Well, Birdie said it really wasn't so bad. Seems this is a city owned home and the inspectors are pretty strict. She was clean and warm and said they feed her pretty good."

"How was she feeling?"

"Just grumpy. Said she's sore and wants to get out of bed as that's what's making her sore. Birdie asked the nurse about getting her up, and the nurse promised to call the doctor before our next visit and ask if she can get up. Birdie was somewhat put out by that. Said they should have already asked and not waited for a visitor to bring it up. Made her pretty determined to visit often and keep an eye on Miss Mona."

"Birdie is a good person. Tell her we appreciate her watching after Miss Mona so well."

"I will and maybe you folks can go see her at the home on Saturday."

"Most definitely. We wouldn't think of not going. Just tell Birdie and the children we'll see them soon."

♥♥♥

Robert received a call on Thursday which advised him that Fulton Engine Company had been awarded a contract with the Morgan Farm Tractor Company. Fulton was to supply engines to Morgan, and the first order was for fifty motors.

The family was jubilant. They were all well aware that the depression still gripped the nation and just having a contract would not guarantee prosperity, but it was a step in the right direction. At least with a contract, when recovery did occur, they would be well prepared. This could be a new beginning for the company, and Molly felt an indescribable surge of relief. She was loathe to close down or sell the factory that had meant so much to her family and this community. She found it hateful to even consider such a move. A collective sign of relief escaped from the workers as well. They had developed deep respect for Robert and

Walter, and were grateful that the company's future was less tenuous.

Robert called Mr. Freedle at the bank to give him the good news. The banker wanted to see them all right away and scheduled an appointment on Saturday to go over the contract and help set up production schedules and plans based on their liquid assets.

It was a happy celebration on Saturday with the Dantons. The women and children crowded into the small apartment at the back of the store while the men and Molly met with Mr. Freedle. Cletus worked out front, waiting on customers, until they returned from the bank

Birdie prepared a meal for her guests.

"I'm sorry we don't have anymore room," she apologized. The men were eating in the store, discussing the findings of the fire investigation, while the women crowded around their small table in the apartment, and the children ate on a quilt spread over the floor.

"Hey, this is great, Miss Birdie," Stephen declared sincerely. "It's like a picnic."

"Yes, you're right, Stephen, and please don't apologize, Birdie. We're just so glad to be with you," Ellen assured her friend.

♥♥♥

The group arrived at the nursing home shortly after lunch. The men and children waited in the reception area while the women went to see if they could bring Mona out front.

"Daddy," Stephen whispered, "this place smells funny."

"Yes, it does, son, but don't say anything."

"What is it?" he whispered once more.

"I'm not sure but whatever it is, there's not much we can do about it."

He sat silently beside his father, a look of misery and suspicion on his face. He wasn't at all sure about this place.

Shortly, the women returned, pushing Miss Mona in a wheelchair. Her white hair was resting on her shoulders, which were more stooped than any of them remembered. Her eyes had lost some of their luster but the old intelligence lingered. She broke into a broad smile as she saw her guests and was soon laughing and talking to all of them as they hugged her awkwardly but warmly as she sat in her chair.

Stephen presented her with his gift of pressed leaves and her hands trembled as she took them from him. Tears streamed down her face unashamedly, causing them all to feel a lump in their throats.

"Thank you, Stevie, thank you so much. These are lovely. The loveliest I've ever seen. Reminds me of autumns when I was a child on the farm in New Hampshire. I miss my folks more'n I have in a long time. Course, I reckon it won't be long 'fore I see them once again."

Stephen wasn't certain what she meant but he made no comment as he looked at his mother's face.

They moved toward a corner where a large sofa set so they could sit and visit with Mona for a while. As they moved by an elderly gentleman sitting in a wheelchair, he raised his head slightly. His eyes fixed on Stephen.

"Tony!" he cried, reaching a thin, frail hand toward the child.

Stephen looked around, further confused by this strange place, and seeing no one else, he glanced up at his father.

"Tony?" the man repeated.

A nearby nurse leaned over and whispered softly, "Tony was his son who died when he was a boy. Mr. Borello doesn't remember that the boy's been gone for over fifty years, but he does remember that he had a son named Tony. I'm sorry, little boy."

"Tony!?" Mr. Borello was sobbing by now.

Stephen hesitated for a moment longer as his family watched helplessly. Suddenly, he moved to Mr. Borello, took his hand and said, "Yes, Papa?"

"Oh, my boy, my boy, I've missed you so long. Where you been? I didn't think you'd ever come to see me."

"I'm sorry, Papa, but I'm here now."

Stephen crawled gingerly onto the frail lap, careful not to injure Mr. Borello. There was a hushed silence in the whole room as the drama of reunion between father and son played out. Stephen sat on his lap, allowing Mr. Borello to hug him and stroke his hair until the elderly gentleman fell asleep.

"Thank you for coming, son. You've made me very happy. I can rest easy now," the gentleman murmured as he drifted off to sleep.

Stephen slipped quietly off his lap and returned to his family. His mother was sobbing silently and his father's eyes were filled with tears. He reached out his arms to his son and lifted him to his chest, embracing him vigorously. He left his father's arms and sat beside his mother, no longer able to crawl into her disappearing lap. She slipped her arm around him, hugged him warmly and planted a kiss on his head.

"We're very proud of you, darling," she whispered hoarsely.

There was not a dry eye in the group. In truth, there were few dry eyes in the room.

♥♥♥

Dooble and Pattie had lunch together while the family was in the city. He brought in a load of wood, as she liked to burn that in the kitchen fireplace rather than coal. It wasn't as warm but it smelled much better, and she liked the sound of it popping as it burned.

They chatted quietly, discussing the weather and the dogs and the work to be completed for the day. They discussed the menu for dinner and the possibility of snow coming soon. When they ran out of conversation, they sat quietly for a few minutes.

"Dooble, do you have any family?" Pattie asked.

"No, not any more. Haven't had one for a long time."

"Are you from around here?"

"Yeah, just outside the city a little ways."

He paused, leaned back in his chair and his eyes glazed over as he began to remember.

"My ma died when I was two, right after my baby sister was born. I had two older brothers, and a sister who died right after I was born. I never knew her. Don't remember my ma. All I remember is that life was real hard.

"Pa ran a sawmill. My brothers helped him even though they were both real young too. Dean was eight when Ma died and Beau was ten. They both worked in the mill with Pa. They didn't go to school very often, just when the weather was too bad to work in the woods. I started when I was six but when I was seven, I started helping with the trees too. I was too little to help cut them down but I could help run them through the stripper in the mill. It took the bark off'n the trees so they could be sawed up into planks.

"Anyway, Pa died the year I turned ten. Beau was 16 and he left home to make it on his own. He promised to help us all he could but I never saw him again. Me and Dean and Marybeth were sent to live at the preacher's house. He felt it was his Christian duty to take in orphans. Truth was, we were little more than slaves. I fared better than Dean and Marybeth as I lived in the barn with the horses and cows. It was my job to keep the barn clean and the preacher's wife didn't want me in the house because I smelled like a barn. They didn't heat the house except the front room where the preacher and his wife stayed. Dean and Marybeth had to stay out of there so they were shut up in a cold house, but the heat from the animals kept me pretty comfortable.

"Food was pretty scarce so I took to scavenging wherever I could. The kids were given scraps off'n the preacher's table but the good preacher and his wife rarely remembered there was somebody in the barn that needed feeding too. I would manage to get some milk from the cows before the preacher milked. I 'spect he woulda throwed me out as a thief if he'd known I was taking a little milk once in awhile. Some of the ladies at the church would come by and bring a little food. I would always run out to meet them when I saw them come up and Dean and Marybeth would run outside if they could. The ladies would hand the food to me if the preacher didn't get there quick enough and I'd run hide as much of it as I could. I don't know if they ever suspected what was going on but they could tell we was hungry.

"One lady was a school teacher and she asked the preacher why we weren't in school. He said there was no money for clothes to send us to school so the church brought us some clothes and we went to school a couple times a month after that. We liked that because we was always fed when we were there. The teacher from the church saw to it that we got a good lunch.

"The preacher and his wife left the church the year I was 15 so I lit out on my own to make my way in the world. Dean had already left and he came to see us right before the preacher left. He was working in the coal mines of Pennsylvania and wanted us to come live with him. I went up there after we was homeless and took Marybeth too. She wasn't old enough to make her own way so my brother took her in. I guess she's still there.

"After times got hard, I lost my job in the coal mines and I drifted around for awhile. I ended up back at Issaqua Harbor and don't rightly remember how it happened but anyway, here I am. I lost my brother's address and didn't never try to contact him after I left Pennsylvania. I hope they're okay. I have to believe they are anyway."

"Oh, Dooble, I'm so sorry. It must have been so hard on you. How brave you are to be such a good man after all you've been through." Pattie was sincerely touched by the story of his past.

Dooble slowly reached across the space between their two chairs pulled side by side in front of the fireplace. He very gently took her hand into his and pressed it to his lips. She could feel the stubble on his chin, but what she felt more intensely than that was the soft kindness of his mouth. He dropped her hand and reached up to touch her hair as he had on that breathless evening that seemed like eons ago to the lonely woman.

She leaned into his hand and he slipped his arm around her shoulder, pulling her close to him. She rested her head in the hollow of his shoulder until he pulled away, placed his hand under her chin, gently lifted her face, and kissed her lips. She breathlessly kissed him back.

"Pattie Darby, will you marry me?" he whispered huskily.

"Yes! Oh, yes, yes, yes, Dooble Howell! I will marry you!"

He kissed her hand. "Floyd."

"What?" She was caught off guard by his remark in her flustered state.

"My name. It isn't really Dooble. That's a nickname from who knows where. My name is Floyd. You will be Mrs. Floyd Howell."

She laughed and cried and threw her arms around him, clinging happily to him.

Chapter 14
A Wedding

Robert gave details about the fire inspection report on their way home from the city. Cletus had saved the newspaper clippings, and they were passed to the back seat as he talked. There were pictures of the burned apartment, Mr. Minson, and the absent owner who lived in New Jersey.

"It seems that the owner, Mr. Kinton, had been sending money to Minson for repairs that were never done to the building. Minson had been landlord there for five years and three years ago, money was sent to repair the heating system. According to the investigation, it amounted to nearly $500.00. As we all know, the repairs were never made.

"They also instructed him to make any needed repairs to the electrical wiring or plumbing, and when someone would report a problem, Minson would collect the money for the repairs from the owner and never have them done. In hindsight, the owner admitted he should never have sent money without a receipt showing that the work had been done, but he trusted Minson.

"Kinton said he had no idea that one of the fire escapes had collapsed. That was the one outside the Dantons old apartment where the three men died."

"Those poor souls," Ellen lamented.

"Shameful." Molly shook her head in anger and disgust.

"And that's not all. Of course, the worst thing is that those people died, but Minson was only supposed to charge $7.00 a month rent. He was taking $1.00 each month from every tenant in the building and lining his pockets. That was in addition to the salary he was drawing.

"The owner had an established policy that anyone who was late paying their rent had 30 days to get it paid before eviction processes would be started through the judicial system, but Minson was throwing people, even those with children, onto the streets on the day the rent was due if it wasn't paid."

"Mr. Kinton gave a heartfelt apology to the city and all his renters," Ellen reported as she read one of the articles.

"That's well and good but it doesn't bring back the dead or right the wrong to all the people Minson stole from," Robert pointed out. "There's going to have to be a reckoning in this instance. I don't think owners should be so callous as to never check on the condition of their property. He's going to have to take some responsibility for these events just as well as Minson."

They finished reading the articles as Walter drove until it became too dark to read anymore. They approached the estate entrance and were glad to be home.

"I hope the Dantons will be able to spend Thanksgiving with us," Ellen remarked as they entered the gate.

They had been invited that afternoon with the promise that Walter would pick them up, but they were delaying a decision until they knew the plans of the Schmidts. Cletus wasn't certain whether the store would close that day or remain open.

♥♥♥

The family gathered around the dinner table for a particularly elegant dinner that evening. Pattie was radiant, smiling easily throughout the meal. Dooble was quieter than usual but even the men noticed how his eyes followed Pattie's every move.

They sat enjoying a cup of rich coffee before clearing the table when Dooble pushed his chair back and slowly stood up. He cleared his throat and everyone looked his way.

"Miss Molly, Mr. Robert, everybody – uh, I wanted to let you good people know, uh, that, uh…that is, I have asked Pattie to be my wife and she accepted." He sat down quickly as those words sprang quickly from his lips.

An impassioned riot reigned. Gimpy jumped up from under the table, startled by the commotion, and Patches, waiting outside the kitchen door, began barking, uncertain as to what was transpiring in the house.

It was several minutes before things settled down enough for an intelligible conversation to be conducted.

"When do you think you'll be getting married?" Molly inquired, her head already filled with ideas for a small and lovely wedding.

The two looked at each other and then laughed.

"We haven't discussed it," Dooble admitted.

"How about Thanksgiving," Pattie suggested.

"Wonderful idea! Now the Dantons have to come here for Thanksgiving!" Ellen said excitedly.

"Would you like to get married here at the manor?" Molly offered. "It would be a blessing to have a wedding in this house and would be the happiest event we've ever seen here."

"Oh, Miss Molly, that's a beautiful idea," Pattie gasped happily. "I love this house, and I love everyone here so it would be like being married at a beloved home place. Thank you so much. And it would be more convenient too, especially for Miss Ellen. Since I don't have any real friends in the village, would the two of you be my attendants?" She turned toward Molly and Ellen.

♥♥♥

The flurry of wedding plans consumed the household for the next month. Thanksgiving was a mere five weeks away from the engagement announcement so there was much to do in a short period. Robert and Walter were grateful to escape to the haven of the factory each day. They were required to work extra hours frequently in order to implement the contract with the tractor company, and neither of them complained.

The women made another hurried trip back into the city in a determined search for just the right wedding dress. Dr. Sheffield gave Ellen permission to go but ordered no more traveling after November 1.

They discovered a small bridal boutique near Macy's Department Store. Mrs. Stickler, the shop owner, was a kind and gentle lady who made all of the dresses. Her prices were extremely fair, especially since everything was handmade, and the women were thrilled with the selections. Mrs. Stickler stood quietly by, smiling as the ladies looked through her inventory, trying not to stare at Pattie's birthmark.

Such a lovely child, she thought. *It's a tragedy that mark is on her face. It sure doesn't seem to bother them though!*

Pattie tried on several dresses and stepped out from behind the screen wearing one that was cream colored and draped with fine, Victorian lace. It had a gentle round neck with lace falling from the shoulders to form soft sleeves striking her arms just below the elbows. The skirt flowed gently around her ankles and was lined with dusty blue satin. As soon as she heard the audible gasps from everyone, including Mrs. Stickler, she knew that she had found her dress.

"Does it look okay?"

"Oh, my dear, you're an angel! You look positively ravishing!" Molly gushed.

"How much is it?" She looked uneasily at Mrs. Stickler.

"Please, my dear, let me give this to you as a wedding gift. It's priceless on you and you have to have this dress. It was made for you."

"Thank you, Miss Molly. You have been so good to me and Dooble."

"Nonsense, child, each of you bring me great joy, and it makes me happy to do something special for you."

"Do you have any shoes?" the bride asked.

"No, but they have them right up the street at Macy's. Just ask for the satin slippers for brides. They'll be able to fix you right up. And while you're up there, I'll wrap the dress up real nice for you."

They entered Macy's and Ellen was aware of people turning to stare as Pattie walked by. Pattie, however, was oblivious to it, and Ellen soon quit noticing too. It simply didn't matter.

They located the shoes in just a few minutes. The perfect pair was cream colored satin with one inch heels. Ellen found a lovely lace handkerchief with tiny, embroidered blue flowers. She bought it as a gift for Pattie and slipped it discreetly into her bag so as to surprise her friend later.

"We have a little time left so why don't we do a little Christmas shopping while we're here?" Molly suggested. "We probably won't have another opportunity."

There were a surprising number of affordable gifts available at the huge department store and soon they had made numerous selections. They paid for their packages, and as they prepared to leave, Molly turned to Ellen.

"Ellen, I would very much like to buy a bicycle for Stephen's Christmas. There's a bright red one in the toy department with a wire basket on it so he can put Gimpy in it when they ride. Do you mind if he has one?"

"No, Miss Molly, we don't mind if he has one but we don't expect you to buy it."

"I know you don't expect it, but it will make me very happy to do it."

They soon had the limousine loaded with packages, and the bicycle was tucked safely into the trunk. They stopped at Schmidt's store to visit their friends. Birdie was very excited about the upcoming wedding, and they were going to be able to be at the manor for Thanksgiving and the wedding. Mrs. Schmidt was getting worse and Mr. Schmidt had decided to take her to visit her sister on Thanksgiving while she was still able to travel. He would close the store and they would spend the night in Brooklyn at her sister's home.

A brief visit was made to the nursing home. Mona was very weak and was in the bed, but she smiled warmly at her visitors. They gave her gifts of bath soap and perfumed talcum powder.

Her gratitude for the gifts was touching, and they were glad they had taken the time to visit with her.

Ellen stopped a nurse on the way out of the nursing home.

"Nurse, where is Mr. Borello? I'd like to say hello."

"I'm sorry, ma'am, but he died."

"Oh, no, I'm so sorry."

"Yes, ma'am, so are we, but it was a peaceful death. I talked to him right before he went to sleep that night. He told me his son Tony had visited him that day. He said he hadn't seen him in a long time and now he was at peace, knowing that his Tony was okay. He died in his sleep that night."

Thanksgiving Day dawned bright and clear, the sun glittering off the frost covered limbs, grass and windowpanes.

"God sprinkled diamonds for your wedding day, Pattie," Stephen said as he gazed out the kitchen window.

The wedding was set for 10:00, to be followed by a traditional turkey meal for the wedding guests. The couple was to be picked up by a car at 3:00 and transported to Wedding Falls Resort in the mountains two hours away for a honeymoon weekend. Walter returned from the city with the Dantons at 9:00 and Birdie hurried to Molly's room upstairs to help the bride get ready for the ceremony.

The scene she encountered when she entered the room took her breath. Pattie was standing before the full view mirror, her dress nestled comfortably around her. Her thick, shiny brown hair was piled elegantly onto the top of her head. She sat down for Ellen to place on her head the small lace cap with the fingertip veil of illusion attached. They had discovered the veil when they unpacked the dress after their trip to the city. Attached was a note from Mrs. Stickler.

Please accept this gift with my blessings for a long and happy life together.

Molly brought out a bouquet for Pattie to carry. There were no flowers blooming on the estate so they had gathered evergreen boughs and dried rose hips as well as bunches of Nandina berries.

The bright leaves that Stephen had pressed for her were tucked into the greenery as well. The curves and twists of the rose branches added a simple, earthy eloquence. Molly attached it with cream colored ribbon streamers to a prayer book she had owned since she was a child. The streamers cascaded down and swayed gently as Pattie moved.

"This is something borrowed," she explained to Pattie as she had placed the prayer book in her hands.

"And this is something new." Ellen slipped the handkerchief with the embroidered blue flowers into her friend's hand. "It also has something blue on it with the flowers."

"We need something old," Birdie realized. She reached onto her shoulder and released the clasp of a small cameo resting there.

"This belonged to my grandmother. I would be honored for you to wear it, Pattie."

"Thank you, Birdie; I'll take good care of it. Thank you, everyone. You have been so kind to me, and I love you all. This is the happiest day of my life." She lost control and began sobbing softly.

"Now stop that, child!" Molly admonished. "You'll have us all crying and besides, you'll ruin your makeup."

They all hugged warmly before stepping back to view the bride.

"You're a vision, my dear, you really are." Molly stated with admiration.

Pattie slipped her feet into her new satin slippers in preparation of descending the stairs to begin her new life.

♥♥♥

Father Branson stood before the large fireplace in the front parlor. Dooble stood nervously to his side, his dark blue suit accented with the new gray and burgundy tie Walter, his best man, had given him. Robert had tucked a white handkerchief into the pocket of Dooble's coat, and he looked quite dashing standing there, waiting for his bride. His special shoe allowed him to stand straight, giving no visible evidence of his handicap. Walter stood beside him, offering support to his nervous friend.

The church organist began playing the wedding march on the small pump organ brought in for this special occasion. The guests, which included the Carvers, Dr. Sheffield, and even the Howard brothers all dressed up and looking uncomfortable in stiff collars, turned as the strains of the wedding march filled the room.

Stephen entered, carrying two gold bands on a blue satin pillow. Julie followed, carrying a small wicker basket of dried rose petals that she scattered on the Oriental rug. Molly entered the room next, escorted by little Carson. Ellen entered alone, dressed in a navy blue dress with long sleeves and a white collar nestled around her neck. She carried a bible topped with evergreen boughs, also clipped from the front yard of the manor.

The march increased in volume and the guests stood, excitement electrifying the room. Pattie, escorted by Robert, stood in the doorway, her face covered by the gossamer veil, her right hand tucked under Robert's arm and her bouquet held at her waist.

Everyone in the room gasped at her beauty, and Dooble's eyes filled with tears.

Robert escorted her down the aisle and slipped her hand into Dooble's, as he gave her in marriage to that good man. He moved away and took his place beside Ellen, his hand resting gently on her arm.

Father Branson charged the couple regarding their responsibility to God and to each other and began repeating the vows.

"Do you, Floyd, take Ellen…?"

Stephen glanced around in confusion, looked over at his mother and asked, "Who's Floyd?"

His mother shook her head quickly so he became immediately silent. The bride and groom smiled fondly at their ring bearer.

♥♥♥

All the guests enjoyed the turkey dinner and took turns toasting the happy new couple with champagne brought in for just this occasion. The two were overwhelmed by all the attention and the toasts were given by each guest in the room, one by one.

When it became Stephen's turn, he stood, raised his glass of grape juice, turned to his friends and asked, "Who's Floyd?"

Through their laughter, Pattie was finally able to explain.

"Floyd is his real name, Stephen. Dooble is just a nickname, and we wanted to use his real name in the ceremony. He's still the same person."

"Oh." The child was obviously relieved. "I thought maybe somebody else got married."

The couple opened their wedding gifts, thanking all their friends graciously. Molly had crocheted her a beautiful shawl, made with thread almost as fine and lustrous as a spider web.

"But you've already given me a wedding gift, Miss Molly," Pattie objected as she touched her wedding gown gently.

"Yes, but this was something from my soul, made with my own hands, so it's more special than something made by someone else."

Pattie ran across the room and hugged her benefactor gratefully.

At 3:00, the car from the resort arrived at the front door to transport the happy couple to their hideaway. The guests lined up on the walkway off the porch and tossed birdseed at them as they ran toward the car.

"Why are we throwing birdseed?" Stephen asked.

"Because it is a wish for their happiness and good luck," his mother explained.

"I think their happiness is going to be a sure thing," Roy Howard remarked as he overheard the conversation between the young boy and his mother. "Don't think I've ever seen two people anymore in love."

♥♥♥

Wedding Falls Resort was stunningly beautiful, and the young couple was deliriously happy in their luxurious room overlooking the falls. They ignored the stares from strangers as they entered the dining room, too happy to be concerned about insensitive looks and whispers.

They sat at a table for two before the large dining room fireplace on Saturday evening, eating their meal. A man, woman and a young boy of about nine sat near them.

They kept staring, but Pattie and Dooble had eyes only for each other.

Suddenly, the little boy pushed his chair back and walked over to their table, standing beside Dooble.

"Are you two circus freaks?" he asked and then he began to laugh, pleased at his joke.

Pattie and Dooble sat in stunned silence and shock while his parents made no move to retrieve their rude son.

Jefferson Milworth, the manager of the resort, witnessed the outburst and hurried to their table.

"Young man, that's enough. Go to your table right away or you can leave this room."

"I don't have to. My mama and daddy are here and they can buy this place!"

"Maybe so but while I'm manager here, your rudeness to other guests will not be tolerated. Now do as I say."

He went wailing back to his parents' table and his mother stood up.

"Well, I never!" she hissed indignantly. "How dare you shout at our son while you let monsters like that in with decent folk!"

"Ma'am," Mr. Milworth stated, struggling to maintain control, "you and your family have exactly thirty minutes to vacate these premises. Our staff will help you pack and you needn't worry about the bill. We don't need your money."

"Vernon, are you going to let him talk to me like that?" She turned to her husband, fairly sputtering with rage. "How dare you speak in such a manner to me. I have never been so insulted!"

Her husband made no move to come to her rescue and sat there, crimson with embarrassment.

"You now have twenty-nine minutes, ma'am. Do I need to call staff to remove you from this area?"

"Well!" she snorted as she stormed out of the dining hall, her squalling son in tow and her husband following meekly several lengths behind.

Mr. Milworth turned his attention to his insulted guests.

"I am so deeply sorry for that unmerciful and uncalled for attack on you good people. Please accept my sincerest apologies and understand that they will never again be guests of our resort. We do not in any way support or tolerate such a cruel outburst and most certainly do not share his vicious opinion."

"Thank you, sir," Dooble replied graciously. "It's quite all right and we certainly don't hold you responsible. He's just a child and it really isn't his fault."

"Well, it was obvious where the fault is," he responded. "It was still quite unpleasant and we don't want anything to be unpleasant in our inn. If there is anything that we can do to make reparation, please just ask."

"No, no, that's quite all right. We're fine, really we are."

As they returned to their meal, one by one, the other guests in the room stopped by their table to greet them kindly and congratulate them on their marriage. One gentleman sent a bottle of fine wine over to them and another sent a cake.

♥♥♥

Jefferson Milworth ascended the steps to the room of the evicted guests to make certain they did not overstay their deadline. He knocked loudly before opening the door to announce, "You have ten minutes."

As he entered the room, he saw the woman stuffing towels from the bath into her bag.

"And leave our towels, please." He glared at her coldly and exited, closing the door firmly behind him. He stood there for a second, trying to stop his angry shaking.

He glanced around quickly, making certain no one was standing in the hall to see his next action. He then stuck out his tongue at the closed door and walked down the hall to return downstairs.

He stopped two staff members as he descended the stairs.

"Go stand outside Room 107 and make certain they're out in nine minutes. Then escort them out the back door. I will have a car waiting there. The sooner we get them out, the better."

♥♥♥

Mr. and Mrs. Floyd Howell left the inn the next day to return to their new home in the cottage behind the manor. It would also be Patches' new home too as she was welcomed into Pattie's house as a family member.

Their nearly perfect weekend was not spoiled by the one unpleasant incident which had occurred the previous evening. They would both hold the happy memory of their honeymoon in their hearts for a lifetime.

Fearless Heart

Chapter 15
A Birth

The household settled down after the wedding and adjusted to Pattie's move from the manor. Patches had no difficulty at all adjusting to the change and Gimpy had no concept of it since Pattie still spent her days in the large house, and he spent his nights in Stephen's room.

Christmas decorations were located in the attic and brought out for the first time since Molly was a child. There were boxes and boxes of fragile ornaments, delicate angels carved out of clay and baked in kilns, large blobs of what were once candles but were now melted masses, and crocheted snowflakes created by Molly's mother and grandmother. She touched them tenderly, remembering, and aching to see once more those whom she had loved so dearly.

The halls were draped with long garlands of cedar cut from the grounds and woven together in unbroken lengths. Holly with bright red berries was harvested from the numerous trees growing in the surrounding woods and slipped in among the cedar to add a splash of seasonal festivity and color. Garlands were also wrapped snuggly around the banisters guarding the huge staircase descending from above. Red bows and clay angels were tucked into these stair decorations with large vases of holly flanking the steps in the foyer. A clump of mistletoe hung provocatively over the large doors entering the parlor, causing Stephen to make a wide sweep in order to avoid this dreaded spot. He had no desire to be kissed by anyone, especially Julie when they visited for Christmas.

"Yuck!" he declared in disgust. "I don't want any girl kissing me!"

Dooble laughed, promising him that he'd change his mind soon enough.

A tall cedar tree nestled in the corner of the parlor away from the fireplace. Glass ornaments, more clay angels and crocheted snowflakes gave it an air of excitement and life. There were even some of Stephen's pressed leaves hanging proudly from the boughs.

"We need a tree topper," Pattie observed, standing back to view the decorations.

"It's a lovely tree, dear. You did a beautiful job decorating the whole house. It won't be a tragedy if we don't have a tree topper. I can't recall having one when I was a child so I doubt that there's one in the attic anywhere."

"We used to have an angel topping ours," Pattie remembered. "Grandmother made her out of cornhusks and painted her dress with purple poke berries. I can remember getting them all over my hands, and it was days before the stain came off. As I recall, my fingernails had to just grow out to get all of it off of them."

"How about your wedding veil?" Stephen suggested.

"That's a wonderful idea, Stephen!" Pattie exclaimed. "Thank you, I'll go get it right away."

"Are you sure, dear?" Molly was concerned. "We don't want anything to happen to it."

"I'm certain it'll be fine way up on top of the tree. Besides, I'm going to try and make an angel out of cornhusks this next year. I'm not certain I'll be able to figure it out but I'd really like to try."

"Maybe we can all figure it out if we work together," Molly offered.

She climbed up the tall ladder Dooble had brought into the house for decorating and placed her beloved veil on top of the tree. The lace cap nestled at the top like a tiny dove. The illusion cascaded down, giving an ethereal look to the tree.

"There, that's better. But it's still not quite right." She studied for a few minutes and then put her coat and boots on to go outside.

Dooble caught her behind the cottage, pulling dried honeysuckle vines off the stone wall in the back.

"What're you doing, love?"

"I'm going to wrap these around the Christmas tree. I think it'll give it a more completed look. It looks a little sparse right now."

He smiled at his wife, pride and love shining from his face, his eyes, his voice.

♥♥♥

Everyone was raving at the dinner table that night about the beautiful decorations, and especially the tree. The honeysuckle vines twisted and braided together were really lovely.

"I think it's the prettiest tree I've ever seen in this house," Molly declared.

"There's still something missing and I can't quite put my finger on it," Pattie pondered.

She was deep in thought during dinner and afterward as she cleared the dishes.

"Can I have some popcorn?" Stephen asked.

"May I," his mother corrected.

"Huh?" he asked in confusion.

"That's it!" Pattie shouted. "Strings of popcorn! We used to string popcorn and drape it around the tree. That's what's missing! Thank you, Stephen!"

She took her hands out of the water and rushed to put some corn in the wire basket. She held it over the fireplace and soon had mounds of white kernels in a large bowl. She repeated her actions and filled yet another bowl. She took some out of the second bowl, poured melted butter over it, salted it and handed it to Stephen.

"Okay, sweetie, here's your popcorn. And while you eat it, you can string the rest to be put on the Christmas tree." She retrieved a needle and thread from the sewing basket which rested in the corner cupboard near the fireplace. She showed him how to do it and got him started as she completed the dishes.

Soon the whole house was stringing popcorn and in short order, the job was completed. They hurried into the parlor and Dooble climbed the ladder while Pattie directed him as to where the popcorn strings should be placed.

"Now. That's better," she declared with satisfaction as she stood back to admire their work.

♥♥♥

Ellen made a visit for her regular checkup to Dr. Sheffield the week before Christmas.

"Everything is just fine, Ellen. Looks like you're going to be right on schedule around the first of the year."

"That's great, doctor, thank you. I'm ready for it to be over. It's getting a little difficult to move around."

"I can just imagine," he agreed.

"No, you can't, John," Molly corrected him. "No man can. By the way, would you like to have Christmas dinner with us? We'd be pleased to have you."

"Why, thank you, Molly, that's most gracious of you but I'm going upstate on Christmas Eve for Christmas with my brother and his family. I'll be back on December 26 but if it weren't for that, I'd love to celebrate with you and your family."

"What if I have the baby while you're gone?"

"I don't think that'll happen," he assured her, "but if you're worried, I'll alert Hattie Mae. She's probably delivered more babies than I have."

"Well, that would make me feel much better."

"Consider it done," he promised.

♥♥♥

The next day, they received a call from Cletus. Mona Dorsett had died the night before. The nursing home had notified them as they had no other family listed for her. The welfare people were giving her a small, inexpensive funeral, and she was to be buried in the city cemetery near the park.

Ellen was distressed that she could not attend the funeral but Robert, Walter and Molly traveled to the city to pay their respects. Stephen did not go as they felt he was too young to understand the finality of the situation. They stopped by Schmidt's store and picked up Birdie. Carson and Julie stayed at the store with their father.

It was a simple but eloquent ceremony. Mona's friends from the Salvation Army filled nearly two pews in the nursing home chapel and looked quite dashing in their uniforms. Even Officer Dan and his wife came.

The group moved quietly to the cemetery, and the Salvation Army played the hymn "Just as I Am." They prayed the Lord's Prayer together and sadly left their friend, the pots of poinsettias brought by each mourner bobbing brightly in the cold winter day.

"That was a beautiful service," Birdie remarked. "Miss Mona would have been pleased."

"Yes, I agree," Robert stated.

"I'm afraid Mrs. Schmidt may be next. She's not doing well at all. Mr. Schmidt may be forced to put her in the hospital or a nursing home." She sighed deeply as she thought of her friend at the store.

♥♥♥

Walter and the Dantons arrived at the manor shortly before noon on Christmas morning. It had snowed on Christmas Eve but fortunately, it was a light snow so there was no problem with the roads. The children were excited to distraction, running happily around the parlor, Stephen being careful to avoid the dreaded mistletoe looming ominously over the doorway.

They had lunch and then returned to the parlor to open gifts. There were gifts for everyone, thanks to the generosity and thoughtfulness of all the friends. Birdie had created tiny paper bags for everyone, filling them with nuts and pieces of peppermint purchased from the store. They received very little wages but she had been very careful to save wisely so as to include everyone in her family's gift giving. Carson and Julie had gone to the park and gathered gumballs that had fallen from the sycamore trees, an old wasp nest and an empty cocoon to be placed in Stephen's bag.

He squealed in delight as he pulled these treasures out of the bag. He looked at the cocoon curiously.

"What's this?" he asked.

"It's a cocoon," his mother explained. "That's where a butterfly comes from. A caterpillar will eat and eat until it gets really fat, and then spins a cocoon around himself. He stays inside for a while and when the spring arrives, the cocoon splits here at this end that's open and a beautiful butterfly wiggles out."

"Wowww!" Stephen breathed. "Has the butterfly already come out of this one?"

"Yes, dear, that's why it's open. This is an old one, probably from last spring. You never want to get one that's closed as it'll kill the butterfly."

Stephen thanked his friends warmly, and they were soon outside with his new bicycle, taking turns trying to ride it.

"Looks like we'll have to have some riding lessons this spring," Dooble observed.

♥♥♥

The women remained inside, clearing wrapping paper and enjoying the warmth. Ellen began to squirm in her chair somewhat.

"Something I ate didn't agree with me," she declared. "I have indigestion."

Molly, Birdie and Pattie moved to her side at once.

"Are you sure it's not something else?"

"I don't think so. I hope not."

"I'm going to have Walter go get Hattie Mae just in case," Molly stated with worry in her voice.

She went to the door and called Walter, and he was soon on his way to the village while Robert rushed to Ellen's side.

Pattie and Dooble took Cletus, the children and Gimpy to the cottage.

"What's wrong with Mama?" Stephen was visibly shaken.

"She'll be fine, sweetheart," Pattie assured him. "It may be time for the baby to come so we need to wait here. We'll know when Hattie Mae gets here so please don't worry."

"Is it like the butterfly coming out of the cocoon?" he asked.

Pattie and Dooble looked at each other and Dooble said, "You're right and that's a beautiful way to look at it, Little Man."

♥♥♥

There was a tap on the door a short time later and Stephen rushed to the door behind Dooble, anxious to hear anything about his mother. Walter stood there, smiled down at Stephen, and announced, "Looks like you're going to be a big brother in a little while, son."

"Please, Walter, have Daddy tell Mama I love her."

"Okay, Pal, I'll do it for certain," he promised the small child.

He came into the cottage to speak with the Cletus.

"Looks like it might be a long night, Cletus. Do you want me to go ahead and take you back to the city or do you want to spend the night?"

"Well, I hate to impose on you good people but I know my woman ain't gonna want to go nowhere with that baby on the way. I 'spect the best thing for me to do is call Mr. Schmidt and see if it's okay for us to stay over. I know he wants the store open tomorrow but Mrs. Schmidt may not be in any condition for him to leave her so I'll just have to get his thoughts on it."

"Come on over and make the call and you know you're more than welcomed to stay here the night. We have plenty of room and Birdie being here is probably very comforting to Ellen right now."

Cletus called Mr. Schmidt and advised him of what was happening.

"Oh, I'm sorry to hear that, Mr. Schmidt. I sure hope she's gonna be all right.

"Yes, uh huh... yes, sir, we will. You too. I'll talk to you tomorrow."

He turned from the phone and said, "Mrs. Schmidt is in the hospital. They had to take her this morning. So Mr. Schmidt said for us to go ahead and stay the night. He'll be fine but we really need to get back pretty quick. I know he'll want to get to the hospital."

Suddenly, a pain-filled cry echoed down the stairway into the foyer where they were standing by the phone. Cletus reached out and grabbed Robert by the arms as he attempted to bolt upstairs.

"No, Buddy, stay here. She'll be fine but we just have to wait. Why don't you come on over to the cottage with us?"

"No, I'll stay here.... I'm sorry, Cletus, I didn't mean to snap at you. I can't stand this."

"I'll run over and tell them we're staying the night and then I'll be back to sit with you. Walter will be here with you until I get back. Are you gonna be okay?"

"Yeah, thanks, I'll be okay. I'll just be glad when it's over."

"I'm sure Ellen will be too," Cletus commented as he moved toward the cottage.

♥♥♥

The men sat silently, Robert jumping up occasionally to pace nervously around the parlor, wringing his hands and running his fingers through his hair. The cottage settled down for the night with quilts spread on the tiny floor and little heads peeping out from under the covers. Pattie and Dooble went to bed but didn't get much sleep. They watched their guests, making certain they were well, and worried about their friend in the manor, bringing a new life into the world.

Cletus and Walter were dozing in the large chairs around the fireplace in the manor parlor and Robert was stretched out on the sofa, trying to rest, when he heard someone running downstairs. He burst through the door into the hall to see what was wrong. It was Birdie, on the way to the kitchen to retrieve hot water.

"What's wrong?" He was alarmed.

"Everything's fine, Robert. It's just about time and I have to get some hot water upstairs. Can you help me get some poured into a bucket? It has to be a clean bucket too."

There were several kettles of water steeping on the kitchen stove and Robert pulled a bucket out of the pantry. He poured some water into it, swished it around to cover the whole interior, and then poured it out. He then filled it with more hot water and carried it upstairs with Birdie.

She stopped him outside the door to Molly's room where his beloved lay in agony. She took the bucket from him, entered the room and closed the door behind her. He stood helplessly outside in the hall, his heart breaking as he heard his wife cry out in pain.

"Come on, Buddy," Cletus appeared behind him and took his arm gently. "Let's go back downstairs. They'll come get us when it's over."

Walter sat up as they entered the parlor. "What time is it?"

Cletus looked at the clock on the mantle. "It's nearly 2:00."

"What's happening?" He was sitting up now as he questioned Cletus, concerned about the look of terror on Robert's face.

"It's almost time. Birdie came downstairs to get some hot water and she said it won't be long now."

"Are you okay, Robert?" Walter moved to his side, trying to find some way to comfort and reassure his friend.

"I don't know. I just don't know. This is difficult. She's laying up there hurting and it's my fault and there's nothing I can do about it. This is torture."

♥♥♥

Robert was sitting on the sofa, his head in his hands, and Walter and Cletus were dozing once again. He looked up at the clock. Nearly 3:00. He put his head back into his hands and prayed silently. He raised his head as he heard movement on the stairway and jumped up to exit the parlor. Walter and Cletus awakened and stood up, ready to support Robert in any way they could.

Robert pulled the door open just as Birdie reached the bottom of the steps.

"It's a girl," she smiled.

He pushed by her, racing up the stairs. Cletus hugged Birdie and Walter slapped him on the back as they watched their friend hurry to his family.

Soon everyone was deep in exhausted sleep, including Robert as he sat by his wife's side, his head resting on her bed. Their daughter slept peacefully in the small crib near the hearth of the fireplace.

♥♥♥

Robert came after Stephen at the cottage early the next morning. Pattie and Dooble didn't know if the baby had been born yet or not. Stephen had just finished breakfast and was asking about his mother when the door opened and his father entered.

"You have a baby sister, son," he said proudly.

"Yayyyyyy!" he shouted joyfully. "Can I see her? How's Mama?"

"Mama's fine, and yes, you can see your sister for a minute but we can't stay. Mama's really tired."

They crossed the drive to the manor and were soon running upstairs. They entered the darkened room quietly and Stephen tiptoed to his mother's side, noticing with relief the birdhouse nestled securely on her bedside table. Beside it, also, rested the tiny music box he had given Miss Molly as a gift not long after they arrived at the manor. He kissed his mother gently before peeping into the crib at the tiny bundle lying so still.

"What's her name?"

"We don't know yet, Stephen. We were hoping you could help us come up with one."

"Why don't we name her Molly Elizabeth? After Miss Molly. She told me that's her whole name."

The two adults looked at each other and smiled.

"Thank you, Stephen," his mother agreed. "Her name will be Molly Elizabeth."

Fearless Heart

Chapter 16
The Revelation

The Fulton Manor was filled with activity, especially after the arrival of tiny Beth. It was decided to call her Beth in order to eliminate confusion, and Molly was enraptured by the tiny addition. Every move, every sound Beth made was reported nightly at the dinner table, with everyone listening patiently and kindly. The Blairs were warmed by the love and acceptance shown by Molly to her namesake.

January was a particularly bitter month with deep snow and blustery winds. The family was grateful to stay inside, but Robert and Walter were forced to spend several nights at the factory. It was a short five miles from the manor to the plant but much of the route would be impassable following a particularly brutal snow. Ellen and Molly hovered carefully over both the children, wary of any signs of sniffles or fever. They wanted no repeat performance of the year before when Stephen contracted pneumonia. The memory still terrified all of them.

As January ended and February progressed, a respite in the weather was awarded to the countryside. The winds ceased and the sun began melting the snow somewhat, causing enormous icicles to form on the eaves as nighttime temperatures dipped to freeze the daytime thaw.

Molly sat silently in the parlor, her crocheting lying unattended in her lap. Her mind moved to another time, another place, another life.

♥♥♥

She leaped off the train as it pulled into the station at Issaqua Harbor, looking around for an automobile to deliver her to Fulton Manor. Her spirit was high and her face was covered by a smile that the discomfort of the train trip from the city couldn't erase. The conductor pulled her trunk off the train onto the platform and ran over to a car waiting at the curb, signaling to the driver. Soon her trunk was loaded into the vehicle and she climbed into the front seat.

The driver, familiar with the Fulton family, tipped his hat to her, ground the gear shift into first and pulled away from the depot.

"How you doing, ma'am?" he questioned cordially.

"I'm wonderful, sir, and thank you for asking." Her smile radiated throughout the automobile. He smiled in response, her happiness impossible to ignore. He whistled softly as they rode through the countryside toward the manor. She looked eagerly out the side window, willing the vehicle to reach her destination as quickly as possible.

She quickly exited the vehicle as it stopped at the front door of the large mansion and ran to the front door. The driver unloaded her trunk, placing it on the front steps. As she reached the front door, it opened and a man stepped out.

"Mr. Monroe, please take care of the driver for me. And, hello, it's good to be home."

He smiled at her greeting as she brushed past him into the hallway.

"Welcome home, Miss Molly," he said to the back of her head as she disappeared down the hall.

"Mother!" she called out as she peeped inside the parlor off the hall. She glanced up the wide marble staircase. "Mother! Where are you? I'm home. And I have some wonderful news! Where are you?"

♥♥♥

The two women sat together on the parlor sofa as Molly continued to joyfully tell her mother about her fiancé. Her mother was stunned into silence by Molly's sudden announcement of her upcoming wedding.

"He's wonderful, Mother. You're going to love him too, I just know you will. He's a doctor and will have a practice here in Issaqua Harbor. He has just gotten his license, and he's so handsome. I can't wait for you to meet him. We're going to get married as quickly as possible."

The older lady sat silently, her hands folded in her lap, a slight frown furrowing her forehead. She raised her eyebrows at the last remark.

"I know, I know," Molly noticed her mother's expression. "You wanted a really big wedding but this will work better for us, I assure you. Davis is going to be opening his new practice and that will take up all our time and resources so a small wedding in the chapel at St. Christopher's is all we need. Or even a small ceremony here at home. That would be lovely if you and Father would let us."

Molly was so excited, she hadn't yet noticed her mother's silence. She jumped up as she heard her father coming down the hall.

"Father, come inside quickly! I have some wonderful news I just shared with Mother….I'm going to get married. He's a wonderful man and I'm sure you'll like him very much. He's a doctor and we plan to marry right away and…"

She was stopped by the look on her father's face. He stepped inside the parlor and closed the door behind him.

"No." He did not look at his daughter as he moved to the fireplace. "You will not marry anyone that we do not know. You will marry someone who is acceptable and suitable to the standing of our family in the community. It will be someone who will come to work in our company and keep it running. You are certainly aware that has always been the plan."

"But I love him, Father," Molly insisted, her heart suddenly sinking.

He waved his hand in her direction.

"Love. What do you know of love? We're talking tradition, duty to family and that's what is important. Love fades and then what do you have? Nothing, that's what. Commitment to the family and to our company is what you need. The company is your responsibility and your inheritance. A doctor can't run a steam engine business. No, it's out of the question. You'll marry someone more suitable."

She stood stunned and in shock until she could compose herself enough to speak. When she did, she spoke softly and with deep determination.

"You don't understand, Father. I love him and I will marry him. I hope it will be with your blessing."

"Never!" He spun around to face her and she was frightened by the dark anger on his face. Her father had always been stern but she'd never seen this look before. Of course, she had never before defied him.

"You will do as you are told."

She squared her shoulders and clenched her jaw.

"No, Father." Her voice remained quiet and steady. "I will marry Davis. We are going to have a child and we will marry as soon as he arrives in Issaqua Harbor. He is traveling by steamship from Maryland and will take a car here as soon as the boat docks in New York."

She thought that her father might strike her as he clenched his fists and his eyes filled with fury.

"How dare you bring shame to this family?"

Her mother finally moved from her spot on the sofa and approached her daughter. Her husband reached out and stopped her as she moved past him.

"No, leave her be. She has brought shame and dishonor on this family. As soon as you marry this – this – *doctor*, you will leave our home and you will not return. You have made your decision and you will have to live with it." He turned and stormed out of the room, slamming the door behind him.

Molly stood in disbelief, sorrow and anger gripping her heart. She hurried out of the parlor to a small powder room off the foyer.

She was physically ill as she realized the depth of what had just happened. She knew her father well enough to know he meant what he said.

❤❤❤

The next week seemed to last forever as Molly waited for Davis' arrival at Fulton Manor. Her father had denied her access to the family dining room and she had retreated to the kitchen with Mrs. Monroe, the housekeeper, and her young son Walter. Mr. Monroe took his meals with his family in the kitchen so they enjoyed being with Molly after she was banished from the dining room. They had always loved her and were glad for her presence among them.

Molly knew that Davis was to arrive sometime in the afternoon of Thursday so she anxiously watched the driveway all day, hoping to see a car pull up to the manor. As she glanced outside shortly after dark for at least the hundredth time, she was relieved to see the lights of a car moving up the long, winding driveway. She ran to the front door and waited anxiously on the porch for its arrival.

She ran excitedly to the car as it stopped, her face lit with a wide smile, expecting to see Davis exit. She stopped short as two strangers, one wearing an official uniform of some kind and the other wearing a suit, stepped into the drive. She stood silently as they approached her.

The man with the suit removed his hat.

"Excuse me, ma'am. We're looking for any family of Davis McLean."

Terror gripped her heart as she struggled to speak through her lips, paralyzed with fear.

"I'm his fiancée. Is there something wrong?"

The two men glanced at each other and the uniformed officer said, "I'm sorry, ma'am, but there's been an accident." He looked over at his companion with a helpless expression on his face. His friend took up the conversation.

"The ship that was coming from Baltimore hit a barge while trying to dock in New York, ma'am. Several people were knocked overboard, I'm afraid. Mr. McLean was one of them."

She stared at them in disbelief.

"What are you saying?" she asked quietly, her voice not betraying her anxiety.

"I'm afraid Mr. McLean was swept overboard," he repeated as he fumbled clumsily with his hat. "We, uh ... we recovered the body but..."

She heard nothing else as the night closed in on her and she fell to the driveway in unconsciousness.

♥♥♥

Molly snapped back to the present, the memory of that long ago event still too painful to recall. She wiped the tears from her eyes, her hands shaking with emotion and sorrow from her mind journey back to that fateful night.

The men arrived home from the plant later on that dark, cold afternoon. Molly was uncharacteristically quiet during dinner that evening. She seemed strangely preoccupied. After dinner, she approached Walter, pulling him to the side.

"Walter, may I see you in the library for a moment?"

He followed her into the front room and the door shut behind them. He remained there for nearly thirty minutes before emerging and returning to the kitchen. He glanced briefly at Robert but made no comment.

"Is Miss Molly okay?" Ellen inquired, an edge of concern in her voice.

"Yes, yes, she's fine. No need to worry."

♥♥♥

As the men drove from the manor the next morning, Walter turned to Robert.

"Robert, Miss Molly would like to speak to you tonight after dinner, in private, if you don't mind."

"Is something wrong?"

"No, no, I assure you, everything's fine. She just has something to discuss with you. Just understand how much she cares for you and your family. And trust me, it'll be fine."

Robert was curious but not worried as they approached the plant.

♥♥♥

"Look at those long ice things, Miss Molly," Stephen pointed out.

She smiled at his lapse of memory about the name of the frozen object. "Yes, they are quite long, aren't they? Reminds me of elephant tusks."

"Yeah, they do. Except they ain't curved."

"Aren't, Stephen. My goodness, we never use that word! It sounds really rude."

"But that's what Dooble says." the child pointed out.

"That's true and I certainly mean no insult to that fine gentleman, but that's part of his language, and we don't want you to adopt it as part of yours."

"Okay," he whined, soon forgetting the scolding as he watched the water dripping off the trees and icicles. He would laugh aloud as an occasional icicle snapped and fell away or a large sheet of snow slid off a roof or crashed from heavily laden tree limbs. It looked as if winter was losing its grip on the manor, one icicle and one sheet of ice at a time.

"Do you think Daddy and Walter will get home okay today?" he turned to speak to Molly. She was leaning over the crib to pick up Beth when she suddenly stopped. She had a stricken look on her face and she clutched her left arm, her breath gasping.

"What's the matter?" he asked with alarm. "Miss Molly, what's the matter?"

He received no answer so he ran out of the kitchen in search of his mother and Pattie. He found Pattie first, in the dining room next door, dusting the shelves of the china hutch. She looked up with surprise as he burst into the room.

"Come quick, Miss Molly is sick!"

She dropped her dust cloth, scrambled off the ladder and ran with Stephen back to the kitchen. She shouted for Ellen as they ran down the hall.

"Miss Molly?" she cried, her voice tight with apprehension, "what's wrong? Are you okay?"

Molly looked up at her, still clutching her arm. "Hurts," she gasped. "Can't breathe."

Ellen rushed into the room, fearful that something was wrong with one of the children. As she saw Molly's distress with Pattie leaning anxiously over her, concern took over.

"Oh, my God, Miss Molly, what's wrong? Pattie, please go call Dr. Sheffield at once."

Ellen quickly pulled a chair over for Molly to sit in and loosened the buttons at her throat. "Stephen, honey, get me a glass of water please."

He scurried to follow his mother's instructions.

After what seemed like hours but was actually only a few minutes, Pattie returned. "He's on the way," she breathlessly explained.

They managed to get her into the small bed in the cook's quarters off the kitchen in hopes of making her more comfortable. Ellen rubbed her forehead with a moistened cloth even though she had no signs of fever. She didn't know what else to do.

Stephen kept running to the front window, searching down the drive for the doctor.

"Stephen, do you think you can call the factory and get your daddy on the phone?" his mother asked.

"I'll try. Can you write the number down for me so I can give it to the operator?"

At that moment, Beth awakened and began fussing. It was time for her feeding.

"Come on, sweetie," Pattie took his hand. "I'll write it down for you. You make the call please, while I feed little Beth. Just tell your daddy and Walter to come home. Miss Molly is sick and the doctor is on the way."

♥♥♥

Walter and Robert arrived right behind Dr. Sheffield. They all rushed into the kitchen, looking for Molly. Pattie pointed to the room, and Ellen looked up as the doctor hurried inside. She moved away to give him space to examine and stepped outside to wait with the others. They stood fearfully wringing their hands and pacing during the examination, all focusing undivided attention on Dr. Sheffield as he came out of the room.

"Looks like she's had a heart attack," he announced.

Ellen and Pattie cried out, placing their hands over their mouths.

"Oh, no. Please, no," Robert prayed.

"I don't think it's very bad, not to minimize her condition. It's difficult to know for sure but she's conscious. I gave her a sedative so her breathing will be more even and relaxed now. I want to call for an ambulance to take her to New York Memorial as soon as possible. They may not be able to get here before morning and tonight could be critical."

"Can we take her?" Walter inquired.

"Why, yes, if you're willing to try it."

"Of course. What do we need to do?"

"Let's get her wrapped up good and we need something to carry her out to the car. I want to keep her as straight as possible but we don't have a stretcher."

"How about the ironing board?" Pattie suggested.

"Excellent. That'll work. We need to wrap her very warmly too. She doesn't need a shock from the cold when we take her out. I'll ride along in the back with her and direct you to the hospital."

Walter had already run outside to warm up the car. He advised Dooble of her illness as he walked over, curious about all the activity. He hurried inside to see if he could do anything, and stood beside his wife, holding her closely as she trembled with fear and concern.

Ellen had run to the telephone, called the number Dr. Sheffield had given her, and advised the nurse who answered that a heart attack patient was coming into the hospital.

"They'll be there in about two hours, or hopefully less!" she explained.

♥♥♥

The limousine pulled into the hospital entrance less than two hours later. Robert leaped out of the front seat, rushed inside to get help, and a stretcher soon carried Molly Fulton into the hospital, Dr. Sheffield at her side. The two men stood helplessly by, looking at each other, not knowing what to do or where to go. Robert was suddenly overcome by emotion, and began to weep.

Walter put an arm around his friend in comfort and felt like crying himself.

"I'm sorry, Walter. I don't know what came over me. It's just that she's so important to me, to us. I can't explain my feelings because I don't understand them myself. You must think I've lost my mind, carrying on so, but we do love her so very much, Ellen, Stephen and I."

"I understand, Robert. Probably much better than you do. Please, come over here and sit down. I have something to tell you."

He sat down on the large, leather sofa, cold and hard, and struggled to regain his composure. He settled down and sat quietly as Walter pulled a chair over and placed it in front of Robert so that he could maintain eye contact with his friend.

"I don't know how to say this, Robert, except to just say it. You see, Miss Molly wanted to talk to you tonight about something very important to both of you. She has been agonizing over it for months and wasn't sure how or if to tell you. She was afraid if she told you, you'd be angry and leave, but she feels you have a right to know. She loves you and your family very much and would never want you to be hurt. You are the most important person in her life." He glanced nervously down at his clasped hands.

"Robert," he continued, taking a deep breath, "Miss Molly has been searching for you for all of your life. You see, she is your natural mother." He held his breath as this shocking statement entered into his friend's perception.

Robert sat numbly, paralyzed by the words. Confusion swirled through his rattled brain. He shook his head to clear his ears, not certain of what he had just heard.

"What?" he muttered, his lips barely able to move through the shock gripping his body.

Walter grasped Robert's forearms to steady him, as he was swaying, and, he feared, about to pass out. He made no further comment, waiting for the impact of those powerful words to sink into Robert's awareness.

After a few minutes, Robert managed to regain control. He breathed a shuddering sigh which seemed to tear from his very soul as he ran his trembling fingers through his hair.

"But, how...?" he asked, throwing his hands outward in confusion.

"I don't know the full story. Most of what I know is just kitchen talk and gossip, and even though Miss Molly has told me that you're her son, I don't know the full particulars. I would rather she tell you, and I hope you hold no hard feelings toward her."

"Oh, God, no. Of course not. But I just don't understand..."

"I'm sure you don't. All I know is that she was engaged to be married and the man she was to marry died. Her father sent her away and when she came back, she was somehow different, and her father never accepted her again as his daughter. She had me hire a Pinkerton detective some years ago, trying to find you. That's how I knew for sure that she really did have a son. It was difficult because all the court records are sealed. The detective learned your adopted name somehow and tracked down your family in Pennsylvania. By then, your parents were dead and you had left the steel mill to move to New York. I searched for you in Pennsylvania and New York for two years. All we had was your name and age, and New York is a huge city.

"I finally got lucky when I began checking the docks. I talked to a man with the railroad and he was familiar with a man named Josh Bennett who was supervisor on the docks where you worked. He told me Mr. Bennett might be able to help me. I was afraid if I asked for you by name, he'd mention it to you and scare you away so I began to follow the men who worked at his dock. I spoke to Miss Mona about a week before Christmas and put a face with the name. I had to be careful how I asked as she was an incredibly intelligent person, so I sat with her one evening and we just talked. I would ask her the name of people as they came by, genuinely impressed that she knew so many. I saw you cross the street and asked who you were. I now knew who you were but I still didn't know where you lived.

"The next time I came back, Miss Molly insisted on coming with me. We sat on the street waiting for you to appear, hoping and praying that you would. That's the day she offered you a job. It was quite difficult for her to maintain her composure when she saw you. She cried all the way home."

Robert sat in deep silence, trying desperately to let the force of these incredible words penetrate and register. His entire life was forever changed with the uttering of these remarkable facts, his stable and solid past suddenly in disarray and dissonance.

♥♥♥

Walter called the manor to report to the others that they had arrived safely.

"I don't know how long we'll be here, Ellen, but please don't worry. We'll call back as soon as Dr. Sheffield gives us a report on her condition."

"Can I speak to Robert?"

"He's taking this illness pretty hard, Ellen. Let's give him a little while to settle down and he'll call you soon."

"Oh, okay, I understand. Just tell him we love him." She couldn't hide the disappointment and concern in her voice.

♥♥♥

Dr. Sheffield appeared after a very anxious hour spent in the waiting room.

"She's stabilized, gentlemen. They have a heart expert here and he looked at her. Said it doesn't sound like she had much damage and her heart beat sounds good now. Her blood pressure is still a little high but it's settled down quite a bit from when we first arrived. He really thinks she's going to be fine."

"Thank God." Robert breathed with relief.

"Yes, that's right, Robert. Thank God. I think it'll be all right for all of us to go back home and come back tomorrow. It'll be dark soon but we'll still get back early," the doctor suggested.

"You two go on back, but I'm staying," Robert stated. "I want to be here in case she needs anything. I'll call Ellen and let her know and tell her that you're on your way back."

Dr. Sheffield was somewhat surprised by Robert's decision to stay but did not question him. Walter seemed fine with it and expressed no surprise, so, as odd as it seemed, the doctor made no comment.

Ellen was disappointed that her husband was not coming home with the others, but she understood.

"Just take care and try to get some rest, dear," she urged him.

"I'll give the Dantons a quick call also and let them know what's going on."

She hesitated briefly. "I wasn't going to say anything but, earlier today, Mr. Schmidt called Cletus from the hospital where you are now. Mrs. Schmidt died this afternoon, dear."

"Oh, no, I'm so sorry. How is Mr. Schmidt? And Birdie?"

"He seems to be fine but Birdie is taking it pretty hard. She was really close to Mrs. Schmidt. He's going to call us back after all the funeral arrangements are made, and Mr. Schmidt is going to close the store for a couple of days until after the funeral."

"Wow," Robert sighed. "It's been a rough day, hasn't it?"

"Yes, dear, but try not to worry too much. It'll all work out. Just give it to God."

"I'll give them a call and try to get by there tomorrow if everything is stable here. I love you, Ellen."

"I love you too, sweetheart. And I'll see you soon."

♥♥♥

Robert sat quietly by Molly's bed all night, checking her every move or sound anxiously. It was nearly midnight when she stirred, a weak moan escaping her lips.

"Are you in pain?" he asked, his voice heavy with worry. "Do you need a nurse?"

"Robert?" she whispered plaintively.

"I'm here..."

She opened her eyes, looked at him, and smiled through the tears in her eyes.

"I wanted to talk to you today, Robert. I have something very important to tell you and I don't know how you'll take it or..."

"Yes, I know, and it's fine." Robert interrupted her. "Walter told me. I don't know everything but you can explain all that later. After you get well."

"Are you okay with it?"

He laughed gently, his own tears spilling onto her sheets.

"I'm okay with it," he assured her. "We'll talk as soon as you're able."

♥♥♥

Ellen, Dr. Sheffield and Walter arrived at the hospital early the next morning. Walter had brought a shaving kit and Ellen had clean clothes for Robert. He was relieved to see them and quickly explained that Molly had had a good night. Ellen and Walter sat with her while Robert found a shower and some breakfast, and Dr. Sheffield conferred with the nurse and heart specialist.

"I'm happy to report that the specialist says it looks like Molly dodged the big one this time. She's very lucky and if she continues to do as well as she is now, she'll be able to go home within a week," he reported to the anxious group.

"Thank heavens." Ellen smiled. "Did you hear that, Miss Molly?"

"Yes, I sure did, dear," she replied weakly, "and it sounds wonderful except for the part of having to stay here a week. I miss my...I miss the children."

"And they miss you too." Ellen's joy and relief were evident in her voice.

Robert returned and was likewise relieved by the news. He took his wife's arm gently and asked, "Can we go outside for a minute, sweetheart? I want to talk to you."

♥♥♥

Robert dropped the bombshell on his unsuspecting wife as gently as possible, and reached out to steady her as she swayed in reaction to the shocking information.

"Are you sure you understood this right?" she asked incredulously.

He hugged her tightly. He understood her disbelief and shock as he too was still coming to grips with the astonishing revelation. It sounded like some colossal fairy tale.

She stood motionless for a few minutes, digesting and processing this unbelievable knowledge. She looked up, a flash of enlightenment crossing her face.

"That means our children are her grandchildren."

"Yes, that's right."

"Our children have another grandmother." Wonder filled her voice. "That's why she's always loved Stephen so much and why she was so excited when we named Beth after her."

"Yes."

"Oh, I'm so glad we did. Do you suppose God gave Stephen some knowledge that we lack? Maybe that's why he thought about naming Beth after Miss Molly."

"Maybe so. But remember that we have a very thoughtful and caring son." He stood patiently as his beloved processed all the ramifications of their incredible conversation.

"And what do we call her now?"

"I plan to call her Mother."

"And what about the children? What should they call her?"

"Why don't we ask her in a few days when she's better able to discuss it?"

She looked into her husband's eyes, and threw her arms around his neck.

♥♥♥

Robert reluctantly agreed to leave the hospital that afternoon to return home with the others.

"You're needed there, and at the plant, Robert," Molly reminded him. "I'm going to be fine, and as soon as I get home, we'll sit down and have a long, long talk. There's so much I want to tell you and that you need to know." She looked deeply into his eyes, a look of profound sorrow on her face.

"I can't get over how much you look like your father. He was a wonderful man and was the love of my life. I wish you could have known him. I wish..." She began to weep as the painful memories of things she could not change came crashing in on her.

Robert soothed her, alarmed by her tears.

"Now, now, please, just settle down. I don't want you making yourself sick. We'll talk when you're able. We'll have plenty of time." He leaned over and kissed her tenderly on the cheek as he left her side to return to his duties with a new commitment and sense of duty.

Walter stopped at Schmidt's store before they left the city. Birdie and Cletus were grateful for their concern and glad to see them.

"The funeral is tomorrow at the Salvation Army Chapel and she'll be buried in City Cemetery," Cletus explained.

They approached Mr. Schmidt and gave him their condolences.

"I really appreciate you good people coming by. I don't know how I'm going to make it without her. It just doesn't seem possible that she's gone. Sorta like a bad dream but I know I'm not going to wake up from it. I feel like a ship without a rudder. I don't know which way to go."

"It takes time, Mr. Schmidt," Ellen comforted him. "She was a wonderful lady and the two of you had some beautiful memories, I'm certain. Please concentrate on those and your faith to get you through this difficult time."

"Thank you, little lady, thank you kindly. I'll try."

♥♥♥

Stephen was ecstatic when his parents returned home. Pattie had taken good care of him but he missed his parents. They had decided to tell him about his grandmother after they had dinner. It was heavy on their minds as they pondered how to breach this sensitive subject without confusing their son.

As soon as Pattie and Dooble left the manor to return to their cottage, the parents sat down side by side in two chairs and Robert pulled his son into his lap.

"We have something to tell you, son," he began.

"Is it good news? Or bad news?" Stephen was suddenly suspicious. "Has something happened to Miss Molly?"

"Oh, no, sweetheart, she's fine, truly she is." his mother hastened to add. "And this is really wonderful news."

Robert cleared his throat, fidgeting somewhat, not knowing where to start.

"Do you know what a grandmother is, son?" he finally began.

"Of course, Daddy. Don't you know? Grandma Sims is Mommy's mother and my grandmother."

He responded nervously. "Yes, I know but I'm trying to tell you something without confusing you."

"Why don't you just tell me and then I'll tell you if I'm confused."

"Okay, it's a deal... Well, it seems that Miss Molly is your real grandmother."

The child delayed his response only momentarily.

"Yayyyyy! That's great, Daddy! And why would that confuse me?"

He relaxed somewhat as he began to realize that maybe this wasn't going to be as hard as he had first imagined. Their son had an uncanny ability to accept situations as they were without questioning or analyzing them to death. He would understand more as he matured, and it wasn't necessary to go into all the details at this stage.

"I thought it might confuse you because I always talked to you about my mother and your mother's mother as being your grandmothers. And now I have to tell you that Miss Molly is my real mother."

"Now I'm confused," the child admitted. "How can you have two mothers?"

Robert took a deep breath. Here we go, he thought to himself.

"Do you remember when little Beth was born the day after Christmas?"

"Sure."

"Well, Mommy is her birth mother. She's the one who brought her into the world and she will take care of her forever, just as she'll take care of you forever. But sometimes when a child is born, the mother can't take care of him or her for whatever reason, so another very nice, unselfish lady will take that child and adopt him and raise him as her own – just as if she had given birth to him. My mother had adopted me like that and loved me for the rest of her life, just as if she had given birth to me. And to me, she was my real mother, and she was your real grandmother."

Stephen looked perplexed as he listened intently, attempting to follow his father's explanation.

"Now I have learned that Miss Molly was actually my birth mother and she was unable to take care of me because my real father died before I was born. So she gave me to my adoptive mother because she knew that I would be cared for and loved in a way that she couldn't do at that time. But Miss Molly never stopped loving me and she never stopped looking for me. And my adoptive mother never stopped loving me and she never stopped taking care of me."

"Wow." Stephen replied in wonder. "How lucky. You had two mothers to love you. And I have two grandmothers."

The parents glanced at each other. "I don't know why we ever worry about you, Little Man." His father repeated Dooble's name for him. "You are wiser than all of us put together."

"But why couldn't Miss Molly take care of you?"

"I'll explain all that to you another day, son," his father concluded.

"I know. When I get older." Stephen said, rolling his eyes in resignation.

♥♥♥

Robert was very silent after dinner as he and Ellen sat in their apartment. Stephen and Beth were settled down for the night and

Robert peered into the fireplace, his eyes not focused on the flames. His mind was obviously somewhere else.

"Are you okay, dear?" Ellen asked kindly as she gently touched his arm.

"Yeah, I'm okay. Just... It's just hard to grasp, Ellen. I can't help but wonder what happened to make her give me up. And what happened to my father? Why couldn't Miss – uh, Mother's father have helped her? They certainly had the means. My life would have been so much different if she had raised me. I don't want to sound ungrateful but..."

"Just wait, Robert, until she can explain everything to you. We've always believed that everything happens for a reason and you certainly had a good life with your adoptive parents. They never hid the fact that you were adopted and I'm certain they would have told you anything that they could have. You know that adoptions are always secret. That's the law."

He glanced over at his wife, smiling weakly at her assurances.

"Besides," she continued, "if you had grown up here, we never would have met and we wouldn't have our two beautiful children."

He leaned across the sofa and hugged her warmly.

"How right you are, sweetheart. And that would really have been a tragedy."

♥♥♥

Two days later, Cletus called Robert at the manor, and Robert listened and spoke fervently for a few minutes, laughing and obviously excited. He hung up the phone and returned to the kitchen, looking overjoyed.

"What is it?" Ellen asked, his excitement contagious.

"That was Cletus. Seems that Mr. Schmidt has decided to close his store down and move to Philadelphia with his sister. She and her husband own a shoe store and he can work with them. He said his heart is just broken about his wife, and he just can't stay in that store any longer."

"That's wonderful. I mean, for the Dantons, not Mr. Schmidt. Are they coming here? Miss Molly told them sometime ago they could come anytime their situation changed."

"Yes, and I went out on a limb and told him that, so I hope I didn't overstep my boundaries. I'd prefer that Mol...uh, Mother was here to give her stamp of approval. I'd be mortified if she decided it won't work out since she's gotten ill. That means there will be four children in this house, and that can get pretty noisy." He frowned as he began to doubt his decision.

"I don't think you have anything to worry about, dear. Besides, you're going to see her tomorrow and you can ask her then. When is he leaving?"

"As soon as the Dantons can find a place to go. He's ready now."

"Well, personally, I think this is the best news I've had in a long time. I can't wait for Birdie to get here, and I was worried about how Pattie was going to be able to handle all the work since I've got my hands full with the children and Miss Molly's household books. And Stephen will have some playmates his own age and take some of the pressure off Miss Molly. She's been his playmate since the first day we arrived."

"Yes, it will be wonderful to have them here, and I want Cletus to work at the factory with us. We really need the help and Cletus is pretty smart about mechanical things, I believe.

"Oops! I got so caught up in the excitement of our friends coming here that I nearly forgot to tell you. Cletus said the newspaper reported yesterday that Minson is going to be tried for fraud and extortion. The state is asking for the maximum twenty years on each charge and wants the prison time to run back to back. That means he's looking at 40 years in prison. There isn't anything the state can charge the absent owner with but New York has promised changes in their regulations governing all owners of rental property."

"That's truly tragic, dear," Ellen responded, "and I'm sorry but Mr. Minson brought it on himself. It's regrettable that the owner doesn't have to be held accountable too but maybe some good will come from all this loss if the regulations are changed. Very sad, very sad indeed."

♥♥♥

"Oh, Robert, that's absolutely delightful! Of course, the Dantons are welcomed into our home! And don't worry about the children. I thrive on their energy. I'll just have two more grandchildren!"

Robert hugged his mother affectionately.

"You're a remarkable lady, Molly Fulton."

"It runs in the family." she winked at him.

And so it was, that when Molly Fulton was returned to her home at the manor three days later, the car contained the Danton family and their few belongings as well. The Blairs waited anxiously at home for their arrival as there was not room enough for everyone, even in the large limousine. No one missed the wonder of the situation, as the two families began an intense adventure into a life that none of them had ever expected or dared to dream.

Gail Cauble Gurley

PART IV

LEGACY

Gail Cauble Gurley

Chapter 17
The Legacy

All efforts and attention for the next several days were placed on keeping Molly comfortable. She refused to stay in bed, so as a compromise, Robert carried her downstairs each morning and back up at night to alleviate the stress of climbing and descending the stairs.

She sat in her rocking chair by the fireplace, playing "Button, Button, Who's Got the Button" with the three older children. When they tired of playing sit-down games, Dooble took the young trio to the cottage to play with the dogs so as not to disturb Molly or Beth with their squeals and running. Carson had been enrolled at the school in Issaqua Harbor and Julie and Stephen would start there the next fall. Julie and Stephen anxiously awaited Carson's return each day and would watch in awe as he completed his "homework." Carson felt very mature and experienced as the two younger children watched him in amazement as he carefully wrote down numbers and added them together and moved his fingers along pages as he read the words printed on them.

The children usually went to the cottage after Carson completed his school work and before dinner was ready. They loved to visit this magical place and would play there at every opportunity. They were alone in the cottage, exploring the loft area around Dooble's and Pattie's bed one afternoon.

"Hey, look at this!" Stephen shouted.

Carson and Julie ran to the side of the bed where he sat on the floor and crawled into the tight space to reach him.

"What is it?" Carson asked.

"It's a secret hiding place!" He had pulled at the baseboard when he saw a slight crack in it and it lifted up and off easily. After removing it, he slipped one of the bead board wall panels and it too lifted off. It was a narrow space, barely 6" wide and was very dark inside.

"Maybe there's a treasure hidden inside." Julie hoped.

"Yeah, maybe so." Stephen agreed. "But we'd better go get Dobble so he can look. It's dark in there and I don't want to stick my hand in."

Soon Dooble arrived, being trapped and pulled away from his chores by three excited explorers. He moved the bed out of the way so he could get into the small space and held a lantern close to the opening.

"Well, I see some spider webs and dust balls but nothing else. It looks like it's empty, kids."

"Ahhhhh."

They could not hide their disappointment and none of them could hide their enthusiasm as they shared this discovery with everyone at the dinner table that night.

"You know," Walter remembered, "I had forgotten about the secret hideaways in the cottage. There's several more throughout too and I'll try to remember where they all are. My father showed them to me when I was about your age, but they were all empty except for spiders so I never bothered them again. I didn't like spiders. Still don't. But I'll try to help you find them if you'd like."

"Yes, please. Can we go now?" Stephen pleaded.

"No, no, not now. That's Dooble's and Pattie's home. We'll look one day when the plant is closed if it's okay with them."

So the mystery of the secret cubbyholes kept the children entertained for several days, imagining all sorts of mysterious happenings and goings-on. They entertained themselves for hours, imagining pirates stowing their gold, women hiding jewels or secret plans stashed by the military on strategy to fight the Indians and the British.

"Maybe someone hid love letters in there," Julie sighed.

"Yuck! Girls!" Carson exclaimed in disgust.

♥♥♥

Several days after returning home, Molly asked Robert to join her in the parlor after dinner. She felt that it was time to explain his heritage to him.

"It's been a little hectic for the last couple of days, hasn't it?" she laughed good-naturedly, making small talk.

"Is it too much noise for you? Are you okay?" Robert asked, concerned.

"Oh, mercy, no, it's not too much noise. I love every minute of it. I just wish I could play with them. I think you are too worried about me. But anyway, that's not what we're here to discuss. I'm sorry. I suppose I'm somewhat worried about how to tell you."

"I understand." He remembered how he had struggled when he told Stephen that Molly was his grandmother. He was also dealing with his own issues of confusion, anger and even resentment. He was anxious to hear the story of why and how his mother was forced to give him up for adoption.

"Robert, I can't tell you how happy I am that I finally found you and your wonderful family. The only time that I can remember being this happy was when I was engaged to your father.

"His name was Davis Edward McLean and we were very much in love. He was incredibly handsome and intelligent, and was planning to be a doctor. He had completed his studies and was going to open an office in the village after we were married.

"Sometimes when you enter a room, I catch my breath because you look so much like him. And you have his intelligence as well.

"But my father didn't approve of him because he had no interest in coming into the family business. Davis was a doctor and that what he wanted to do. I think Father finally realized that

I was going to marry Davis with or without his approval, especially when I told him that we were going to have a child. You. Father used to call me 'a very obstinate female.' Personally, I think that's a good thing." She smiled at her son.

"My father was from the old school where women were subservient and obedient, and neither my mother nor I ever subscribed to that school. I'm certain it was hard for him to try and deal with independent females. It was especially difficult for him to realize that I was with child and he knew the finality of my decision. No matter how much he wanted to change things, the final decisions had been made and it was hard for him to accept this.

"Davis had completed his residency at Johns Hopkins Hospital, and we were to be married in two weeks at St. Christopher's. I had wanted to be married here at home but Father refused. He swore he would not even attend the wedding.

"Davis was returning to me by riverboat. It was one of those gray, foggy days in early September, and according to some of the other passengers and crew, most everyone was standing on the deck, waiting to dock into the docking area in New York. They suddenly hit a barge that was tied up off the shore instead of being tied at the dock as it was supposed to be. The captain of the riverboat didn't see the barge in the fog, and wasn't looking for it there anyway, so, according to all reports, it was a strong jolt.

"Several passengers and one crew member were thrown overboard. Davis was one of the passengers. They recovered all but two bodies, but Davis was recovered, thank God.

"I was quite concerned when he didn't arrive on schedule as he was very punctual and was never late. I saw lights coming up the drive early that evening and ran out to greet him with great relief. To my horror, it wasn't Davis but some strangers dressed in a suit and a uniform. I think I knew at once, and I stood there, more in shock than anything else and waited to hear what they said. When they told me, I fainted.

"Father talked to them and Walter's father carried me upstairs to my room. Father tried to open my bedroom door where I had barricaded myself in, somehow thinking that the locked door could keep out bad news. He beat on the door loudly and demanded that I open the door.

"I finally let him in and I'll never forget what he said. 'Well, girl, it seems your doctor isn't coming to marry you after all. He's fallen over the side of the boat and is gone.' I swear he was gloating. At any rate, I heard nothing else he said as I fainted dead away again. It was such a cruel and horrible thing to say, even though I knew it was true. When I regained my senses, Mother was leaning over me as I lay on the floor. She was sobbing and Father was standing behind her, his legs spread, his arms crossed across his chest. He saw that I was awake and he bellowed, 'Get up, girl. You're a Fulton and it's time for life to go on.'

"I can remember being blinded by grief and rage. I struggled to my feet and struck out at him by screaming horrible things. I told him I hated him and I'd never forgive him and I believed that he had killed my Davis. I also told him that I'd always belong to Davis. Even death wasn't going to change that. Our baby would keep Davis alive for me.

"He had such a terrifying look on his face that for a second I truly thought he was going to kill me. I thought it would be merciful if he did, and then I was determined to live so that you would live. You were a symbol of all that had ever been beautiful and good in my life so I shut up and remained silent.

"Mother and I slipped out of the house to make the funeral arrangements for my beloved Davis. He had no other family, and so we gave him a Christian burial at St. Christopher's and buried him in the cemetery behind the church. I was numb throughout the whole procedure, and there's very little of it that I even remember. I guess that's a merciful thing.

"In less than a month after Davis died, Father packed me up and sent me to a home for unwed mothers in Wisconsin. It was a despicable place. The women there were treated worse than animals, and we were constantly told how common and trashy we were. Two of the girls committed suicide while I was there, but I was determined not to allow them to break my spirit. I used to talk to you every night and I promised you that no matter what, someday I'd find you.

"The hospital staff kept calendars away from us so we'd not know the birthdays of our babies. It was all a way of making it impossible for us to ever find them, but I had a tiny calendar that Mother had given me when they took me away. I hid it carefully and marked each day off so that I would at least know the date you were born.

"We were all put to sleep when we delivered so that we could be better controlled, and we were never allowed to see our children. The only way I knew that I had a boy was because I wasn't as drugged as they thought, and I heard one of the nurses mention that you were a male.

"They were very cold to me in the hospital and would do nothing for me. I was just grateful that I had no difficulties because one of the women down the hall actually hemorrhaged to death. I'll always believe it was because she was neglected.

"I crept down the hall after midnight on the day you were born. I found the nursery but there was a heavy shade pulled over the window. There was a small crack on one side of the shade and I strained to peep inside, hoping to catch at least a glimpse of you. It was too far away for me to make out the names on the bassinettes so I was never able to pick you out from the six babies in there that night. I made a promise, standing at that shaded window. I promised you that I would find you if it took my whole life and that you would always be in my heart. I tried to sneak down again the next morning but was caught, and they tied me into my bed so that I couldn't escape again."

She paused to regain her composure and Robert sat in front of her, holding her hands firmly, his heart aching for what she had endured.

"They kept me tied up until Mother came after me a week later. She was furious and I thought they were going to tie her up too, but she got me out of there as quickly as possible. My wrists were red and raw where I had tried to escape. I just wanted to hurt everyone there. We got on a train and returned home. She hardly left my side for the whole trip. She just held me and cried.

"When we got home, Father would not even come to greet me. He avoided me entirely and had Mother tell me that I would be expected to continue to take my meals in the kitchen from then on. She didn't say it but I heard him tell her that I had no right to be with 'decent folks' and that I was no longer his daughter. He wouldn't kick me out because of the way it would look to the community. He was very cautious about appearances, no matter how things really were.

"The first night I was home, I dreamed of hearing a baby cry all night long. I would wake up, reaching my arms out to hold you, and you would disappear. I finally turned over, pressed my face into my pillow and screamed and screamed and screamed until I was completely exhausted and wet with perspiration.

"Mother hovered closely over me, careful to protect me from Father. She would spend every minute that she could in the kitchen with Sophie and me. Walter would join us often, when Father didn't have him doing something for him so I gradually began to recover. My determination to someday find you kept me going. I visited your father's grave as often as I could and promised him that I'd find you and let you know that you were truly loved.

"Mother, Walter and Sophie were my main contacts with the world. I was a virtual prisoner in my own home with superficial contact with hairdressers or dressmakers only once or twice a year. If I became ill, the doctor came here to see me. I would hear people laughing and talking in the dining room and front parlor and long to visit with them, but I was never allowed to. Soon people quit coming and the silence of the house was nearly unbearable at times. I guess Father's anger toward me soured him toward everyone and people just quit coming to our house.

"I endured that treatment for four years. Then Father became terribly ill and the doctor said he had had a stroke. I tried desperately to make amends with him but he refused to talk to me, so he died without ever forgiving me.

"I went into his room and knelt beside his bed. I took his hand and talked to him, asking him to forgive me for hurting him. He began breathing very heavily and struggling to speak. There was rage on his face, even in his weak physical state and I couldn't help but withdraw for a second. I took his hand again and told him I loved him. He couldn't pull away but I'll never forget the look of hatred on his face. He wouldn't look at me but his feelings were certainly easy to see. The nurse came over and told me I had better leave. She was very kind but she saw that my presence was causing him duress.

"The nurse helped me up. I was crying so that I wasn't able to rise by myself. She gently led me out of the room and made no comment but I did appreciate the kindness in her eyes and the gentleness in her touch as she guided me out. That's the last time I ever saw my father alive.

"I refused to allow him to cause me further pain and guilt, and decided that his behavior was not my fault. It was what he chose to do because he couldn't control me. I long ago forgave him and gave my anger and pain to God. Had I continued to be angry and bitter, I would have certainly allowed my father to control me and he would have won. I concentrated all my energy on finding you, no matter how long it took. And it took longer than I had anticipated."

"Oh, Mother, I'm so sorry for all that you have suffered!"

"No need to be, my son. I feel very blessed to have been loved by such a wonderful and noble man, and to have our son in my life is the ultimate happiness.

"After Father's death, his attorney came to our house. He met with me and Mother in this very parlor, to discuss what Father wanted done. Mother had his will and the attorney asked for it but Mother wisely declined. After a few minutes, we were both very glad that she did.

"The attorney became very angry when Mother refused to give him the will and said that Father had intended to change his will, eliminating me from it entirely. He had wanted the attorney to be the executor so that Mother would be cared for but I was never to receive a penny and when Mother was gone, I was to be removed from the house. The house was to be sold along with the company and the money was to be split between the family business, which I would no longer own, and the attorney.

"Needless to say, the attorney was livid. Mother stood her ground and told him very calmly and assertively that this was her home and her daughter's home, just as the business was hers and mine. He ranted and raved for over an hour and I'll never forget what he said before he stormed out of our home.

"'I'll take you both to court and I'll have you both committed to an insane asylum! You mark my words; no woman is going to take this away from me. I will see you both in court.'

"He left, slamming the front door behind him. We had no doubt that he would do as he had threatened and Mother was very frightened. I tried to reassure her but didn't know where to turn or who to ask for help. I went down to St. Christopher's the next morning and talked to our priest. He promised to go into the city and talk with the attorney on our behalf. He made arrangements to go down the very next day.

"When Father John returned from the city, he advised us that the attorney (his name was Gerald Evans) was sick and was unavailable. Father John left his card with a note for Mr. Evans to call him as soon as possible on a matter of great urgency.

"A week passed and we heard nothing so Father John called Mr. Evans' office. He was informed that Mr. Evans had died of a heart attack three days earlier. As horrible as it sounds, I have to admit that I felt a huge sense of relief. It's sad to feel relief over someone's death but I just couldn't help it, God forgive me. Father John helped me deal with my guilt over that and he helped us get Father's will registered with the courts so that we could close the estate and protect our home from anyone else. Mother sold all of the stocks that Father had owned and put all our money in the banks.

"After Father's death and after we got everything settled, I increased my effort to find you. I had Mother's support and she encouraged me every step of the way. But I found nothing but dead ends and frustration.

"When Mother died, I decided that I didn't want the family's money in banks anymore. I never did trust those institutions so I went into town and drew all the money out. I brought it here and hid it in several safes throughout the house. Not long afterwards, one of the banks' attorneys paid me a visit. He was quite angry that I had closed the account at his bank and he had learned from the other banks that I had closed them there too. He proceeded to call me irresponsible and uncooperative. He even hinted that he thought me to be – let me think, how did he phrase that? – 'slightly touched in the head.'"

Molly chuckled as she remembered this confrontation.

"Finally, he left, realizing he was getting no where. I wasn't sure if he would attempt to go to court or not but fortunately, I never heard from him again. There are attorneys in this world, unfortunately, who make a career of making life difficult for women who find themselves in a place of authority or power. Of course, attorneys aren't the only ones but they do have the potential to create more mischief than most."

Robert smiled at his mother's disdain.

"You have a fearless heart, Mother." He spoke with pride and love.

"I have the heart of a mother who was determined to find you, my dear. It was only three years ago that we finally learned your name and then I really became excited and hopeful that we would find you. I never lost faith, Robert, that I would someday find you. And I never lost the fear that you would reject me. After we learned your name, it was a series of hopes and fears, an emotional rollercoaster, but I never wavered in my determination to keep the promise I had made to you and to your father so long ago. Regardless of your reaction toward me, I wanted you to know who you are and who your biological parents are. I am just so very grateful that you were adopted by a good and kind family who loved you as their very own. God truly had His hand on you throughout your life, my son."

"I don't know what to say to express to you how much this means to me, Mother. You have given me and my family a home and a better life than we ever dared to imagine or even dream of. It's just amazing and almost like a fairy tale."

"And you and your family have given me a life, Robert. I've been so lonely for all of my life since losing Davis and the only thing that kept me going was my determination to somehow, someday find you. I was so afraid of what your reaction would be to the truth and I was torn about whether to tell you or just let things rest. But I knew that you had a right to know and even if it meant losing you, I had to tell you."

"I'm so glad you did, Mother. And I do understand. I'm just so sorry that you have had to suffer and endure through all these years. Your determination and dedication in your search for me make me love you even more. I'm very proud to be your son.

"For all of my life, I never felt complete. Oh, I was loved and cared for but I always wondered about my biological parents. What did they look like, were they alive, why did they give me up? Mama could tell me nothing as all records were sealed and no matter how hard she and my father tried, there was an empty place deep inside.

"The year that I was 12 years old, I went to the drug store to buy my mama a Mother's Day card. I picked up another one and bought it for you. I don't remember exactly what it said but it had beautiful pink flowers all over the front of it and the verse said something about being in my heart. It spoke to me as I did keep you in my heart, even if I didn't know who or where you were or even if you were alive. On the outside I wrote 'To my in-my-heart mother' and I signed it 'Your forever son.'

"I hid the card deep in a box of bubble gum cards and string and other junk that I kept in my closet. I found it a couple of years later and burned it so Mama would never find it and be hurt.

"I felt left out around my other friends who had brothers and sisters. They would fight with them sometimes but I could tell they loved them just the same. My best friend Tommy told me one time that I was very lucky not to have a sister as they were nothing but a royal pain in the neck. I didn't say anything to him but I really didn't feel lucky in not having a sister. So, yes, it's a great relief and a huge burden off my shoulders that you cared enough to keep looking all these years."

He slipped his arm around her shoulders, resting his head on the top of hers.

"Do you know how the detective found out my name?"

"Yes," she replied. "He learned that the law had finally closed down that home for unwed mothers after so many young women died there. There were over a dozen deaths in a two-year period and the state couldn't continue to ignore it so there was an investigation. All of the files were removed and stored in a courthouse in that county and the home was torn down. Nobody who worked there ever went to prison but at least they couldn't hurt anyone else.

"The detective finally learned, after probably 10 years, where the files were stored and he was friends with someone at that courthouse so they would let him in to secretly look through the files. They were in no kind of order but after nearly two years, he found out your name and the name of your adoptive parents.

"You can imagine my disappointment when we hit yet another dead end in Pennsylvania when we learned your parents had died. Fortunately, the detective was a very tenacious man and he kept working until he finally found out from the steel mill in Pennsylvania where you had worked that you had moved to New York. I figured we'd never find you there, since it's so big, but Walter took over the search and wouldn't give up. And I'm so very grateful that he didn't."

They sat silently, Molly's head resting on Robert's shoulder, as they comforted each other, each a victim of a force they could not have stopped. Her silent tears washed away years of pain and anger while his own tears dissolved his internal resentment and aching questions. It was now his wish to comfort and love the one who gave birth to him and then gave him the best, the only, life that she could. Finally, Molly stirred.

"I have some pictures of your father. Would you like to see them?"

"Oh, yes, I really would!"

"They're upstairs in my room so I'll go get them and bring them back here. We'll share them with everyone else later if that's okay."

"Yes, that's perfect but I'll help you upstairs."

"Nonsense! I'm tired of being coddled and I feel fine so I'll just go get them. You wait here. By the way, I guess we'll have to explain to the Dantons and Howells that you're my son. They have a right to know."

♥♥♥

The others sat in the kitchen waiting for Robert and Molly, not asking any questions but curious as to what was occurring. Finally, Stephen looked up from their game of tick tack toe at the table.

"Mama, what are Daddy and Grandmother talking about for so long?"

Everyone looked up at his referral to Molly as Grandmother but assumed it was just a term of endearment as they knew how close the two were. They had heard him refer to her in that way several times since she returned from the hospital.

Ellen seemed somewhat uncomfortable, uncertain of what to say.

The kitchen door opened, and Robert and Molly entered, Robert carrying a flat cardboard box with him.

"Hello, everyone, sorry to be gone so long but Robert and I had some personal business to attend to. We'd like to share some of that information with all of you since you're such an important part of our family now. Robert." She yielded the stage to her son and sat down beside her daughter-in-law, taking her granddaughter into her arms.

"What I have to tell you is wonderful news. I think most of you are aware that I was adopted by a loving family shortly after my birth, and they were the only family I ever knew. I consider myself blessed by the love and care and stability that I received from my parents, but there was always an emptiness inside me, a question and restlessness that I was unable to quench or satisfy.

"It seems that for all my life, there was someone who was feeling this same emptiness and restlessness, someone who devoted her entire life to searching for me, someone who never gave up and continued her quest with the devotion and determination only a mother can possess. That someone is Molly Fulton – my birth mother."

A gasp escaped from every member of the group, and then they all began to smile and talk and move toward the two, congratulating and loving them both. They required no further explanations, and accepted the tidings with non-judgmental approval.

They soon gathered around to view the pictures contained in the cardboard box. It was filled with what looked very much like old pictures of Robert with a much younger, beautiful Molly.

"This has to be your father," Birdie pointed out. "You look exactly like him."

"Yes, that's him."

"You two were very much in love," Pattie stated as she viewed the pictures of Molly and her Davis.

"You're very perceptive, my dear," Molly said. "He was the love of my life."

♥♥♥

The next day, Molly and Robert moved through the small cemetery behind St. Christopher's church. They arrived at the grave of Robert's father. He peered down at the simple marker.

DAVIS EDWARD MCLEAN
October 9, 1882 – September 9, 1906
FOREVER ALIVE IN MY HEART

Robert dropped to one knee, tracing his finger over the letters carved deep into the stone, just as his mother had done so many times in the past. His eyes filled with tears and his mother stood silently, allowing her son time to grieve over the father he never knew.

♥♥♥

There were changes made in the living arrangements within the manor over the next few weeks. Robert and Ellen moved from their apartment into the main manor, and the Dantons moved from the guest quarters into the apartment. The Dantons were thrilled with the new arrangements and loved their new home. Twin beds and a partition placed in the center of the second bedroom afforded privacy for Carson and Julie while providing spacious areas for the two siblings.

Molly spent several days on the telephone in the hallway outside the parlor, making mysterious calls and jotting down notes. She approached Robert after dinner one night and they once again disappeared into the parlor.

"Robert, I've been speaking to Mr. Freedle for the past few days and he recommended an attorney for me to speak with. His name is Sidney Dallas. I have no love of lawyers and certainly have little respect for them, but I do respect Mr. Freedle so I'm as certain as one can be that Dallas is a suitable and trustworthy person for what I want to propose to you."

Robert smiled at his mother's obvious disdain toward attorneys but could
understand, given the history of mistreatment and threats she and her mother had endured during Mr. Fulton's life, illness and death.

"At any rate, I want to make certain that there is never any question that you, Ellen and the children will be my heirs."

Robert was surprised by her statement as he had honestly not even thought of that aspect of his heritage.

"The only way that I can ensure that," she continued, "is to adopt you legally. It's unusual for an adult to be adopted but it isn't impossible. Also, a new marriage license with your name as Fulton would be issued for you and Ellen and a new birth certificate for the children. What are your thoughts on this?"

"I'm…quite frankly, not certain, Mother. I need to think about it and talk to Ellen also. It's a difficult matter to change names as an adult."

"Women are forced by our society to change our last names all the time, Robert," she pointed out kindly. "It's inconvenient but certainly not impossible. I just want the world to know that you are indeed a Fulton. We can't give you the name McLean since your father's name was not included on your original birth certificate but you still have his blood coursing through your veins, along with mine, by the way, and I really want you to have the last name you are entitled to."

"I'm touched by your obvious concern for us but I really don't think you need to worry about that. We'll always be fine and you'll always be my mother, regardless. I would be honored to carry your name, just as I am honored to be your son, as I love you dearly. Knowing my birth mother has eased my mind and doubts regarding who I am, but I can't forget my adoptive parents either. I need time to think and pray about it. I guess this is a problem unique to someone who has been fortunate and blessed enough within a lifetime to be loved by so many genuinely good and decent people."

She embraced her son warmly. "Discuss it with Ellen, dear, and let me know what you decide. I will abide by that decision, whatever it is."

♥♥♥

Ellen stood by her husband, her arm around his shoulders tenderly, after he shared his mother's plan with her.

"You know that whatever you decide will be fine with me, sweetheart," she assured him. "I'm married to the same wonderful man regardless of what our last name is, and I don't think Stephen would object at all. I know Beth wouldn't." She smiled toward their infant, sleeping in her crib, oblivious to the moral struggle her father was experiencing.

"It's just that Mama and Pop were so good to me, loving me as much as if they had been my birth parents, and it seems to me that if I change my name, I'm dishonoring in some way their memories and all they did for me. I feel disloyal by dropping their name as if they didn't even exist."

"But on the other hand, I love Mother in a way I've never loved before. It's as if my soul is finally complete and she was the piece that completed it. I just don't know what to do."

"Suppose we left Blair in the children's names and added Fulton to the end. It would then be Stephen Robert Blair Fulton and Molly Elizabeth Blair Fulton," Ellen suggested.

His face lit up.

"Do you suppose we can do that?"

"I don't see why not. Many women name their children using their maiden names so as not to lose the family name completely. There's no difference in doing this that I can see. And we will, of course, raise the children to understand what the Blair name is and that it is to be always honored. They can even pass it on to their own children if they wish."

"I love you, Ellen." he smiled happily as he embraced her. "Or should I say Mrs. Fulton?"

♥♥♥

Summer arrived at the manor, Beth began cooing and smiling, charming the entire household and Stephen welcomed back the "grass stars," cicadas and tree frogs, introducing his friends to their fireworks and yard symphony. Ellen decided it was time to teach the children their ABCs and numbers as Stephen would start school in the village that fall and Carson would be in the second grade. Carson was a year behind but would catch up soon, they were all certain.

"Birdie and Pattie, I think it's time for us to teach these children a few fundamentals before they start to school, and I see no reason why Julie can't learn also. Would you two be willing to help me?"

They both hesitated somewhat, and finally Birdie confessed, "I don't really know my ABCs so good, Ellen. I can read pretty well but I can't recite the letters by heart. I know numbers okay but I was never very good with arithmetic. I only went through the seventh grade."

"I have the same problem, Miss Ellen," Pattie continued. "My grandmother taught me the best she could and sent me to school whenever possible but we lived several miles from the school, and I had to walk so I didn't get to go that much. I finally gave up when I was sixteen. I can read very well, thanks to my reading to Grandmother almost every night, but it's doubtful that I could write the ABCs in order."

"No need to worry, ladies. We'll get it done. I'll write them down and we'll all work with teaching it to the children. I'll get a blackboard at Carver's in the village and we can practice writing them on that. Truth be known, we could all use the practice anyway. None of us writes as much as we should. I can remember my mother writing letters to relatives almost every week when I was growing up. We depend too much on the telephone now."

The women smiled their gratitude to their understanding and compassionate friend, and were eager to gain more knowledge along with the children.

♥♥♥

One of the first things Stephen wanted to learn was how to write his whole name. So Ellen proudly printed his name across the blackboard: STEPHEN ROBERT BLAIR FULTON

"Wow, that's a long name," Carson noted.

"Yes, but a very proud one," Ellen said.

♥♥♥

The plant continued to operate with the gasoline engines becoming more and more efficient under the keen eyes of Robert and Cletus. Cletus had discovered a bad connection in the carburetors that would cause them to sputter off after several hours use so a longer tube connection had corrected that problem.

They made all the corrections to the engines for the Morgan Farm Tractor Company and filled the first contract. They had a promise of another one shortly but the depression continued to strangle the nation, so they waited patiently. Franklin Roosevelt, a new political voice, was making suggestions so hope was on the horizon.

Molly continued to recover and thrive under the love and attention of her family. She sat on the front porch one evening, surrounded by Robert, Ellen, Beth, Walter, Dooble, Pattie, Cletus and Birdie. Even the dogs lay quietly on the floor as Robert, Carver and Julie chased fireflies and each other.

"I used to worry about whether or not my life would matter for anything," Molly commented softly. "Would the world even notice that I had passed through? What would be my legacy? I have no further reason to worry. All of you are my legacy, my grandchildren are my immortality. There's no need to be concerned about this big house or the factory or any material or tangible article I may leave behind. All of these things are insignificant and unimportant. What's important is the difference that I may have made in the lives of others as well as the difference others have made to me. I am truly blessed by the love of so many good people, and I thank you all for it."

They all smiled warmly at Molly Fulton, as the children continued chasing fireflies, Beth stirred, wanting to be picked up and Gimpy leaped off the porch to chase a squirrel running across the yard to escape the noisy children. Patches looked up, deciding that Gimpy could handle the squirrel situation, and laid her head back between her front paws, content to lie beside her beloved Pattie.

Gail Cauble Gurley

About the Author

Gail Cauble Gurley is a Rowan County, North Carolina native. She has a BA in psychology andMasters in Education from the University of North Carolina at Greensboro. She married EdwardGurley III in January 1971 and they have one daughter, Denise, who lives in Houston, Texas with her three children, Charlie, of the U. S. Marines; Spencer and Madison. Gail worked for many years for the state of North Carolina as an adult probation/parole officer and retired in 1995 to pursue her dream of writing.

She is an award winning writer, worked for several years for two small town weekly newspapers, and has had numerous articles published in magazines. She is employed by the Courier-Tribune newspaper in Asheboro as a feature writer. She is the author of three works of fiction as well as co-author of a screenplay inspired by her racing book, *Red Dirt Tracks*. The movie "Red Dirt Rising" was released in May 2010 and on DVD in January 2011. Her latest book, *Old South Comfort Food*, fulfills a long dream of editing and preserving the recipes of her youth from a treasured church cookbook. *Tales From the Sunroom* as well as *Old South Comfort Food* are available on www.scribesvalley.com. *Old South Comfort Food* is available from the beautiful Carolina Lily on Kern Carlton Road in Salisbury, N. C.

Fearless Heart, her latest work, is the fictional story of a New York City family trapped in the poverty of America's Great Depression; their struggles, faith and ultimate triumph in the face of near insurmountable odds and hardships.

You may reach Gail and at the website www.scribesvalley.com. Gail is also on Facebook.

CPSIA information can be obtained at www.ICGtesting.com
Printed in the USA
LVOW07s1823250215

428347LV00001B/60/P

9 781937 085056